The Spy Who Inspired Me

ISBN: 9782952163859

COVER DESIGN BY RUTH MURRAY

The Spy Who Inspired Me

Stephen Clarke

pAf

ALSO BY STEPHEN CLARKE

Fiction
A Year in the Merde
Merde Actually (US edition: In the Merde for Love)
Merde Happens
Dial M for Merde
The Merde Factor
Merde in Europe
A Brief History of the Future
Death Goes Viral (previously published as Who Killed Beano)

Non-Fiction
1,000 Years of Annoying the French
Dirty Bertie, an English King Made in France
How the French Won Waterloo (or Think They Did)
The French Revolution & What Went Wrong
Talk to the Snail : the Ten Commandments for Understanding
the French
Paris Revealed : the Secret Life of a City
Château d'Hardelot, a Souvenir Guide
The British Invasion (with co-author Valli)
Elizabeth II, Queen of Laughs

ABOUT THE AUTHOR

Stephen Clarke is a British author living in Paris, where he divides his time between writing and not writing.

His best-known novels are the worldwide bestselling *Merde* series, including *A Year in the Merde* (which has sold well over a million copies worldwide) and *Merde Actually* (a number-one bestseller in the UK).

He has also written several non-fiction books, including *1,000 Years of Annoying the French* (also a number-one bestseller in the UK), a biography of King Edward VII's 'éducation sentimentale', called *Dirty Bertie, an English King Made in France*, as well as *Talk to the Snail: the Ten Commandments for Understanding the French*, and *How the French Won Waterloo (or Think They Did)*.

Clarke's book *1,000 Years of Annoying the French* inspired the permanent collection at a French museum, which he curated. It is the Centre Culturel de l'Entente Cordiale at the Château d'Hardelot in northern France.

He has written two stage shows based on his books – an adaptation of his novel *The Merde Factor*, and a words-and-music show in French called *L'Entente Cordiale en Paroles et Musique*.

He also writes jokes for stand-up comedians and song words for singers, and has co-written a French radio sitcom and a radio play. He occasionally performs his own material in music and comedy clubs – but mainly for fun (his own rather than the audience's).

www.stephenclarkewriter.com   @sclarkewriter

This is a work of fiction. It was inspired by a real historical context, but any resemblance to real people, or to other authors' characters, is completely, absolutely and existentially coincidental.

It is true that a famous literary character, Auric Goldfinger, said something along the lines of 'once is happenstance, twice is coincidence, three times is enemy action', but surely there are no enemies in literature. It's all just words, after all.

Night-time, occupied France, early April 1944

Lemming realized that he was genuinely scared of this woman, even though they were supposedly on the same side.

She seemed to recognize the effect that she had on him.

'I don't think you truly understand my job, Ian,' she said. 'A secret agent in the field has only one duty. That is to survive long enough to carry out our mission. And we will do anything, *anything*, to achieve that goal.'

'In that case, don't you think you ought to have tried to –'

The fires in her eyes were burning again.

'Don't *ever* doubt me,' she said. 'Don't *ever* accuse me of doing less than I possibly can for my mission.'

He had frequently thought of himself flatteringly as something of a lady-killer. But this young woman was a genuine lady killer – a female assassin, a feminine bumper-off.

And he was seriously afraid that he might be her next victim.

PART ONE

I

London, four nights earlier

'You have a reservation, Monsieur?'

'Of course. The name's Lemming. Ian Lemming.'

'Ah oui. One table for two, nineteen o'clock. Please follow me.'

The French maître d'hôtel executed a balletic turn on one leg, and then hobbled away between the tightly-packed tables. The majority of the diners, male and female, were in uniform – either khaki, blue-grey or navy blue.

Lemming watched the small maître d' as he swayed between the chair backs, and wondered about the limp. He hoped it had been earned at Dunkirk and not leaping out of a bedroom window.

The maître d' stopped beside an unoccupied table. It stood against a wall, half-protected from the babble of conversation by a carved wooden partition. It was as intimate as you could get in this smoky room in Mayfair.

'Voilà, mon commandant, the best table in the restaurant.'

'Merci, mon camarade,' Lemming said.

'Et mademoiselle ...' The maître d' pulled back a chair with a bow that might have greeted a princess. Bond's date for the evening, a warrant officer in the Women's Auxiliary Air Force, slid into the space, and the chair was eased forward with perfect grace until she was sitting comfortably.

She grinned, amused by the ceremony of it all.

'Bonne soirée, mademoiselle. Mon commandant.' Pausing only to accept the large coins that Lemming slid noiselessly into his palm, the maître d' limped away.

'Oh, this is simply marvellous,' the WAAF gushed. Her consonants were carved crystal, her vowels as tight as a duchess's corset. Lemming supposed she was one of the daughters of minor nobility who populated the various war departments in London.

She was a tall, shapely brunette who had obviously followed the young Princess Elizabeth's cue and had her uniform tailored to fit her admirable bust.

The cut of her jacket, and the surprisingly obscene oath he had heard as she struggled to open her umbrella outside the Houses of Parliament, had been what first attracted his attention to her, two days earlier. He had stepped in to unleash the jammed umbrella, escorted her through the rain to the nearest cab rank, and invited her to dinner.

'Just wait until you've tried the food,' Lemming now said, lighting a cigarette for each of them. 'I'm told they smuggled the chef out of Paris the night before the Nazis arrived, with all his herbs, his knives and half a ton of saucepans. Apparently, they hid him in a crate of garlic bulbs. That's why everything he cooks stinks of the stuff.'

The WAAF warrant officer laughed obligingly and gave Commander Lemming's sharp features an appraising stare. She had been told that, with his gold-braided naval tunic, crisp collar and tie, and worldly-wise manner, he was vying to be more glamorous than the American officers who were stealing most Englishmen's thunder these days. In this, she thought, he had succeeded. No American male would dare to sport a long, silver cigarette holder.

Adding even further to Lemming's sheen, one of her acquaintances had said that the commander was 'something in the special services, but no one quite knows what the special services are.' What few of the WAAF warrant officer's acquaintances knew was that she *did* know. And that she hadn't found any evidence that Commander Lemming, for all his swagger, had seen much action, secret or otherwise.

Meanwhile, Lemming was wishing that he could remember the girl's name. Marjorie? Or was it Margaret? Terribly un-gentlemanlike of him, but he did dine with so many girls. And in his pocket diary, he had noted only 'M'.

No matter, though. By the end of the evening, most of the women he met were perfectly happy to have 'darling' whispered in their ear. Or polite enough to pretend, anyway.

A white-jacketed, black-tied waiter – another Frenchman, slightly younger than the maître d' – came and gave them hand-written menus.

'Bonsoir, mademoiselle. Mon commandant. May I suggest a glass of champagne to begin your evening? One of our last bottles of Taittinger Blanc de Blancs brut 1939,' he added secretively.

'Excellent idea,' Lemming said. 'They say it's as good as the '34. And we must congratulate the viticulteurs for harvesting the grapes even as the clouds of war were gathering overhead. Don't you agree, Mar ... demoiselle,' he corrected himself, making a joke of it.

'Splendid idea ... monsieur,' she agreed, teasing him in return.

'Parfait.' The waiter smiled as though it had been their suggestion.

Watching the Frenchman leave, Lemming made a conscious effort to forgive him for not being in uniform. He was of military age, barely thirty, fully fit as far as Lemming could see. Why wasn't he chomping at the bit to go and liberate his country? Wasn't that exactly why the French loved their patron saint, Joan of Arc? Supposedly she had 'bouté les Anglais' out of France. And those Nazis needed a whole lot more booting.

But then again, Lemming decided sportingly, waiting tables could be defined as essential war work, if it helped to keep up the morale of officers like him.

They perused the menu, which was entirely in French. Marjorie or Margaret let Lemming translate for her, though he suspected that she was feigning ignorance to flatter his masculinity. When the waiter returned with their champagne, served in tall French flutes, Lemming asked his date if he could order the food for them both.

The warrant officer shrugged and smiled, as if to acknowledge that she didn't seem to have much choice.

'We will both have the carottes rapées à la moutarde to start,' Lemming dictated. 'Then mademoiselle will follow with the lamb côtelettes – à point – while I take the Dover sole. Please leave it on the bone. I prefer to carve it myself.' The waiter wrote this down, twitching only slightly as Lemming breathed cigarette smoke in his face. 'To accompany that,' Lemming went on, 'we will have the roasted potatoes and cauliflower florets. And instruct the chef to cook the cauliflower for no more than one minute. Plenty of butter on the vegetables, too, please.'

'Parfait, mon commandant.' The waiter gave a hum of congratulation, as though Lemming had reeled off the correct answers to a series of impossible questions.

Lemming looked to the warrant officer for her approval. She nodded and smiled. In reality, she would have preferred the Dover sole, but had her own reasons for not making waves.

When the sommelier came, it was the same story. To go with his date's lamb, Lemming ordered a half bottle of a young Château Margaux – 'How sweet of you, Ian, to order a bottle with my name,' she said. Lemming accepted the compliment, even though his choice had been a complete coincidence. Luck was with him tonight, he thought.

For himself, Lemming chose a whole bottle of Château Palmer, a white from the same Margaux region, 'so it will feel as though we are in Bordeaux together'.

The sommelier came very close to applauding. Margaux came close to laughing.

12

Left alone, Lemming and Margaux clinked glasses and drank champagne.

'What a simply perfect place,' she said. 'And how clever of you to know about it.'

Lemming bowed modestly, though he was not sure that he had been the one to suggest dining here. When he invited her to dinner, hadn't she mentioned that she would 'love to try that French place near the Mall?' Yes, he was certain that the idea came from her. *Almost* certain. No matter, he always enjoyed flattery of his male ego, however insincere or undeserved it was.

He put down his glass and lit another cigarette. Margaux thought he smoked far too much, probably a sign that he was easily bored. Not with her, she hoped. Not yet, anyway.

'The best French restaurants aren't here just to fill you with enough vitamins to keep your body functioning for the next few hours,' he lectured her. 'They exist to flatter you. You, yes, *toi*, you have shown sheer genius in coming *chez nous*, and in choosing these dishes. And that wine you selected? Brilliant! No one in the history of French cuisine has ever chosen such a perfect wine to accompany their food. This is why we, *les garçons*, will now serve everything with such sweeping, dramatic gestures.' He put on a French accent. 'It is because you 'ave inspired us, monsieur. We feel like singing and dancing for joy. It is so rare that we are lucky enough to be in the presence of such intellect, such effortless good taste, such class.'

Margaux laughed, as she was meant to. She suspected it might be one of the dashing commander's set pieces, but she had to concede that there was something self-mocking about him that made you want to forgive his excess of swagger.

'Last time I was in Paris, the waiters at the Café de Flore made me feel an awful fool,' Margaux said.

Lemming raised an eyebrow, as if he had decided that previous trips to Paris boded well for her lack of morals.

'Oh, I'm sorry to hear that,' he said, 'but, you know, these flattering restaurants are not to be confused with the traditional brasseries where the waiters can make you feel like a baboon fresh from the jungle for not knowing the difference between crème brûlée and crème caramel. I'll wager you were only there for coffee, nothing expensive. Am I right?'

'Yes, and I probably don't look enough like a starving philosopher to get decent service at the Flore. And by the way, what *is* the difference between crème brûlée and crème caramel?'

'Half a minute with a flamethrower, nothing more[1] … Well, I'll be damned!'

Margaux looked around the room to see what might have caused this sudden blasphemy. But the diners were still merrily chattering and consuming, all of them savouring these precious, air-raid-free moments of relaxation.

Lemming began to scribble with a gold propelling pencil into a small spiral notepad. He held up his free hand as if to ward off any questions, so Margaux simply sat back and watched, amused by the mysteriousness of it all. She could make out nothing of his upside-down scrawl except 'flamethrower'. Unless it was 'foam rubber' or 'farm robber', or something similar.

'Yes, it might work,' he said to himself as he stowed the book and pencil in his hip pocket.

'Is it something terribly, terribly secret?' Margaux asked, with what she hoped was the right amount of feminine reverence.

'Yes, sorry, old girl, an idea to share with the admiral. If I told you what it was, you'd have to kill me.'

'Isn't it supposed to be the other way around? Aren't you meant to say, "If I told you, I'd have to kill you"?'

'No, my dear, because if I told you, it would mean I'm a security risk, and the war effort would be better off without me.' He looked deadly serious. It didn't suit him as well as levity.

Their wine came, along with their *hors d'oeuvres*, and Lemming told the waiter to keep the rest of the bottle of Taittinger aside for later. Again, his every word was greeted with admiring nods, as if he was inventing a whole new science of food appreciation.

---

[1] Lemming is mistaken. *Crème brûlée* is based mainly on egg yolks and *crème fraîche*, while *crème caramel* consists mostly of whole eggs and milk.

Lemming joked about this again, as he mixed the mustard sauce into his grated carrots, but then his mood darkened for a moment.

'You know,' he said, 'I think I'll suggest that the admiral takes a closer look at this place. All these men of military age out of uniform. And how did they get their hands on the Taittinger '39? Surely it wasn't ready for shipping until after the Nazis had invaded?'

'It seems slightly ungrateful to enjoy all the trimmings of their hospitality, and then report them to the authorities.'

'You're right,' Lemming agreed. 'So before we report them, we must make absolutely certain we finish that bottle of Taittinger.'

They shared a laugh, and Margaux felt the rasp of Lemming's woollen trouser legs as they gripped her own bare calf, almost brutally. She restrained herself. Her instinctive reaction to such a sudden onslaught would have been to ram the champagne glass into his face. But she took a deep breath and smiled through the smoke of yet another of his pungent cigarettes.

She wondered what to do when, inevitably, he tried to kiss her as soon as they stepped out of the restaurant and into the blackout.

II

Next morning, Lemming sat in his office, Room 7, in the Admiralty. Pale light filtered through the criss-cross paper tapes that were optimistically supposed to reinforce the window against the blast from a thousand-kilogram bomb. The sounds of traffic from outside formed a backdrop to the jangling telephones, urgent voices and thump of typewriters inside the crowded office. His own desk was surrounded by a small fleet of tables and chairs wedged into every available square foot of floor space. Almost a dozen uniformed men and women were constantly going about the business of gathering and (more parsimoniously) re-distributing naval intelligence, in an atmosphere of hurry, smoke and noise. But Lemming had learnt to lock them out of his mind unless he was directly called upon for a reaction.

It was nine o'clock. Lemming had already lost count of the number of cigarettes he had smoked. There was a file open in front of him, but he had read the opening sentence three times without feeling the urgency to go on.

He was bored. If he could have been bothered to read French philosophy books, he would have diagnosed himself with existentialist *ennui*.

The feeling was not new. It was boyhood boredom that had got him removed early from Eton. He had been *victor ludorum* – the most athletic pupil in the school – two years running (and jumping). What more was there to achieve at England's most competitive school? So it was best to move on.

He had loved the freedom of the private school he attended after Eton, which was run by a retired English spy. The school was in the Austrian Alps, and the combination of scaling mountains and dirndls had been perfect for Lemming. For a while.

It was boredom with the repetitiveness and vulgarity of army discipline that had got him sent down from Sandhurst. Well, boredom and a dose of gonorrhoea.

Boredom with money talk had scuppered his banking career. His grandfather had founded a bank, but in Lemming's opinion, money was for spending or gambling, not an object of work or conversation. His job at the bank had gradually turned into one long luncheon appointment, and then he had resigned.

Reporting for Reuters in Moscow had been fun, and his first-hand contact with Stalin's terror machine fascinating. But even that had become routine after Lemming's coup at the show trial of some British engineers, when he had paid Russian runners to ensure that his copy would be the first to reach the telegraph office, outstripping even the most experienced foreign correspondents. He was *victor ludorum* again, and boredom set in.

The war had started well enough. In 1940, he had been sent into newly occupied France to help refugees escape from Bordeaux as the Nazis swept westward.

Lemming's principal role at the port had been to persuade millionaires that their Rolls Royces would not fit on the gangplank. Sweet-talking Europe's chicest had been highly amusing, but short-lived. And besides, it was all schoolboy stuff.

Meeting his first Admiralty boss, Admiral Geoffrey, had been a godsend. Although often aggressive towards people he did not respect, Admiral Geoffrey had always been a receptive sounding board for Lemming's madcap ideas. These schemes had included half-burying himself on a Dutch sandbank to report on Nazi ship movements; ditching a Nazi bomber in the Channel, manned by British troops in disguise, then waiting for a Nazi rescue boat to arrive so that its Enigma machine could be captured; and setting a British corpse afloat at sea, primed with fake intelligence. That last suggestion had actually been used, though the idea was credited to someone else. Even so, Lemming enjoyed the satisfaction of knowing that it had originally been his invention.

The fascination with intelligence-gathering had even permitted Lemming to set up his very own commando unit, 00 Commando. Its purpose was to capture Nazi maps, photographs, code books, memos – anything that would help the Allies to plan future operations. The men would go in with regular commandos and, while the others were blowing things up, they would crack safes and remove vital documents before the whole place was reduced to rubble.

Sadly, 00 Commando's first raid, and Lemming's only taste of real action so far, was best forgotten – he had been on one of the Royal Navy ships carrying troops for the 'invasion' of Dieppe in August 1942. Lemming had watched from half a mile offshore as some 6,000 soldiers, most of them Canadian, had waded up the steep pebble beach to be mown down by Nazi defenders. A tragic waste of life, due almost entirely to faulty intelligence. Air reconnaissance had failed to spot hidden defences. It was even said that some of the planning had been done using pre-war holiday photos – as if bunkers and machine-gun nests would show up on them. It was a basic error that must not be allowed to happen again.

The problem with this potentially engrossing area of Lemming's life was that his protector, Admiral Geoffrey, had now been replaced. Geoffrey's successor as Head of Naval Intelligence, Rear Admiral Rashbrooke, was an aircraft-carrier captain who had been torpedoed, but who had not gone down with his ship. Drowning was not a captain's obligation, of course, but somehow Rashbrooke's survival made him an imperfect war hero. And he was not the gruff old sea salt that Geoffrey had been. Rashbrooke would get your ship where it was meant to go (unless he was torpedoed again), but he would not make a quick diversion to lob a few shells at an enemy frigate. Rashbrooke was a man of routine.

So Lemming was bored again. He was reduced to spending long hours smoking in his office, dreaming up missions for 00 Commando without any certainty that they would be carried out. He felt like a toy soldier. He was always perfectly turned out in double-breasted navy blue, his gold stripes boasting his rank, his broken nose (a football injury) lending him a warrior's mystique, and his air of haughty detachment hinting at secrets untold. At least that part was true now that the great invasion was being actively planned, but he felt very much on the fringe of things.

Lemming was frustrated. He was all too aware that his dashing reputation had been earned without captaining a submarine, piloting a Spitfire, or even carrying out one of his own commando missions. Hence, he felt, his need to win battles with women, to raid their defences and come away with their vital secrets, or at the very least a mental map of their vital statistics.

Many of these women were married, and though a wedding ring had never been a real obstacle in Lemming's circles (he had once had an affair with a baron's wife whose regular lover was a lord), it did add a tinge of guilt to some of his victories.

That was what had annoyed him about Margaux last night. She was unmarried, a mere warrant officer in the WAAF, but she had refused his generous offer to taxi her to his bed.

He had argued forcefully in favour of a night, or at least a late evening, of shared physical pleasures: 'What if there's an air raid tomorrow, and we both get blown to smithereens? In that last instant, wouldn't you regret missing the opportunity to live life to the full tonight?'

'That's a very persuasive argument,' Margaux had replied coquettishly, 'but on the other hand, abstinence tonight would mean that our maker would have one less sin to forgive tomorrow.'

'If He's going to forgive us anyway, where's the objection?'

'So you admit it would be a sin?' she had asked, with an infuriatingly provocative smile.

'We're at war, the lines between sinner and saint are being redrawn every minute,' Lemming had replied with what he hoped would sound like the authority of a blooded soldier.

But she refused to relent, which had the predictable, but no less annoying, consequence of making him want to see her again as soon as possible. Damn the woman and her steely self-control.

The phone rang shrilly by Lemming's right hand. Shaking his head to clear his mind of extraneous thoughts, he answered.

'Lemming.'

'Good morning, commander.' A female voice. 'Would you come and join the rear admiral in the third-floor conference room? Immediately, please.'

Orders were usually polite in this building. Those given to Lemming, anyway.

'I'm on my way.'

Oh well, he thought, it might just be something urgent enough to take his mind off Margaux.

III

Except that there she was, sitting in the conference room, staring straight at him. He saw the flicker of an amused eyebrow, and quickly stifled his gasp of surprise, giving her a small nod before closing the door behind him.

'Ah, Lemming.' Rear Admiral Rashbrooke was sitting at the head of a long wooden table. He gestured towards the chairs arranged along either side of it. The two seats immediately to the left of the rear admiral were occupied by an Air Force group captain and an Army major. Opposite these two officers, facing the door, sat Margaux.

'Good morning, sir,' Lemming said. 'Gentlemen. Warrant Officer Lynd.'

The rear admiral glanced at Margaux, then at Lemming's face. He gave a minute shrug, as if resigned to the fact that half of the women in London were personal acquaintances of his well-groomed assistant.

'Take a seat, Lemming.'

Lemming went to sit next to Margaux, remembering with a jolt of regret that his old boss Admiral Geoffrey had often called him Ian. They had been a team.

'Major Maclean has just joined 00 Commando,' Rashbrooke said, nodding towards the young army officer who had a face prematurely aged by a high forehead. He wore the crossed-knife badge of the commandos but looked as though he might have been a history teacher in civilian life. Maclean smiled easily. He held a pipe in his fist, and Lemming thought he detected Turkish tobacco, his favourite. The man must have a private supplier, he thought. Unless he had been to Turkey in person recently.

'And Group Captain Basil.' Here was another man who had seen action. A slight facial tic hinted at terrors barely survived. Basil had a thin, studious face that seemed accustomed to analysing everything around him at top speed. He looked Lemming straight in the eyes as he acknowledged him.

'Warrant Officer Lynd you seem to have met already,' Rashbrooke said.

'Yes, sir,' Lemming answered.

'Have you read the file you found on your desk this morning?'

'No, sir. I didn't realize it was that urgent.'

'Everything is urgent,' Rashbrooke said, unnecessarily in Lemming's opinion.

'I've been working on a new idea, sir, that I'd like to discuss with you after this meeting, if you have time.' He regretted saying it instantly. It felt like an excuse. Lemming hated excuses.

'Yes, yes, we'll see. Now, please run us through the basics of the mission, major. For those who have not yet had time to read them.'

Lemming tried to exchange a knowing glance with Margaux about the rear admiral's obvious pettiness, but she was already looking towards the major.

Maclean began to speak, and Lemming found himself concentrating in equal measure on the outline of the mission, and that of Margaux's profile. She was leaning forward attentively. Lemming admired her long, straight nose, her slightly parted lips – was that really a touch of lipstick? – and the cut of her tunic. She was listening impassively, as if she had attended many such meetings before. He began to wonder how that could be, for a woman in her mid-twenties at the most, a humble warrant officer in the WAAF.

'Operation Grab is a fairly standard night op,' the major was saying. 'Six men and myself, landed from a submarine, will paddle ashore east of Dieppe.'

'Dieppe.' Lemming was unable to prevent himself repeating the name. He swore silently. He was sure it was the woman's fault, distracting him.

'Yes, Dieppe,' Rashbrooke said. 'This is where you come in, Lemming. Some of 00 Commando made it ashore in '42 and got back in one piece. We want all the reports you have.'

Lemming knew that the rear admiral had been misinformed. In fact, back in August 1942, 00 Commando's landing craft had been hit by a shell a few yards off the beach, and the only survivors from the unit had been the men who swam back out to sea. No enemy intelligence had been retrieved from Dieppe. Lemming did not want to reveal all this now, however, and show up his boss's ignorance.

'Very good, sir,' was all he said.

'We'll be tackling part of the Nazis' Atlantic Wall,' Major Maclean went on. 'Impressive chain of gun emplacements and bunkers. But it has its weaknesses. East of Dieppe the cliff is soft, and there's a spot where it's collapsed, giving us a lesser slope to climb. Or so we think, judging by the latest reconnaissance.' The major waved his pipe meaningfully towards Lemming, the intelligence man. 'At least one of their lookout posts is teetering on the edge of the cliff, and doesn't seem to be used any more, for the moment at least. So this is our chance. The men will land and enter an artillery command post nearby, where, according to our information, they will find documents related to planned reinforcements and the location of ammunition dumps in the area. Maps and code books too, of course. Meanwhile, Warrant Officer Lynd will link up with the local Resistance.'

Lemming could not stop himself staring at Margaux for a moment. So that was it? She was going undercover? He felt suddenly ashamed. He had underestimated her. He had assumed she was an earl's daughter, doing war work to prove that the aristocracy did its bit. But she was a woman of action. Perhaps it wasn't even her first mission. Those trips to Paris she had mentioned – they might have been undercover outings into enemy territory. And the previous evening he had hardly asked her about herself. He had been too content to chatter self-mockingly about his own history. Had she been pumping him for information? If so, she had done a masterly job. Now he definitely wanted another dinner. If there was time.

'When is all this to happen?' Lemming asked the room in general.

'You leave from the Sussex coast in about 36 hours,' Rashbrooke said.

Again, Lemming brought all his self-control to bear. 'We?' he wanted to ask. But surely he would not be going ashore? Not that he was afraid, of course. Just under-prepared. He hadn't paddled anything more than a Serpentine rowing boat since his basic training. And he certainly wasn't cut out to sneak up on sentries and slit their throats. There would probably be no smoking during a night raid, either. It was unthinkable.

'You will accompany the mission until the commandos leave the sub,' Rashbrooke told him. 'Give them the latest reconnaissance info. Run through the types of document they need to look for, common hiding places, that sort of thing. They have prepared for the mission, naturally, but they'll need to be kept occupied during the crossing. They might be cooped up below the surface for more than 24 hours if the first attempt at a sortie has to be called off for any reason. We don't want them to go stir-crazy.'

Lemming thought that he might well be tempted to lead the commandos in a stir-crazy choir of claustrophobic howling, but he dared not say so.

'You're looking perturbed, Lemming,' Rashbrooke said. 'I know you haven't been on any active missions recently.'

Everyone was staring at Lemming, so he squared his jaw and said, 'Looking forward to it, sir. It will be good to get out of the office and do my bit.' But he felt the need to explain any discomfort he might be exuding. 'One thing is bothering me, sir,' he added.

'Yes?'

'The name, Operation Grab. If I may say so, it doesn't feel right.'

'Doesn't *feel* right?' Rashbrooke frowned in disbelief, but Lemming had stuck his neck out and did not want to retreat.

'No, sir. It sounds like "crab". Or "drab". It could be misunderstood.'

'Misunderstood by whom exactly? Do you think we'll be broadcasting about it on the wireless?'

Margaux was now watching Lemming intently. Perhaps, he thought, she wanted to see whether he would back down.

'Grab sounds clumsy, sir,' he went on. 'Almost unplanned. Common thieves grab. Might I suggest something more positive, like ...' He said the first thing that came into his head. 'Forget-me-not.'

For some reason he found himself looking at Margaux when he said it, which was embarrassing.

Rashbrooke almost guffawed. 'You want to change the name of the mission to a *flower*?'

'I hope this isn't because there is a lady present,' Margaux said, with enough irony to wither any blooms within a mile.

'No, no, of course not,' Lemming stuttered, his brain working fast. 'I think it would send a positive message to the men. It suggests that the sub will be waiting for them when they return. Good for morale.'

'It's much too late to change the name of the mission now,' Rashbrooke objected.

'If I may interject, sir,' Maclean said, 'Commander Lemming has a point. Dieppe has unfortunate associations. We need to show the men that we're not sending them on a repeat show of that mess-up. Every little counts when it comes to morale.'

'Yes,' Margaux said. 'And the name will sound like a homage to the men who were lost on the '42 mission. They haven't been forgotten.'

Rashbrooke considered this.

'Very well, then, if everyone agrees,' he said. There were nods around the table. 'Operation Forget-Me-Not it is. I'm just thankful you didn't suggest Operation Pansy.'

Rashbrooke picked up a pencil and wrote the new name on the cover of his file.

'The Air Force, meanwhile ...' he said, handing over to Group Captain Basil.

'We shall do a bit of discreet patrolling overhead,' Basil said, making it all sound very casual, 'but our main contribution will be a diversionary night raid on one of the other harbours in the vicinity.' His jaw clenched involuntarily, no doubt at the memory

24

of previous raids back in the days when the Luftwaffe had dominated the skies. 'Can't tell you which one yet, but it won't be Dieppe. And if required, we will also be on call to provide air cover when our chaps withdraw. And our lady, of course.' The three men nodded gallantly towards the only woman in the room.

In reply, she shook her head.

'I shan't be withdrawing. I shall be staying on,' she said.

'Of course, of course.' The group captain looked uncharacteristically flustered. He was probably not used to having women in on the planning stages of missions. To be fair, Lemming thought, nobody was – except when they were there to take minutes.

'Warrant Officer Lynd will be using the raid as cover,' Rashbrooke said. 'Is it all right to reveal the bare bones of your mission, warrant officer?'

Margaux nodded. 'Although I'd prefer it if the other men were kept in the dark about what I'm going to tell you,' she said. 'If one of them is captured and tortured ...'

'Yes, yes, total secrecy, gentlemen,' Rashbrooke agreed.

'To put it succinctly,' Margaux went on, 'there's a problem with the local Resistance. Either they have a double agent or the Gestapo is making somebody sing. Things have gone ominously quiet there. I'm going into Dieppe to do some snooping.'

'It's a highly perilous job,' Rashbrooke said.

Lemming saw Margaux shake her head again, as if she resented the special consideration she was getting.

'All our jobs are dangerous, sir,' she said, 'mine no more or less than anyone else's here.'

'You're right, I simply meant ...' Rashbrooke trailed off helplessly, and Lemming permitted himself the slightest smile. This girl didn't let herself get pushed around. He promised himself that he would ask her on another dinner date, for that same evening if possible. Now that there was a chance they were going to die within hours, surely she would agree that there was all the more reason to indulge in some forgivable sin?

The meeting got down to detailed planning, which bored Lemming. He enjoyed the creative side of a mission – the concept, the target, the methods and equipment to be used, and yes, the name – but he despised the minutiae. At exactly what minute something would happen, what to do if something went amiss. He was more of a lone gambler, weighing his own odds, throwing everything he had at an opportunity, accepting the personal loss if his gambit failed. He was no longer a team player. Since he had given up school sports, the biggest team he was actively involved in was a bridge pair. And even then he got bored when his partner was bidding.

He forced himself to listen carefully, though, as Maclean and Basil explained with matter-of-fact coolness how they intended to proceed. To hear them, you would have thought that the whole of Nazi Germany was no more than an irritating farmer who wanted to stop them scrumping his apples.

Rashbrooke gave his approval, promising them 'all the extra information at our disposal. You'll have it by ...' He looked at Lemming. 'Two this afternoon?'

'Two, certainly, sir,' Lemming confirmed. 'And I can answer any further questions when we're on the submarine. We have some excellent land maps of that whole coastline,' he added as an afterthought. 'In case Warrant Officer Lynd would like to consult them ...'

'Thanks awfully, commander,' she said. 'But you know, I've been studying the area intensely for the past week. I could probably recite the menu of every surviving restaurant within ten square kilometres of our landing point – from memory.'

So she *had* been pretending that she couldn't speak French at dinner. She must have been making fun of him all evening.

Lemming felt a sudden craving for yet another cigarette, and a whisky.

IV

After the meeting, Lemming stayed with Rear Admiral Rashbrooke for a debriefing. Both of them stood up to stretch their muscles. Rashbrooke permitted himself a discreet yawn. Fresh fruit and real coffee weren't the only commodities in short supply in London. For a man with the rear admiral's responsibilities, a full night's sleep was as rare as a banana.

'Bit of a bad show, not reading the file,' Rashbrooke said, stuffing his pipe.

'Sorry, sir. Perhaps there should be a priority system for intelligence files? Most urgent and all that. Colour coding, maybe, according to status.'

'Yes, yes, yes. What did you think of it all?'

'Sounds very watertight, sir, if that's not a bad pun.'

'And I take you know Miss Lynd?' Rashbrooke asked, holding a burning match in place and sucking on his pipe between words.

'Yes, sir. Funny thing, now that I think of it. A couple of days ago I ran into her not far from here. She was struggling to open an umbrella, so I stopped to help her.'

'Yes, yes, all very Sir Lancelot –'

'What I mean is, sir, bit of a coincidence, don't you think? I meet her by accident, we go to dinner, then she turns up here. Do you think she already knew I would be involved in the mission?'

'Well ...' Rashbrooke considered the question while he inspected the state of his pipe.

'And that's another thing, sir. I'm almost certain it was her suggestion that we go to a French restaurant in Mayfair. But during dinner she implied that it was *my* idea. Excellent food and wine, and they have a fine cellar, but it's a suspect kind of place. They had a '39 Taittinger Blanc de Blancs brut.'

Rashbrooke was clearly not worldly enough to see the significance of the vintage. He squinted at Lemming through a

27

thickening cloud of pipe smoke. Definitely not Turkish tobacco, Lemming decided. More like Welsh seaweed.

'And the waiters were military-aged Frenchmen,' Lemming went on. 'Very bizarre.'

'Bizarre ...' Rashbrooke seemed to be musing on the foreignness of the word. Lemming guessed that, when the rear admiral wasn't captaining aircraft carriers, he preferred to stay within British territorial waters.

'I mean, it's as if the waiters were undercover, sir,' Lemming said.

'Oh, I think they are.' Now Rashbrooke was smiling. 'It was Le Rose de Picardy, am I right?'

'Yes, sir, La Rose de Picardie.' Lemming could not stop himself correcting the rear admiral's French grammar and pronunciation.

'We know all about that place. Most of the waiters are De Gaulle's men. Not spies exactly, but informers. The *général* ' (Rashbrooke attempted a French pronunciation again, and failed as miserably as before, beginning the word with a very English 'jay') 'feels left out, and the Rose is one of the London locales where he's trying to pick up gossip. Oh yes, we know all about that place. Apparently its nickname is "Le Fleur du Mall". Some sort of French pun, I'm told.'

Lemming was so offended at being left in the dark that he did not enjoy the joke[2], or even correct the rear admiral's mistaken gender. *Fleur* was feminine; it should have been *la Fleur*.

'But surely I should have been told about the place, sir?' he asked.

'It was probably in a memo you didn't read, Lemming. And I trust you implicitly. No danger that a man like you would ever reveal anything sensitive in public. I have our people lunch and dine there regularly, staging fake conversations, spreading false rumours. Any truths those waiters might overhear will be

---

[2] The nickname is a pun on the title of the poetry collection by Charles Baudelaire, *Les Fleurs du Mal* – usually translated as *The Flowers of Evil*.

submerged in nonsense. By now, De Gaulle probably thinks we'll be invading France through Belgium, Italy and even Sweden. He'll be convinced we're using hot-air balloons, a cross-channel railway bridge and trained elephants. He'll be expecting an army of fighting bulls crossing the Pyrenees.'

Lemming had to laugh. It was exactly the kind of ploy he would have come up with. Perhaps, he thought, he'd even suggested it, in one of his memos.

He, like the whole of the British intelligence community, knew that De Gaulle and his men were not to be trusted – ever since September 1940, when De Gaulle had revealed an upcoming raid on Dakar by going to a London outfitter's and ordering a safari suit, explaining to the tailors exactly why he needed it. Surprise, surprise, when the British and Free French attacked Dakar, its defences had been reinforced. And now, with the big invasion of Europe brewing for some time in 1944, it was even more vital to keep all secrets from De Gaulle.

'But what do you think, sir? Could Lynd be a crypto-Gaullist?'

Rashbrooke pulled his pipe out of his mouth.

'First time anyone has implied that. She's been very successful so far. Highly spoken of. Disciple of that Polish woman agent, you know, Christina something.'

'Krystyna Skarbek,' Lemming said. The name was well known in intelligence circles. This was a woman who spoke fluent English and French as well as her native Polish, and who had seen action right across Europe since the very start of the war.

'No questioning Skarbek's loyalty,' the rear admiral said. 'But I suppose you might be right about Lynd,' Rashbrooke said. 'It's a risk. Can't have her wading through our Resistance contacts and giving all the names to De Gaulle. He'd be sending them dinner invitations within the week. I'll have somebody double-check Lynd's record and her known contacts. Meanwhile, Lemming, you'd better stick close to her until it's time to leave for Sussex. All night, if necessary. You're good at that sort of thing, so I hear.'

'Very good, sir,' Lemming said. He blushed. 'What I mean is, yes, sir, very well, understood.'

'You won't let her know that it's because we doubt her in any way, will you? Try to convince her it's all about security. Or sex.'

'If you say so, sir.'

The war seemed to be taking a turn for the better.

V

Margaux was still in the building. Lemming found her sitting at a desk with a Wren, a chief officer called Sylvia Trench, who had spent most of 1942 and 1943 as Lemming's secretary.

Both women were surprised to see him.

'Ian?' Sylvia said.

'Commander Lemming?' Margaux added.

'The rear admiral has asked me to sit in,' Lemming explained. He looked around in vain for a chair. 'Or stand in, anyway.'

The office was an airless windowed cubicle in the heart of the Admiralty, one of a dozen in this corridor. The decor, lit by a bare electric bulb that hung on the end of a frayed cable, was wall-to-wall filing cabinets. Sylvia Trench was now a communications officer, keeping records of contacts with agents abroad. No one without sufficient clearance was even permitted within the corridor, which was guarded by a sentry at all times.

Lemming leaned against a filing cabinet and listened as the two women ran through some details of Margaux's planned attempt to rendez-vous with a French agent who had, until very recently, been a radio operator. Now that owning a radio transmitter in occupied France carried the death sentence, as did simply listening to the BBC, the lives of these people had become all the more precarious.

30

'If you see no activity after dawn,' Sylvia said, 'assume the worst. Her husband was killed in '40. She's always up early. If the house looks unoccupied, you'll have to judge whether it's safe to break in and look around. And if there are any Jerries about, watch out. There are no soldiers billeted in the house. We've had no intelligence from the area for more than a week now. One of our signals was acknowledged, but without the safety signal. It looks bad.'

Margaux nodded silently as Sylvia continued the briefing.

Even just listening, Lemming could feel the hairs on the back of his neck tingle and rise. It all felt very real, very threatening. Exciting, certainly, but deadly, too. A quiet stroll along a Normandy road could get Margaux shot. In a matter of hours, the young woman he had dined with, propositioned, warmly but frustratingly kissed, could be bleeding out on the floor of a French café, or screaming for mercy in a disused farmhouse as her neatly trimmed fingernails were ripped out. It was all a very long way from London, from civilized life.

Almost none of the women he knew had ever been in action. Only some of the nurses had seen the real effects of battle. Everyone had been on the receiving end of air raids, of course, but that was different. Margaux was about to go deep into the fighting, unarmed and behind enemy lines. He felt guilty for having doubted her true motivation. Even if she was working for De Gaulle, she was on the right side. It was just that she might be, from a British viewpoint at least, on the wrong side of the right side.

On the other hand, she could pose an unwitting danger to other agents – to the whole war effort – if she revealed too much to le général. It was tragic to doubt your allies, but this seemed to be the way the war was developing. It had always seemed only natural to doubt Stalin, but now De Gaulle, the man who had been protected for four years by the British, was suspected of putting himself and his political future above all else.

'Anything to add, Ian?'

Lemming realized he had stopped paying attention.

Sylvia was looking at him indulgently, as if she knew his dreamy ways. Margaux seemed less patient.

'Nothing,' he answered.

'Well then, thanks awfully, Chief Officer Trench. I'd better be going,' Margaux said, and stood up.

'I'm coming with you,' Lemming told her.

Both women looked as surprised as when he had first walked in.

'Why?' Margaux asked bluntly.

'Rear Admiral Rashbrooke has ordered me to protect you.'

Sylvia suppressed a laugh at this Aesopian irony. It was the wolf and the lamb all over again.

'I don't need protection,' Margaux said.

'Orders are orders.'

'Do you mind if we get verbal confirmation? I wouldn't want to be the victim of faulty intelligence.' Margaux reached for Sylvia's phone and handed the receiver to Lemming.

'Lemming here, get me the rear admiral. It's urgent,' he told the operator.

As the line clicked and hissed, he fully expected Margaux to give in and tell him to hang up. He had called her bluff. But she stood silently, waiting for the call to go through.

'What is it, Lemming?' Rashbrooke did not sound pleased to be disturbed.

'Sorry, sir, I have Warrant Officer Lynd here. She doesn't seem to believe that I've been assigned to ensure her safety before the mission.'

'Put her on.'

He gave her the phone.

'I'm very sorry to disturb you, rear admiral,' Margaux said, sounding not at all apologetic, 'but I would like your personal confirmation that Commander Lemming has been ordered to ... *protect* me.' During her meaningful pause, she stared sceptically into Lemming's eyes.

Lemming didn't hear the reply, but he watched Margaux's growing irritation as she listened.

'Yes, sir, very good sir,' she said, and hung up. 'You win,' she told Lemming, and pushed past him out the door.

'Tally ho,' Sylvia laughed as he followed.

VI

Trafalgar Square was jammed with buses and lorries. The air stank of their exhaust. The occasional motorbike swerved and grumbled between larger, gridlocked vehicles. From the top of his column, Admiral Nelson looked calmly down on the congestion. For the whole war, just as he had done during his career, Nelson had stood tall during the heaviest bombardments. His unthinking bravery had cost him an eye in Corsica, an arm in Tenerife and his life at Trafalgar, but so far the Nazi bombers had never managed to touch him. Rumour even had it that the Nazis wanted to leave Nelson intact so they could take him to Berlin if they won the war.

More than 150 feet below the admiral's lookout post, Margaux was striding through the crowds of men on leave or on duty, their shoulder-slung gas mask cases the only common feature in the tapestry of different uniforms.

As Margaux progressed, she attracted admiring remarks in almost every accent and language in the allied canon. A pair of Scots Guards, some Czech airmen, a gang of very young GIs, what sounded like Scandinavian sailors – they all wanted to stop and chat with this determined beauty. Even a trio of scruffy boys in tattered hand-me-downs looked up from the drawing of Churchill that an old man was chalking on the pavement, and whistled delightedly.

Margaux ignored them all. Like the other women pedestrians, both civilian and uniformed, she remained resolutely eyes front, a vital technique in these male-deluged streets.

'You might as well tell me where we're going,' Lemming said, relishing his brisk walk in the April breeze. He was keeping pace at her right shoulder.

She stopped suddenly, and he collided with her, instinctively gripping her arm in case she fell. She shook herself loose. He saw a flash of anger in her eyes before she regained control. Lemming had to grin. It was very rare that a beautiful, angry woman was forced to remain in his presence for so long.

'If you must know,' she said, lowering her voice because she was attracting the attention of half a dozen men, 'I'm going to Soho. An area you probably know quite well.' Soho was infamous for loose morals of all inclinations.

'As a matter of fact, I don't really know it at all,' Lemming replied, unruffled. 'Cheap sleaze has never attracted me. I'm rather surprised that *you* would find it interesting.'

'I don't. But I am going there because I have to collect ...' She paused, checked that no one was listening, and said in a low voice, 'some intimate, foreign-made garments. Second-hand clothes are not what I usually wear, but I shall be needing them over the next few days.' She spoke the last few words through gritted teeth, clearly furious at this man's intrusion into her planning.

'Ah, I see,' Lemming said, feeling slightly guilty.

'I'm so glad you understand at last,' she replied. 'And if you are *really* determined to attract the attention of everyone in London, why don't you dress up as a Royal Navy intelligence officer and march into an intimate, foreign-made ladies' garment shop?'

'Hmm.' She had a point.

'Of course, there are places in Soho where it would not be at all unusual for a man to be seen, even a smart officer like yourself. They cater for all tastes. Even yours.'

Again, something made him enjoy the sting of her anger. But now he had begun to think fast.

'Come with me,' he said. Before she could object, he grasped her by the elbow and marched her past the National Portrait Gallery and over Charing Cross Road. They entered a gents' outfitters, its window space divided equally between uniforms and civilian suits. Barely three minutes later, they emerged, Lemming's uniform now hidden beneath a long, pale-grey raincoat. On his head, an anonymous trilby. He carried his uniform cap wrapped in a newspaper parcel under his arm. He was feeling foolishly proud of himself, as though the mission had already begun.

'Better, I suppose,' Margaux said. 'Now you look like a South African diamond merchant, here to supply Hatton Garden with cheap engagement rings.'

She leapt between two buses and crossed Charing Cross Road again, on her way to Soho.

Margaux told him to wait for her in a basement club. She would come and fetch him there in twenty minutes. But Lemming opted not to go in. For a start, he was not at all sure he could trust her to turn up, and anyway, it was barely credible that a lone WAAF would come looking for a man in a club called Adam and Eve's. The entrance was protected by a rampart of sandbags, which hid most of a picture gallery of burlesque photographs, but the lamp over the entrance, with a red heart etched into each of its four sides, gave the game away.

Even from street level, the club downstairs reeked of cheap, stale cigarettes and ancient beer. Lemming loitered outside by the sandbags and smoked, filling his nostrils with sweet Turkish incense.

'You goin' in, chum?' An infantry corporal, his forage cap askew on his forehead, wanted to get past. He had another ordinary soldier with him.

'I'm not your —' Lemming was about to object to their lack of respect for an officer. 'No, sorry, you chaps go in,' he said, getting out of their way.

'You don't know what you're missin', mate,' the corporal said. The men ducked past the sandbags and went down the steps.

It was now fifteen minutes since Margaux had left Dean Street and gone around the corner into Saint Anne's Court, an alleyway of workshops where, supposedly, a French seamstress had prepared a small selection of underwear. Nothing too racy, Margaux had explained, just an ordinary silk selection that a middle-class woman could be wearing in Normandy. Silk might seem excessively chic, she said, but in wartime London, lesser stuff was hard to come by – if you insisted on genuine French merchandise.

Lemming reasoned that if any Nazis or Vichy militiamen started questioning the quality of Margaux's underwear once she was in France, the game was probably up anyway.

Now he was getting impatient. He was on his third or fourth cigarette. He had long got fed up of the men eyeing him as they walked by, probably wondering whether he was police, pimp or black marketeer. The women passers-by, meanwhile, either noted his presence and looked away – these were the ladies on an innocent shortcut to or from Oxford Street – or lingered, waiting for a proposition.

He ground out his latest cigarette butt beneath his shoe. Where was the dratted girl? Had she given him the slip? Surely not. She knew that he had the authority to stop her getting on that submarine.

He felt that he had been an incompetent watchdog. Tailing someone was more of a science than he had imagined. When he had the time, he would write a manual on the subject: discreet observation, with techniques to ensure that one never lost contact with one's subject, even when he or she was out of sight. A vital skill in the intelligence services.

Almost twenty minutes now. Perhaps she had telephoned someone from the seamstress's workshop and organized a brief rendez-vous there. A Gaullist part-time waiter, maybe. He cursed himself for not keeping the whole of Saint Anne's Court in view. An amateurish mistake.

'Lookin' for business, sonny?' A cracked female voice whispered in his ear.

'No. Now will you –' Lemming turned to find Margaux grinning at him. She held up a cushion-sized brown-paper parcel, neatly tied with string.

'You're very easy to sneak up on, you know,' she said, as she turned and walked away towards Shaftesbury Avenue.

'Where are you going now?' he asked, catching up.

'You'll see.'

VII

'You probably don't think women like me do much in wartime apart from make tea, type, bandage wounds and relieve their soldier boyfriends' tensions –'

'I've never thought any such thing,' Lemming said, reminding himself that Englishwomen exactly like Margaux also did sterling work operating radar, sending messages, no doubt cracking codes. He had even heard of one young Englishwoman who flew fighters, piloting them from the factory to the airfields. But as far as he knew, there was no real British equivalent of the brigades of female Soviet soldiers, or Polish and Czech partisans. Murderous ladies, by all accounts.

'Admit it, Ian, you've never thought that an Englishwoman as young as I am, with an accent like mine, might do anything violent.'

Lemming looked at her, admiring again her perfect skin, generous lips and teasing eyes. She really was what people called an English rose. Or a Picardy one, perhaps.

'Touché,' he finally admitted.

'At last, an honest officer in London,' Margaux laughed.

They were sitting at the corner table in a tea room in Shaftesbury Avenue, huddled together in subdued conversation. There were empty tables all around them, but you could never be sure. The other customers were four middle-aged women, a few young couples – men in uniform, girls in civilian clothes – and a family group consisting of an Air Force officer, his wife and two pre-adolescent daughters, their conversation stilted, probably afraid to discuss the man's uncertain future.

'You have to believe that I am genuinely good at what I do,' Margaux said, lowering her voice even further.

Lemming still wondered if she was skilled enough to have made some kind of contact in Saint Anne's Court.

'Does that include being good at entrapping male officers by means of stubborn umbrellas?' Lemming asked, watching her closely for any hesitation.

'I was wondering the same about you,' she said. 'This morning, when I was told that you would be joining the meeting, I was sure you'd picked me up deliberately that day. A sort of male honey trap. What would you call that? A chap trap?'

Lemming had to admit it was a good answer. Either it was true, or it was well thought out.

'But when I saw you come in the room,' she went on, 'I was almost sure that was genuine surprise on your face. And now I'm convinced of it. You're very easy to read, you know. You're a book waiting to be written. A manual for women on how to fend off predatory men.'

She took a reluctant bite of her sandwich. They had ordered a round of ham, and both had regretted it with the first mouthful. Lemming had managed to wangle some mustard, but now he was resigned to filling his stomach and nothing more, as so often in this war.

He chewed mechanically, wondering whether to ask Margaux about the French restaurant, but quickly deciding against it. To ask would give away his suspicions about her loyalty. The pick-up with the umbrella was an inevitable question, he thought, but the choice of restaurant would be too much.

'I imagine you have to fight off a lot of predators,' he said. 'For instance, you said you were in Paris? That must have been hell for a young woman like you.'

'You're right. By the time I got home, I knew how my brother had felt when he was caned at Harrow. Black and blue.'

Lemming raised his eyebrows. When a young woman started talking buttocks, anything could happen. But he kept his mind on the job.

'Was this in wartime? Your visit to Paris, I mean.'

Margaux looked around the tea room, and knitted her brow.

'You don't expect me to answer that, do you?' she said, any warmth now gone from her voice.

'Sorry.' Lemming cursed himself. Everything about this field agent business was much harder than he had imagined. 'Tell me about your brother,' he said. Girls usually liked to talk about their brothers.

'I prefer not to talk about him,' she said.

He gave up on the sandwich and lit a cigarette, his main form of nourishment. He began to sift through potentially safe topics of conversation. Pickings were slim.

'All right,' he said. 'Tell me why you pretended you needed help with that French menu.'

Margaux thought about this, her sandwich held in mid-air. She put it down and pushed the plate away.

'I assumed you would like it,' she said.

'Do you always do what you assume men would like?'

'Only if it amuses me.' She finished her cup of what had libellously been called coffee. 'Let's go,' she said.

'Where?'

'Are you going to pay or shall I?' was all she answered.

Lemming was suddenly angry with himself for being so passive. This girl – woman – was giving him the run-around. It was as if she held all the trumps and was forcing him to play out every losing hand.

'Where are we going?' he demanded.

'Back to the office, of course. We both have preparations to make and people to see. Have you already forgotten the information the major asked for? About your unit's trip in '42?'

Lemming ground his teeth and threw some change on to the table. Sometime very soon he was going to make her pay for this insolence, this disrespect for his rank. No, not for his rank, for his manliness. Yes, that was it. She was what a New Yorker had once described to him as a 'ball-buster'. Well, he told himself, no woman had yet succeeded in busting his, but she was getting close. The effrontery of the woman, pushing him to the edge in this way –

Suddenly his anger evaporated as quickly as it had arisen. Yes, that was it. Margaux, in Latin: *margo*, the edge. To which she was pushing him. Or *margo*, the border. Over which she was planning to go, into France. It all fitted. Third declension. *Margo, margo, marginem, marginis, margini, margine.*

He congratulated himself on this classical joke, while pulling open the package that contained his cap. He was going to go back to the Admiralty in full uniform. He had had enough of skulking about.

As he stood up, taking off his trilby and raincoat, he saw Margaux staring at him. And not with any kind of admiration at the fine military figure before her.

'You're changing your identity *again*, in full public view?' she said, in a low but firm voice. 'Why not just wave a flag and announce to everyone that you're doing something terribly secret?'

Lemming stood there in shock. She was right. He had forgotten already. Thank heavens I'm not going ashore, he thought. I'd have the Nazis on my back in minutes.

'Why weren't you ordered to stick closer to the major or the group captain,' Margaux asked. 'Why did it have to be me?'

'Self-sacrifice,' he said. 'Anything for the war effort, you know.'

She shook her head and made for the exit.

VIII

They were on the train to Brighton. Dawn had broken softly, the morning was almost warm, and the window of their first-class compartment was open. Lemming was sitting beside it, smoking, but he would have bet half a crown that there was exactly as much smoke coming in as going out. The train was still speeding up as it cut through the bomb-ravaged suburbs south of the Thames, and the locomotive was working hard. There was the occasional jolt whenever a burst of steam drove life into the engine's straining pistons, and with each new thrust, a dense cloud of smoky vapour billowed along the length of the train.

Lemming and Margaux were both in uniform. Lemming had left their suitcases by the door to discourage anyone from joining them in the compartment. They might have been lovers on their way to a seaside hotel.

Rather distant lovers, though, any observer would have decided. Margaux sat in the middle of the compartment, not quite opposite Lemming. Her top half was hidden behind an open newspaper. He read the headlines. If they were to be believed, the Russians were making progress in Crimea and Romania. German U-boats seemed to be sinking like stones. In the light of where he was due to spend the next 36 hours or so, he hoped it was not true of submarines in general.

'Charlie Chaplin has been acquitted,' Margaux said, her first words since Victoria.

'Not for making Modern Times, I hope. Awful tripe.'

Margaux ignored his joke.

'He was accused of taking that actress across state boundaries to have his way with her.'

'Seems rather a lot of effort to go to.'

'Poor girl is pregnant. She's thirty years younger than he is. I mean, I don't think he should be put in prison for getting someone pregnant, but it's a sordid affair.'

Lemming did not comment. He felt the jibe about age differences, even though he was only ten years older than Margaux. Well, twelve to be exact. He had now had time to read her file.

It had revealed little out of the ordinary. Education: minor girls' public school, then finishing school in Belgium, hence the fluent French. Father: a stockbroker now working for the RAF in Scotland. Mother: a mother, still at home in Hampshire. One brother, Patrick, two years younger than Margaux, who had been serving as a navigator in a Mosquito night fighter when he went missing over France – in March, less than a month ago. That was probably why she didn't want to talk about him. The unbearable anxiety of not knowing whether he was dead or alive. It was the fate of so many sisters. Brothers, too. Lemming's own youngest brother, Mark, had been wounded and taken prisoner at Dunkirk. He had subsequently died of his wounds. The grief was horribly painful, but at least the doubt was over. Margaux was still suffering the torment of uncertainty, and it was admirable, Lemming thought, that she was going ahead with her mission.

Accordingly, he had slipped a note to a colleague asking if there was any news of a Patrick Lynd. The reply was that the lad seemed to have been sent to a Stalag somewhere in Germany. Lemming passed on the news to Margaux, who simply thanked him, and made no more comment. He understood: Stalags were not necessarily good news, and not the kind of subject anyone wanted to banter about.

Of Margaux's service record, her file had only good things to say. She had joined the WAAF in 1940 as a radar operator and plotter – one of the women who tracked the progress of allied and enemy planes during operations. A year later, she had been 'recruited'. The file did not specify who had recruited her, but Lemming knew that it was the SOE, the Special Operations Executive. This was Churchill's espionage outfit that Lemming knew pretty well, largely because his brother Philip was a member. Of course, as far as individual operations were concerned, his knowledge was very shady. That was the SOE's strength, staying in the shade.

According to her record, Margaux had been involved in operations called Housekeeper, Seamless and Sophie. Naturally, there were no details about what each mission had entailed. They all sounded very feminine, he thought, so Forget-Me-Not was quite in keeping for her. Though Lemming knew that a name meant nothing – that was the point. An operation with a prim name like Housekeeper might mean something violently untidy like blowing up a destroyer and all its crew.

He and Margaux had spent most of the previous day at the Admiralty, each making their final preparations. Lemming had commandeered an office where they could be alone. Margaux had set to work, her desk facing his. She had scrutinized documents almost the whole time, and not once tried to contact anyone outside the building. She had written two letters, but did not object to their being sent to the censor. When Lemming made discreet inquiries about the contents, he was told that she was passing on chatty news to her parents, the kind of girlish stuff that any London-based WAAF would write: shows and films she had seen, a chance meeting with an old school friend, reassurances about the depth of London's air-raid shelters.

He wrote up a brief report for the rear admiral about Margaux's trip to Soho. He confessed that he had been unable to ensure that Margaux had not communicated with anyone except the seamstress, and suggested that the woman's workshop should be put under observation. Anyone dealing in French silk underwear was bound to come into contact with French officers, he wrote, even if De Gaulle himself was famed for his lack of interest in sex.

The locomotive wheezed and whistled. It was stopping. Lemming idly examined the small red-brick station building, with its faded posters advising people to grow carrots and carry gasmasks, and the stark rectangles on the walls where the station's name-boards used to be. He watched a few travellers, mainly uniformed men, get on the train, and he turned towards the compartment door, hoping to discourage anyone from venturing in. A woman in a bright green hat and overcoat came along the corridor and reached up to slide the door open, but caught his eye and recoiled. He laughed as she walked further along the carriage.

It was his first moment of merriment since the previous night, one of the most bizarre evenings he had ever spent in female company. A cross between school detention and a visit to an aged aunt.

For a start, never in his life had he been forced to accompany a lady to the ladies'. At one point early in the evening, Margaux had made for the door of their shared office, and he had asked her where she was going.

'To the lavatory.' No powdery euphemisms.

'I'll show you where it is,' he said, downing his pen and jumping to his feet.

'No need.'

'No trouble.'

A minute later, he found himself attracting bemused looks outside a female convenience. It was worse than Soho.

The absurdity of the situation quickly got the better of him and he returned to the office. After all, he doubted whether there were Gaullist spies lurking behind the ladies' cisterns.

Later, Margaux had insisted on a working dinner, ordered up from the canteen – a boiled lump of an unidentified beast, accompanied by a tepid puree of something that might once have been vegetable but tasted decidedly mineral. After one forkful, Lemming had given up and sent out to Wilton's for mackerel pâté, pickled gherkins, bread, salted butter and two bottles of beer. Margaux had partaken heartily of this edible fare, no doubt conscious that it might be her last decent food for a few days – possibly ever. But after their shared meal she had retreated straight back into the pool of light of her desk lamp.

Sleeping arrangements had been the least embarrassing part of the proceedings. The Admiralty Citadel was the ugliest construction in London, a concrete monstrosity attached like a parasite to the classically elegant Admiralty building. But there was method in its monstrousness – it was designed to hold out even if Nazi tanks were blasting it from Saint James' Park. In consequence, it hosted some of the most peaceful dormitories in the whole city. It would have taken a direct hit from a doodlebug to shake sleepers from their bunks.

Margaux bedded down with the female staff, one of whom had orders to alert Lemming if she attempted to leave or communicate with anyone outside the building. But the night's only disturbances had been Lemming's own dreams, which had woken him sweating three or four times, convinced that a torpedo was sharking silently towards his camp bed.

'Is Sylvia Trench one of your conquests?'

The question jolted Lemming back into the present, on to the train. Margaux had put her newspaper on the seat beside her, and was looking him in the eye.

'Not at all,' he answered truthfully, reaching into his hip pocket for his cigarette case.

'I bet you tried, though.'

Lemming wondered why she was interested.

'Well, funny you should mention bets, because the chaps had a sweepstake. A pound each on who would be the first – you know. She was single, twenty-seven or twenty-eight, and the posting to my department was a lifestyle more than a job. Days and nights on duty, little or no leave.'

'So you men thought you should entertain her. How considerate of you.'

Margaux refused his offer of a cigarette.

'We warned her – she was in peril of turning into a loveless spinster.'

'And which one of you was noble enough to fill this gap in her life?'

'None of us. One Monday morning, she announced that she had married some boffin, a mathematician stationed out in the country somewhere.'

'So you went and drowned your sorrows with the sweepstake money.'

'No, I gave it all to Sylvia as a wedding present. Let no one say I'm a bad loser.'

'I suppose you can take a few losses when you spread your bets so widely.'

Again, despite Margaux's cutting ways with irony, Lemming was flattered that she was so interested.

'You seemed far from unhappy when we kissed the other evening,' he said.

'Yes, I enjoyed it.'

'So did I. Even more than I realized at the time, to be perfectly frank.'

'Are you ever perfectly frank with a woman?' She smiled as she said it, softening the blow.

'Oh yes, all the time.' It was true. Lemming never avoided openness with a woman. Why hide what you would like to do with them? The sooner you told them, the sooner you could begin.

'Funnily enough, I believe you,' Margaux said. 'When you're talking about sex, anyway. As for the rest, who knows.'

'Well,' he said, 'to be perfectly frank yet again, I was hoping that perhaps we might try it again one day. Kissing, I mean.' He looked at her challengingly. She met his gaze, giving nothing away.

'We might,' she said. 'Do you want to bet on it?'

'I'd lose. I think you're the kind of girl who would do anything to win a bet.'

She laughed. 'I don't know whether to take that as a compliment.'

'It is. I'm a betting man. And if you want another compliment, I've come to the conclusion that you're the most courageous woman I've ever met.'

'Heavens, you're going to make me blush.'

Lemming was sure he saw her cheeks flush slightly.

'You're very beautiful, too. And witty. It's a fascinating combination.'

'You sound like half the officers in London, just before they put their hand on a girl's knee.'

'Well, I'm going to do the opposite,' Lemming said, suddenly very serious. 'I hereby give you my solemn promise to abstain from any further attempts at seduction before the mission.'

'That's very saintly of you.'

'I've told you, I'm no saint. So you'll just have to ignore me if I forget myself occasionally and give you a winsome smile.'

'You win some, you lose some.'

'Oh Lord, don't tell me I'm going to be locked up in a submarine with PG Brickhouse.'

This was a writer renowned for his relentlessly witty novels.

They laughed together at last.

'You think he's a traitor?' she asked, as if keen to change the subject. The novelist had been living in France when the Nazis invaded in 1940, and had since been accused of collaborating.

'I don't know why anyone but a Quisling would speak on Nazi radio like he did,' he said. 'Strange, though. He always came across as such a lover of England.'

'I'll be landing not very far from his house. He lived near Le Touquet, just up the coast from Dieppe.'

'Really?'

In fact, Lemming knew this perfectly well. He had spent time in the fashionable resort of Le Touquet in the thirties, as had most people in his circles. It was by a swimming pool there that he had fallen in love with the baron's wife who was also bedding a lord.

The trouble with admitting this to Margaux was that, as far as everyday life was concerned, Lemming had huge problems differentiating between what someone like him, an MP's son who mingled with barons and their wives, knew, and what everyone else might be aware of. Did admitting that he spent summers in Le Touquet make him sound snobbish? Was it common knowledge that Brickhouse had lived there? Could something truly be called 'common knowledge' if it was known to his people, many of whom weren't commoners?

This war was changing England's social order, bringing people into close contact who would barely have spoken to each other before.

'Anyway, Brickhouse has been interned elsewhere now,' Lemming said, 'so I don't think there's much point dropping in for tea at Le Touquet.'

'Wouldn't dream of it. Have you ever drunk the stuff they dare to call tea in France?'

They shared a laugh, and Lemming was reassured: if Margaux was willing to make jokes about the French, she couldn't be as Gaullist as all that.

The train was now speeding through wooded countryside, engulfing trees in its vapour, startling plough horses in the fields, attracting shouts and waves from children on their walk to school. Occasionally, a large country house came into view through the woods – very Brickhousian.

Lemming clicked out of his thoughts about France and Le Touquet and realized that, for the first time ever, he was looking at England with a sense that he might never witness these familiar scenes again. In 1942, he had set out for Dieppe full of absurd optimism. Two years of war later, he, like the country itself, felt very different.

IX

It was at Brighton Station, right before Lemming's eyes, that Margaux stepped out of line. Literally.

He was walking beside her, carrying both their cases. They were in the midst of a dense flow of travellers trooping along the curved platform. They had almost reached the exit when Margaux murmured something to him and stepped to one side, heading for one of the wrought-iron columns that held up the glass station roof.

Standing to attention by the column was a tall man in a dark woollen overcoat that looked too thick for the mild morning. The same was true of the man's grey hat, which was wide-brimmed, somehow foreign. The man wasn't looking directly at Margaux, but he was clearly expecting someone, waiting to be approached.

He was handsome, in a slightly dark, European way. French, Lemming thought – and a wave of almost panicky anticipation hit him in the chest. This was it. Margaux was making contact with them.

She walked straight over to the stranger and made a big show of a supposedly chance encounter. 'What a surprise,' and all that. The man was even kissing her on the cheek.

Lemming put down both cases, almost tripping an elderly lady who was walking just behind him. He marched towards this newly-formed couple.

'Who –?' was all he had time to say.

'Not now, commander, please,' Margaux said, flashing him a disapproving look.

He did not know how to react, and so did nothing.

Margaux and the man moved around to the other side of the column, still going through the public motions of 'how lovely to bump into you!'

Lemming watched as the man spoke softly, and Margaux nodded. She did so several times to show that she had understood. She then kissed his cheek and said loudly, 'Do give my love to Cynthia.' The man walked away towards a waiting train, neither giving Lemming a glance nor looking back at Margaux.

'Who the devil was that?' Lemming asked when he had recovered the cases and his composure.

'If I told you, he'd have to kill you,' she whispered.

'What?'

'Only joking. But you remember where I shall soon be going?'

Lemming found her tone irritating, but grunted 'of course.'

'Well, he was there recently and had some news for me.'

'What news?'

'If you'll wait just a moment, I'll go to the announcer and have him broadcast it.'

Lemming headed through the station exit gritting his teeth.

Outside on the forecourt, there were no military cars waiting for them, so Lemming was able to channel his annoyance into a brusque telephone call to the Admiralty from the nearest public box. While he was on the line, he asked to be put through to Rashbrooke. Again, the rear admiral was not pleased about the disturbance, but listened attentively as Lemming described Margaux's meeting on the platform.

'We'll have a look out for the chap when he gets into Victoria,' he said. 'Meanwhile, you'd better give the young lady a short pep talk about the dangers of Gaullism. See how she reacts. There'll be nothing you can do once she's on the other side, but it can't do any harm to remind her of her loyalties.'

Lemming agreed and rang off.

A few minutes later, he was cheered by a heartening vision. Pulling into the station forecourt in a wide, elegant arc was a 1937 Riley Continental, one of the sleekest cars on the market, its long chassis, low roof and tilted windscreen obviously designed for fast cruising. It was almost a sports car, its rear doors tiny and more suitable for a hastily loaded overnight bag than passengers.

Lemming knew that before the war, this car would almost certainly have been finished in metallic green or blue. It was known as the Blue Streak. However, like so many pre-war vehicles, it had now been clumsily daubed with matt camouflage paint. He hoped that, once the war was over, it would be restored to its glossy beauty without too much damage to the bodywork.

An army corporal got out, saluted and took the suitcases. Lemming noticed a marked limp. A man of action, then, still doing his bit.

'Commander. Ma'am, I'm Pepper. Sorry if I'm a few minutes late. Bad traffic.'

'Don't worry, corporal,' Margaux told him.

The car boot was only big enough for Lemming's bag. Pepper put Margaux's on the back seat, and invited her to get in alongside it.

'Do you mind riding up front with me, sir? Sorry about this. Not much legroom in the back. The only car available.'

Lemming accepted willingly. He would have liked to get behind the wheel.

'Not at all, corporal. Fine machine. Two point five litres, isn't it? Eighty horsepower?'

'Sorry, sir. Couldn't tell you. I just drive it.' He looked sorry to have deflated the enthusiasm of this classy-looking officer. 'Fast, though,' he said, to redeem himself. 'I can get her to eighty, easy, on the London run. In broad daylight, of course, ma'am,' he added, as though Margaux might be scared by the very idea of speed.

'Fast as you like, corporal,' she replied. 'I'll bet you a pound I could take her to a hundred between here and Hastings.'

'Don't bet on anything with her,' Lemming said, more bitterly than he intended.

They set off in silence. Lemming lit a cigarette without offering them around.

The streets of Brighton were busy, mainly with military vehicles. There were uniformed pedestrians everywhere, too, on the pavements and spilling over on to the roads. Lemming thought that if he and Margaux really had been lovers, it might have been very difficult to find a room.

Outside the town, climbing towards the downs, the heavy military presence continued. They passed a school sports field that had been taken over by a tank regiment, its vehicles netted against spying from overhead. The car park of a factory had become an army lorry depot. Men seemed to be training in woodland, crawling from tree to tree. At a distance, their rounded helmets looked American.

A couple of miles outside the town, the car pulled into a gateway guarded by four sentries. Beyond a high double fence, there were a dozen or so Nissen huts, like short lengths of sausage half-buried in the grass. Their semi-circular facades were painted the same colour as the car, and their roofs were camouflaged with yellowing turf. On each, a stubby chimney was smoking. A stand of trees near the road had been thinned out to allow space for parking. Several men were working on a half-track vehicle. Three lorries stood idle.

The whole base was about a hundred yards square, and looked as if it had once been a horse pasture. There were the remains of a jump in one corner, a couple of black wooden trestles and some striped poles. All around the perimeter fence, armed sentries were patrolling. This was high security.

The guards examined everyone's papers and telephoned for instructions before letting the car through. Corporal Pepper then proceeded at little more than marching pace towards the nearest hut, watched closely by the sentries.

The inside of the hut was muggy and smoke-filled. A hubbub of conversation was cut short as they entered. Six men in commando tunics were lounging in assorted armchairs, tea mugs and plates of sandwiches on low tables amongst them. They were at ease yet alert. One of them was Major Maclean, who stood up and saluted.

'Attention!'

The other men followed suit, looking at Margaux with a mixture of lust and respect, and at Lemming with something chillier. He was used to this. His old boss Admiral Geoffrey had told him that 00 Commando's ordinary men had taken against him after hearing that he referred to them as his 'Red Indians'. It was apparently the 'his' that rankled as much as the 'Red Indians'. And the Dieppe debacle hadn't helped. Since then, Lemming's reputation amongst other commandos had spread, and he was, he knew, seen as an aloof cavalier who rarely if ever got his hands dirty.

He did not particularly begrudge the men their coolness. It was true, he was aloof. Even his friends told him so. And his fingernails usually were pristine. This was why he was looking forward to the mission. It would be his chance to show them that he was not above cramming his taller-than-average frame into a submarine.

'At ease, men,' he told them. All except Maclean sat down, but they did not resume talking.

Maclean shook hands warmly with Margaux and Lemming, and introduced his men. Lemming heard the list of names he had seen in the file. All of them, he knew, were volunteers for the mission. But there was one man missing.

'Where is Sergeant Carrell?' he asked Maclean.

'He's bringing the lorry over. Come and have a cup of tea and a slice of the NAAFI's finest fruit cake. Minus the fruit, I'm afraid. No officers' mess here,' he added, as if raisins were reserved for those with pips on their shoulders.

He led Lemming and Margaux to a table by the stove, which was spitting noisily and leaking smoke. A large, flowery enamel teapot on the hotplate lent a homely air to the military scene. The three of them engaged in small talk about the London-to-Brighton train journey while Maclean poured tea into china cups.

The other men were now chatting again. At first sight, they looked an undisciplined lot. Overlong hair, approximately shaven, a couple of them with scruffy moustaches. Two were wearing town shoes instead of boots. But this was not uncommon on a commando mission. The men had to be comfortable. Their packs, piled by the door, were light. The men themselves were all fairly small and wiry. These weren't gladiators. They were brawlers, trained in a dozen ways of silent, dirty killing. They were, Lemming thought, like the archers at Agincourt. Underestimate them at your peril.

The most striking thing about them was that they looked so ordinary. Lemming was acutely conscious that in civilian life he probably would not have given them a second glance. They would have been delivering his wine, painting his front door, announcing his name as he entered some function. The most likely contact Lemming would have had with them would have been to give them a shilling tip for some service rendered.

And yet now, in his presence, they were as self-assured as a group of old Etonians on their way to shoot grouse. For once, Lemming's height and natural breeding counted for nothing. Neither did his military rank. And, he admitted to himself, for good reason – these men were about to land in France, a handful against a whole army.

He was glad that he had taken the time to study the most recent intelligence about their target area. He had plenty to tell them. There were new, reliable air reconnaissance photos, taken no doubt by people like Margaux's brother Patrick. He also had reports about the coastal defences from some French fishermen who had escaped, as well as carefully verified information from POWs. Lemming felt he knew the clifftop intimately without ever having set foot there. He would be able to play his part in the mission, and maybe even put his old reputation to rest.

The door opened.

'Ah, Sergeant Carrell,' Maclean said.

Lemming stood and turned to greet the final member of the outfit. As he did so, what was meant to be an informal half-smile froze on his lips.

Carrell was black.

Lemming was aware of the great service that the Commonwealth troops had given. He knew how many of them had crossed tropical oceans to freeze in the First World War trenches. He knew that hundreds of West Indians had volunteered in 1939, even though they were living thousands of miles away from any direct danger from the Nazis.

It was just that you didn't expect a black man on a commando mission, in the same way that you didn't expect a woman.

'Welcome aboard, sergeant,' he said, as the man saluted.

'Thank you, commander,' Carrell replied, smiling broadly at him, unlike the other men.

Lemming felt the need to maintain the easy bonhomie.

'Well, at least we won't need to black *your* face when you go ashore,' he said.

There was an uneasy silence. Lemming thought he heard one of the other men snigger.

'I'm sure Sergeant Carrell has never heard *that* one before,' Margaux said, and now the men were openly laughing.

X

Maclean insisted that Lemming and Margaux ride in the cab with Carrell for the lorry trip to Newhaven, where they were to board the submarine.

At the mention of Newhaven, Lemming was jolted back to the past – this was where he and his men had embarked for Dieppe in 1942. It was a logical point of departure for this new mission, but he hoped that it was not an omen.

They set off east, quickly hitting the coast road and its long parade of gun emplacements and lookout posts. Tangled mounds of barbed wire blocked every pathway down to the beach. It was high tide, and the rusty posts of tank traps spiked dangerously above the calm grey water.

The traffic was slow-moving. Sitting beside Sergeant Carrell, Lemming hoped he would get the chance to make up for his clumsy, if well-meaning, remark in the Nissen hut.

Margaux opened the way for him.

'Where are you from, sergeant?' she asked.

'Jamaica, ma'am.' The way he pronounced the name confirmed it.

Lemming grinned. 'The most beautiful island in the Caribbean. I was there last year.'

'Really, sir?' Carrell took his eyes of the road for a moment to stare at this man who had been in his homeland much more recently than he had.

'Yes. I was in Kingston for a conference –'

'Should you be mentioning details like that, commander?' Margaux interrupted.

Lemming had had no intention of revealing that he had been meeting the Americans to discuss how to wage war on the U-boats infesting the area. But she was right.

'Thank you, Warrant Officer Lynd,' he said. 'Though I'm sure we can trust the sergeant with our lives.'

'We can never trust anyone with our secrets, commander,' she replied.

'Touché,' Lemming said, stifling his annoyance. 'Anyway, what I *can* reveal is that the Myrtle Bank by the waterfront in Kingston is one of the finest hotels in the world.'

'Sure is, sir,' Carrell agreed, changing gear as he slowed down to let an American Jeep into the flow of traffic.

'You've been there?' Lemming failed to hide his surprise.

'My sister is a chambermaid.'

'Ah, yes. Superb service all round, I must say,' he said, remembering uncomfortably that he had propositioned one of the maids. Unsuccessfully, but even so. 'I didn't actually stay there. We slept up in the hills, much cooler.'

'That's where my mother lives, sir,' Carrell said. Lemming doubted that her home was on the same hill as the mansion he had stayed in. 'Up there by the coffee plantations,' Carrell added.

Oh, Lemming thought, maybe it was the same hill, after all. Just not the same type of house.

'Best coffee in the world,' he said. 'Blue Mountain. God, how I wish I'd brought a few more bags back with me. Cold-pressed, it can't be beaten. Don't you agree, sergeant?'

'We don't get to drink much Blue Mountain coffee, sir. I think it's mostly shipped out to America.'

'Yes, you're probably right.' Lemming felt the familiar discomfort of not being able to banter with ordinary folks.

'Cold-pressed?' Margaux said. 'Then re-heated? Surely coffee is much fresher and tastier if you make it with hot water?'

'Oh no, cold-pressed, that's the traditional Jamaican way, isn't it, sergeant?' Lemming said with a confidence that he wasn't entirely feeling. He tried to remember where he'd heard about cold-pressing coffee.

'Different people make it different ways, sir,' Carrell said, his eyes firmly on the road.

'How long have you been in England, sergeant?' Margaux asked, mercifully changing the subject.

Carrell told them that he had joined up in 1940, coming over on a troop ship with a few hundred other men from the islands. His brothers had stayed on in Jamaica to look after their mother. Their father, a policeman, had been killed while on duty several years earlier. Arriving in England, Carrell had trained as a mechanic, before transferring to the commando unit.

'As soon as I read the racial theories of those Nazis, I wanted to go and shoot at them,' he said. 'Simple as that. Mind you, I had to box a few noses to show some of these fools' – he jerked his head backwards towards where his colleagues were riding – 'that the Nazis hadn't got it right about racial supremacy.'

'Ah yes, fine boxers, the negr –' Lemming was silenced by a jab in the ribs from Margaux.

'Oh man, what in the Lord's name is that?' Carrell moaned.

They had turned off the coast road and were in a lane on the outskirts of Newhaven. To their left was woodland, to their right, fields and a small pebble-dashed farmhouse. Beside the farm gate, a lorry, a delivery vehicle of some kind, was parked across the thoroughfare. A few men in army uniform were loitering beside it. One of them, a tubby-looking officer, was holding up his hand.

Carrell braked gently to a halt, and Lemming now saw that the uniformed men were mostly grey-haired and stooping. Only a couple of them were armed – the tubby officer had a pistol, and an ancient-looking lance corporal was brandishing a rifle, its long bayonet pointing towards Carrell's tyres.

'Home Guard,' Lemming said, fondly. 'My brother Philip set this lot up, you know,' he told Margaux.

Carrell stuck his head out of the window.

'You fellas need a push?' he asked.

'No, we do not need a push, sergeant,' the officer said, irritably. 'This is a roadblock.'

'Well, please unblock it,' Carrell told him. 'Sir.'

The tubby officer bristled.

'We have a Vickers machine gun set up in those woods, sergeant, so I would advise you to show us some identification if you wish to proceed into Newhaven.'

'Sorry but we're not going to show you any identification,' Carrell told him. 'Our mission is secret. You see this badge?' He thrust his shoulder out of the window, pointing at his commando insignia.

'How do we know that's genuine?' the officer demanded. 'How do we know you're even British?'

'Let me talk to him,' Lemming intervened. He was afraid that Carrell might climb out and get himself machine-gunned. Margaux jumped down from the lorry to let Lemming out, attracting a whistle from somewhere in the woodland.

At the sight of Lemming's naval uniform, the Home Guard men got even more nervous. A commando, a WAAF and now a sailor? This mixture of units was disturbingly out of the ordinary.

'The sailor looks foreign,' one of the Home Guards said, a boy about fifty years younger than most of the others.

Lemming ignored him.

'Good morning ... captain,' he said, noting with some surprise the tubby little man's rank. 'Tell me, have you heard of Philip Lemming?'

'No, should I have?' The captain was looking increasingly nervous as this tall officer bore down on him.

'Lemming sounds foreign,' the boy said. 'Ask him if he's Flemish. Or German.'

Again he was ignored.

'He's your founder,' Lemming said.

'Founder? What are you talking about?' The little captain's finger was jittering on the trigger of his pistol.

'Oh, Philip Lemming?' This was said by a Home Guard sergeant who had stepped forward. He was carrying a rifle as though he didn't quite know what to do with it. 'Of course, Esther and Victor's son. Went off to Brazil, didn't he?'

'That's the fellow,' Lemming said. His brother had written a book about his Amazonian adventures.

'Brazil?' Now the captain was totally confused.

'Tell the foreigner to recite a catchphrase from ITMA or you'll shoot him,' the boy said.

'Stupid boy,' the captain told him.

'Philip's my brother,' Lemming told the sergeant, the only man in the whole Home Guard who seemed to be catching his drift.

'You must be Mark,' the sergeant said. 'But I heard you'd died at Dunkirk?'

'Right, that does it.' The captain's pistol was now pointing squarely at Lemming's chest. 'Impersonating a dead British officer. Hands up.'

Lemming had no choice but to obey.

'Make one move and I'll cut you into little English Oxo cubes with my very English commando knife.'

The voice was soft but authoritative, spoken directly into the captain's left ear. Carrell was standing behind him, almost embracing him, his knife drawn. He had snuck out of the lorry under cover of Lemming's diversion. He took possession of the pistol.

'And I've got one question for you before I start cutting,' Carrell added, menacingly. He let the threat hang in the air for a few seconds before adding in a louder and markedly different voice, 'Can I do you now, sir?'

The tension evaporated. All the Home Guard men except the captain burst out laughing. There was even a guffaw from the woods. Everyone loved Mrs Mopp, the charlady in *It's That Man Again*, Britain's favourite weekly radio show. Well, almost everyone. *ITMA* didn't seem to be the captain's cup of tea.

'Now if you'll just move your bloody delivery van out of the road, we'll be saying TTFN,' Carrell said, adding yet another catchphrase from the show. 'Sir,' he added, patting the captain on the shoulder and returning the pistol to its holster.

'Not so fast.'

Everyone turned to look at the ancient lance corporal, who was waving his rifle and bayonet towards Carrell's back from a range of less than a yard. He too had done some sneaking.

'I was in the Boer War,' the old man said. 'You don't catch me out with your Zulu tricks.'

'Oh for God's sake.' Carrell looked suddenly exhausted. His shoulders sagged in defeat.

A second later, the rifle was in his hands and the old soldier was flat on his back.

'Sorry, old-timer, are you all right?' Carrell asked.

'We've still got our machine gun,' the captain said, struggling to get his pistol out of his holster, 'so no more funny business.'

'This machine gun?'

Major Maclean emerged from the woodland carrying the fat barrel of a World War One Vickers, its ammunition belt slung over his shoulder. He had left the tripod behind.

'Now please, captain, let us through before any other vehicles come along and cause a traffic jam,' Maclean said. 'We have a very important rendez-vous to make in Newhaven harbour. And I for one am gasping for a cup of tea.'

Four of the Home Guard men released the van's handbrake and began to roll it out of the road.

Carrell apologized again to the old soldier for having to floor him, and the old man was soon telling him about the colonial troops he had served with in the trenches. Fine lads, he said, fearless fighters. They had been Indians, but the old man did not seem to differentiate between colonials.

Maclean, meanwhile, was suggesting to the captain that it would be advisable to relocate his machine gun for maximum effect.

'Your line of fire between those trees was only a couple of yards wide. Either side of that and you'd have been felling oaks. And in case you hadn't noticed, the warrant officer here had chosen to stand by the fence, right in the Vickers' line of fire. She was blocking the machine gunner's view the whole time.'

'That was very brave of you, Miss,' the captain said.

'Not at all,' Margaux told him. 'I'm sure the Home Guard is much too polite to shoot a lady.'

She shared a laugh with Maclean and the captain.

Lemming heard this exchange and could not prevent himself staring at her. My God, he thought, this well-bred young Englishwoman was willing to stand in front of a machine gun. Had the world really changed that much while he was shut away in the Admiralty?

XI

After the showdown at the Home Guard roadblock, access to the port of Newhaven seemed almost relaxed. White-capped naval sentries checked Carrell's pass and waved them into what looked more like a railway goods yard than a harbour. The lorry bumped across three sets of rails to get into the main dock area. Cranes and ship funnels jutted above the roofs of brick buildings and giant Nissen huts. A goods train was steaming slowly towards the dockside, its open wagons loaded with wooden crates that looked like ammunition boxes. Lemming hoped there would not be an air raid before they left harbour – that train would make quite some firework display.

The lorry edged past an anti-aircraft gun emplacement and right on to the dock. Waved into position by a sailor in an oversized white jumper, Carrel parked between a tall crane and the submarine.

He cut the ignition and announced, 'This is where we transfer to the Queen Mary.'

Lemming got his first close look at HMS Diamond, his base for the next twenty hours or so, if all went well. His coffin for ever, if something went seriously amiss.

The submarine was like a hundred-foot-long metal canoe. It had a flat deck, with radio and radar masts on the prow, and, towards the stern, a tall conning tower fitted with a large cannon. It was as though a destroyer's gun turret had simply been welded on top of a metal tube.

'It looks very top-heavy,' Lemming said. 'As if it might tip over at any moment.'

'If it does, we'll go down with it,' Margaux said. 'You know, there's never been a successful escape from a sunken submarine. If you made it out of one of the emergency hatches, the chances are that your lungs would burst or fill with seawater a long time before you reached the surface. Anyway, the maximum depth used for any of the escape drills is a hundred feet. In reality, the crew stands no chance of escape unless the sub is grounded on a sandbank or within a few yards of the coast.'

As she spoke, Lemming felt her eyes on him, probing for signs of nervousness.

'Then it's lucky for you that you're a fully-trained mermaid,' he replied, reaching for his cigarette case.

A naval captain came striding down the narrow gangplank to greet Major Maclean, who was already out of the lorry. They shook hands and Maclean gestured over his shoulder towards Lemming and Margaux, who were getting down from the cab.

Lemming lit his cigarette and sucked deeply.

'I think I'd prefer to get changed before we go aboard,' Margaux said.

'Me too,' Lemming said.

'You're getting changed?' She looked surprised.

He had been warned that the cramped conditions of a sub were not the safest place for an expensively tailored Admiralty get-up. So he had brought along an older, rougher uniform.

'Yes. I'll clear the men out of the lorry and you can change in there,' he told Margaux.

The commandos started boarding. Lemming stood guard while Margaux donned her French outfit. The submarine captain finished talking to Maclean and came over. Lemming was relieved to see that he too was wearing slightly worse-for-wear clothing, including a short battledress tunic, exactly what Lemming had brought with him.

'Strangeways, sir. Good to have you aboard.'

'Lemming.'

They shook hands. The captain's hand was dry and gripped firmly. Lemming had a violent allergy to limp handshakes, and was instantly reassured. Strangeways looked battle-hardened. He was around thirty-five, with a glint of humour in his eyes, but a steely calmness about him. A good man in a crisis, Lemming decided. He was predictably pale compared to a sailor who served on the surface – submarines usually surfaced only at night. There was no danger of sunburn, even for a sub crew patrolling in the Mediterranean.

'How long have you served on HMS Diamond?' Lemming asked.

'Couple of years, mostly North Sea and the Arctic. They've brought us back to calmer waters now, though. She's getting a little fragile in her old age.'

Lemming gulped, silently he hoped.

'How old is she?' he asked.

'Oh, she just turned twenty-four, but we hope she'll last forever. You know what they say about diamonds.'

'Yes, yes. How many crew can she hold?'

'Thirty-six. But only twenty on this run – reduced manpower because it's just an out-and-back job. You're lucky, you'll have something almost like a cabin to yourself, not too close to the engine room. Same goes for Miss Lynd.' Strangeways gestured towards the interior of the lorry. 'Oh, and, touchy subject ...' He lowered his voice. 'I should warn you – if possible, try to make sure you won't need the latrine for anything more than, let's say, light relief. Pretty horrific place. There are facilities in the railway building over there, if you need them. Or Miss Lynd does ...'

'Well, I ...' It was not a subject Lemming had ever broached with a lady. Even walking her to the conveniences in the Admiralty had been a mild form of torture for him.

The back awning of the lorry opened, and Margaux jumped down in civilian clothes, looking every inch the average French *mademoiselle*. She was wearing a navy-blue skirt suit that had seen far better days, a cream blouse and thin black tie. A grey coat was folded over one arm. Her dark hair was parted in the centre and held in a low bun by a plain blue headscarf. She was carrying a small, rigid leather bag, a cross between a suitcase and a briefcase. She looked as though she might be on her way to apply for a job as a *notaire's* secretary, a few hours' journey from her home town, with overnight things in case she was asked to start straight away.

'It's all right, gentlemen, I overheard,' she said. 'As far as I'm concerned, we can board immediately.'

While Lemming got changed in the truck, Strangeways introduced himself, shaking her hand.

'Thank you so much for allowing a woman on board,' Margaux said.

'You're not our first,' Strangeways told her. 'We ferried a woman to Norway last year, when it was still taboo. Had to disguise her as a boy. But that mission went rather well, so the men are less nervous of female company. For a few hours, anyway. Beyond that it would get uncomfortable for all concerned.'

'Well, this girl will try to be HMS Diamond's best friend,' Margaux said.

They moved towards the gangplank, which was just that, a plank. It sprang under Lemming's feet like a diving board. Once they were on deck, standing below the conning tower and its cannon, he could feel that this was a very small vessel indeed. He had been on larger boats for a day cruise to the Thames Estuary.

They had to wait their turn to climb down into the nearest hatchway. One of the commandos was passing down Tommy guns and packs before he disappeared into the hull.

'What's life like on a sub, captain?' Margaux asked.

'Oh, for myself and the other officers, intense concentration 24 hours a day. For the men, it varies. I'd say, 95 per cent routine boredom, two per cent the thrill of the chase, and the rest is blessedly short periods of utter terror that the hull is about to split open and drown them in freezing seawater.'

'Sounds just like the Admiralty,' said Margaux, who had been watching Lemming during Strangeways' short speech.

'There's probably less hot air in a sub,' Lemming said.

'I don't know about that. Overheated air is the main problem with a tub of her age,' Strangeways said. 'Still got her ancient ventilation system.'

Lemming felt his throat tighten.

'Can't you carry oxygen with you to renew the supply?' Margaux asked.

'That wouldn't be practical. Pumping in new air would increase the pressure inside the hull. If we weren't careful, we might explode. And releasing spent air would create bubbles that might get us spotted. That's why we often surface at night, to let some fresh air in. The danger being, of course, that we'll be shot at and sunk.'

Everything Lemming heard about life below seas added to the impression that he was about to spend the worst few hours of his life, but he was determined not to let it show.

It was their turn to descend.

'I'll go first,' Strangeways said. 'Follow my lead. Take it slowly, one step at a time. And please wait until my head is well out of your way before you start coming down.' He stepped on to the ladder in the narrow hatchway.

'You go next,' Lemming told Margaux. 'I'll pass your bag in.'

'All right.' She gave his hand a quick squeeze, and they exchanged an encouraging smile. He liked to think that it was because she was nervous, and not because she thought he was.

XII

As soon as night fell, the submarine began to glide out of the harbour and into the Channel. The grinding vibration of the hull did not alter, but Lemming heard the note of the engine change and sensed that they were moving.

The submarine was going to travel for the next eight hours or so at ten knots, slowly but surely getting closer to occupied France. Assuming no Nazi ship or plane decided to interrupt its leisurely crossing.

Lemming asked to start the journey in the control room. He wanted to share the immediacy of going into action. It would be the stuff of reminiscences that he could later share with his London friends. But Strangeways told him regretfully that there was no room in there for extra hands, and a seaman escorted Lemming and Margaux to their bunk spaces.

It was like clambering deep into the guts of an engine. As you moved along the submarine's main passageway, you were continually ducking or swerving to avoid a protruding pipe, bulkhead or some other murderous metal extrusion. There ought to be a rule, Lemming thought: no submariners over five foot six.

Lemming's 'cabin' was curtained off, and he shared it with a dozen crates, stencilled 'OXTAIL', 'HAM', 'PEAS', 'POWDERED EGG' and suchlike. It was still fiendishly cramped. There was not enough headroom to sit up on his bunk. He had to lie down or risk braining himself against the hull.

Even worse than the lack of space was the stink. It was multi-layered, and the diametric opposite of a good wine: first to hit your palate was the sickly scent of diesel. Then came the heady aroma of unwashed bodies. Finally there were subtle notes of stagnant water, in which someone had long ago dumped a cargo of cabbages. All this with an ambient metallic aftertaste, like something Lemming had once experienced after food poisoning. A decent cigarette would at least dull the foulness, he thought, but one spark and the heady blend of chemicals in the atmosphere would probably combust.

He left his bag on a box marked 'LARD: TINNED' (he knew how it felt) and went off in search of Margaux.

He did not have far to clamber. A few yards further along the passageway, he found her standing in a tiny alcove, beside a fold-down bunk that was held in place by grimy canvas straps. She was rummaging through her suitcase.

'If you have any extra perfume, I'd love to borrow a couple of drops,' he said. 'One under each nostril.'

She turned and smiled, wrinkling her nose.

'It's the only thing that makes me grateful I won't be here for the return journey,' she said.

'As soon as you send word to us, someone will be over there to fetch you,' Lemming replied. 'You know that. Forget-Me-Not, remember?'

'Yes, thanks.' She continued rummaging.

'Have you forgotten something?' Lemming asked.

Margaux shook her head. 'I'm just giving my kit a final check. Making double-sure there's no trace of Blighty. One English maker's name on a button or a pencil and I won't be coming home.'

'Good idea,' he said, deeply relieved that he did not have the same worry. 'In ten minutes I'll go for'ard and start my lecture to the men about the local tourist attractions. I'll pick you up on the way.'

'If I'm not here, I'll be aloft on the sun deck.' She returned to the minute inspection of her luggage.

Maclean and his men were in the torpedo room. As this was not an attack mission, only the bottom rungs of the torpedo racks were occupied, one on each side of the hull. Even so, Lemming was going to be giving a lecture in the same room as two unexploded bombs.

There was space here for eight bunks, seven of which were occupied. When he stepped through the hatchway, Lemming thought the commandos looked like human torpedoes, waiting to be fired at the French coast.

'No need to get up,' he joked, and was glad to see a couple of the men grin.

Margaux lay down on the free bunk and Lemming stood hunched beneath the low metal ceiling, intensely aware of the thin atmosphere in this confined space, nine bodies consuming more of its oxygen with every nervous breath.

He proceeded to give a detailed lecture about the coastal features that they were to expect, handing round photographic prints and charts to stress certain points. Most of it was a re-run through information that the men had studied for the previous few weeks, but Maclean had insisted that every new version of old facts helped to imprint them accurately on the men's brains.

Lemming also showed them carefully censored papers that had been retrieved on previous commando missions. He gave them key words to look out for: 'V1' and 'Fi 103', for example, the technical terms for the doodlebugs that were plaguing southern England. Another one was 'Vergeltungswaffe' – revenge weapon, the official Nazi propaganda name for the V1. London also suspected that a newer rocket was in development, Lemming told the men, 'so lift anything marked "geheim" – secret – even if it looks like the recipe for schnapps. We want to know what delights the Nazis are cooking up for us.'

The men listened avidly, as did Margaux, and for the first time Lemming felt as if he was really playing his part. He was still conscious, though, that of all the people crammed into that tiny compartment, he was the odd one out, the lucky man who was running the smallest risk. He was like a mountain guide pointing up to a precipitous, unclimbed peak that everyone except him was going to scale.

'One last point,' he said. 'It may sound obvious, but it's worth repeating. If you run into any of the natives, beware. The gendarmes are just as likely to hand you over to Fritz as they are to help you. As for civilians, tread very carefully. Don't reveal anything, even to someone who has convinced you they really are in the Resistance. The networks run by De Gaulle are as fiercely anti-Nazi as anyone, but their set-up is vulnerable.' This was addressed to Margaux more than the others. 'They're often centrally controlled, so individuals may know too much about each other. Catch one and torture him or her, and you can catch them all. And some of them may put French interests before the overall war effort. So don't entrust any un-coded secrets to anyone, not even so they can radio them back to us. They might radio them to De Gaulle as well. And *le général* doesn't need to know anything about what you're getting up to over the next few hours, even if you will be tramping through his back garden. Everything you learn will be going directly to Churchill and Eisenhower. Anything to add, warrant officer?'

He had been watching Margaux as he spoke, and had seen no reaction to his message about De Gaulle.

'You're right, commander,' she said. 'Careless *parler* costs lives.'

The men laughed. It was a good note on which to end the lecture.

A few hours later, Strangeways came to rouse Lemming from troubled sleep with a round of corned beef sandwiches and some pears in syrup, to be eaten straight from the tin. Lemming forced himself to take a few symbolic mouthfuls of the unappetizing food. He was more grateful for the generous tot of rum.

'We never let supplies of that get short,' Strangeways told him. 'It's our only anaesthetic on board in case of injury.'

Comforting news, Lemming thought.

'In twenty minutes we should be in position to drop off our passengers,' Strangeways said. 'Do you want to come up top and say au revoir?'

'Certainly.'

When Strangeways left him, Lemming ducked and wove his way along the passage to Margaux's bunk. She was lying down, her eyes open, lost in thought.

'I just thought I'd have a private word before you get going,' Lemming said.

'Please don't say anything silly, Ian,' she replied, smiling but obviously anxious. 'I need to concentrate. So no promises, no demands.'

'All I wanted to say was good luck, and I'll be thinking of you.'

'Well, that's very kind of you, but I can't promise I'll have time to think of you. Sorry.'

'I understand.'

There were other things he wanted to say, but too many of them would have fallen into her 'silly' category.

'Are you sure you've got everything?' was one.

'Don't take unnecessary risks' was another.

He could opt for a joke: 'Be careful crossing the road. The French drive on the right, but only when they can be bothered to choose sides.'

But he said nothing more and left her in peace.

Up on deck, the sea was fairly calm, but small waves were slapping noisily against the hull of the submarine. A chill breeze picked up droplets of spray and spat them intermittently into tense faces.

It was pitch dark. The only light was coming from the horizon to the west. It was as though someone over there was taking flash photographs of the coastline with a giant camera. The RAF had kept its promise and was bombing a harbour. There was no sound, just the white-orange flashes, which gradually began to meld into a reddish tinge on the skyline, a beautiful yet unnatural dawn.

It was the opposite of the London air raids Lemming had lived through. In the bomb shelters, all you got was noise and vibration. Here, it was only light.

Lemming was standing at the foot of the conning tower. Towards the prow, almost invisible in the darkness, sailors were silently checking over two of the dinghies that they had inflated. One of the boats was already in the water, almost directly below Lemming.

Margaux was beside him, dressed in dark oilskins over her French clothing, and waiting for the signal to clamber in. Maclean and his men were also on deck somewhere, standing in the gloom.

Margaux gripped Lemming's arm and breathed into his ear, 'Thanks for coming this far.'

He clamped a hand on hers and squeezed in return.

'Cigarette?' Lemming whispered, lighting one for himself.

'No thanks. Not sure it's wise, you know.'

Everything was unexpectedly peaceful.

Then Lemming noticed a strange phenomenon on the surface of the water.

It was as if someone was skimming stones. There was a series of ten or more splashes, in a straight line parallel to the hull of the submarine.

Before he had time to analyse this vision, he was hit by a roar of sound. First the rattle of a machine gun, then the crash of a bigger gun, almost immediately followed by a much larger and noisier splash just a few yards astern of the submarine. This one rocked Lemming almost off his feet, and sent a stinging jet of spray into his eyes. He thought he saw one of the inflatables leap into the air like a kite.

He instinctively clutched Margaux close to him, as all around them, men shouted and ran along the deck.

One of the commandos began firing his Tommy gun into the darkness.

Lemming was watching all this with uncanny calm, like a distant observer, when something caught him on the side of the head. He heard, rather than felt, a loud clonk on his skull, before noises began to blur, and the already dim light faded to black.

PART TWO

I

He was definitely going to speak to the nurses about leaving the window open. A man might catch pneumonia in a draught like this. They would have to bring him another blanket right away.

And should a nurse really be slapping his face?

'Wake up. Wake up.'

He didn't want to wake up. His head hurt. He was still dizzy, and his bed seemed to be rocking. Did hospitals have hammocks?

'Ian. Ian.'

Such familiarity, he thought.

Then he opened his eyes and saw a familiar face. Blurred, and dark, but recognizable. If only he could put a name to it.

'Ian,' the face said. 'Quickly, you have to get out of there.'

It was Margaux. Not in a nursing uniform, but a black oilskin jacket. And they were not in a hospital. They were outdoors. And he was in a boat.

'Give me your hand.' She was speaking softly but insistently. 'You have to come and lie on the beach while I stow the dinghy. Quickly. Don't go back to sleep.'

She slapped him again.

Blinking hard, trying to clear his vision – which was difficult to judge in the dark – Lemming let himself be lifted, first into a seated position, then standing up to his ankles in freezing water.

'Is this Hastings?' he asked, optimistically.

'No.' Margaux led him three steps forward, and told him to sit. He sank heavily onto what felt like a mixture of damp sand and large pebbles.

'Brighton?'

'No.'

'Oh no, not Bognor?'

'It's France. We're at the planned landing point.'

'Oh. The others?'

'No sign of them.'

'What happened?'

'Be quiet and stay here.'

Still dazed, he did what he was told, and listened as Margaux dragged the dinghy up the beach towards the low, whitish cliff a few yards away. He tried to remember how he had got into the boat. And why. What the hell was he doing in France? It was mystification as much as fear that hit him. He wasn't supposed to be on a French beach. He was meant to be in the submarine. What had gone wrong?

Margaux came back and held up a hand in front of his face.

'How many fingers?' she asked, still whispering.

'Twelve?'

'This is serious. How many?'

'Four.'

'Near enough. Let's get off this beach.'

'Leave me here,' he said. He felt too weak to climb the cliff and go rambling around the French countryside.

'I can't. If you're captured, you know far too much.'

'I'd never talk.'

She grunted a mirthless laugh.

'Ian, you have no training. Once the Gestapo get started on you, you'll tell them the code to your mother's chastity belt. You'll have to come with me. Or perhaps I should just shoot you here and now.'

Despite his wooziness, he could hear from the tone of her voice that she was not entirely serious. Or so he hoped.

She grabbed him under the right arm and heaved. He got to his feet, relieved to feel that his head was clearing slightly. He was beginning to see and think again.

'To the left,' he said. 'Easiest way up. No minefield.'

They came to a place where the chalk had collapsed, as predicted by the air reconnaissance photos. The slippery cliff face was encrusted with boulders. It was relatively easy to use them as stepping stones and handholds up to the grassy ridge above. Lemming went first and lay on his stomach, looking out into the French darkness. He saw nothing except lifeless black shapes, heard nothing but his own breathing and the rhythmic wash of the small waves on the shoreline behind him.

Margaux came to lie alongside.

'Did you manage to stow the boat?' he asked.

'Yes, it was exactly as you told us on the sub, a tidal cave.'

'Did you tie it up securely?'

'I filled it with stones and jammed the anchor between some rocks. I have trained in this sort of stuff, you know.'

'Of course, sorry. How long before the rendez-vous?'

'Which rendez-vous?'

'With the sub. It's re-surfacing just before dawn for the commandos. When it's time, we have to paddle back out to sea. What's the time now?'

He heard Margaux sigh deeply.

'Ian,' she said, 'for all I know, the sub might have been sunk.'

It seemed hard to believe. Strangeways and his crew could be lying drowned in their metal coffin?

'If not, it'll be back,' he said. 'Or another sub will. Operation Forget-Me-Not, remember.'

'In any case, I'm going ahead with my mission,' she said. 'It's what I came all this way for.'

Once more, Lemming was stunned by the fortitude of this young woman. He was angry at himself for feeling so weak.

'Can you walk?' she asked. 'We ought to get moving. Someone might come looking for us.'

'Yes. The devil of a headache, but I'm OK,' he said. 'Let's go. Dieppe is to the right.'

'We're not going to Dieppe.'

'We're not?'

'No, I'm afraid Naval Intelligence doesn't know the whole story about my mission.'

This took Lemming's breath away. So he had been right. She was a double agent, working for De Gaulle instead of Churchill?

She went on. 'You didn't expect me to tell every Tom, Dick and Harry where I was really going, did you? Intelligence is like one of your cigarettes, Ian. The fewer people you share it with, the better.'

'So you're not working for us?' he asked.

'What exactly do you mean by "us"?' She sounded aghast. 'No, don't answer that. Let's go.'

Crouching low so as not to be seen against the relative brightness of the sea, they moved off into the Norman night, away from Dieppe.

After several minutes trudging along the fringe of a ploughed field, they arrived at a hedgerow. They slid down into the ditch at its foot and listened.

The sea was still the loudest sound. The softest of breezes caused trees to flutter now and then. Somewhere a dog barked and was answered. The two animals challenged each other for a minute, and then felt silent.

Lemming was conscious that his feet were wet and cold. He would have liked to wring out his socks. But that was the least of his problems. He was still frantically trying to work out who exactly he was in France with. And the only result was an increased headache. He put his mouth close to Margaux's ear.

'I'm sorry, I'm not used to being lied to by my own side.'

'Lied to? Surely you understand the concept of secrecy, Ian. Anyway, if you're going to tag along, you have to trust me.'

Lemming did not see that he had much choice.

'What happened out there?' he asked.

'A German torpedo boat, I think. Something hit you on the head. You grabbed me, and we fell right into the dinghy. Damned lucky. You were out cold. There was a lot of shooting going on, so I started to paddle for all I was worth, out of the firing line. Bullets and shells flying everywhere. There was an explosion, but I'm not sure who it was. Then it all went dark. I kept my head down and made for shore, as per the original plan.'

Lemming thought about this, sorry and yet simultaneously relieved to have missed the action.

'You think the Jerries were waiting for us?' he asked.

'Who knows? I damned well hope not, otherwise my whole mission will be compromised.'

'What about the commandos?'

'I didn't see any other dinghies.'

'God. If they didn't make it, we're on our own,' he said, feeling the full import of the fact in his gut.

'Well, not exactly alone. There's the whole Nazi army over here, too.'

II

They skirted a hamlet and headed eastwards, where there was still no sign of dawn. The fields all seemed to be long strips, some planted, some not – an ancient layout, Lemming thought, perhaps dating back to the days of William the future Conqueror.

They met few roads, and each time they paused for a long minute, listening.

'There are so many gun emplacements in the area that there have to be large troop numbers,' Margaux whispered. 'Patrols, changeovers, sentries. And the gunfight and explosion offshore will have made the occupiers especially jittery.'

Once, they heard a bicycle approaching, its chain creaking and, from the sound of it, one wheel out of alignment so that it squeaked against the frame. They ducked down, hidden behind a grassy bank, and listened to the laboured breath of the cyclist.

If it was a Nazi soldier, he sounded promisingly unfit. Unless he was so loaded with weaponry that his weight had doubled.

They carried on through the damp but mercifully rainless night, and Lemming was relieved to feel his headache dulling and his sight becoming clearer. His night vision was good.

Suddenly, he felt almost exhilarated. It was absurd, but this nocturnal creeping about reminded him of the nights when he used to sneak back into Eton after an illicit encounter with a girl. If anything, he felt less afraid of bumping into a Nazi now than he had been of getting nabbed by his housemaster. No German was going to give a British officer six of the best on the backside – he hoped.

In such silence and darkness, it was the smells that swamped the senses. Out in the fields it was all damp earth and vegetation. Near to houses, he enjoyed wafts of wood-smoke from fireplaces left burning at night. He was surprised to recognize a sweetly fermenting compost heap, and then a sudden blast of pungent cowshed, all hay and dung and bestiality.

Margaux put an arm out to stop him. They were on the edge of a village. From memory, he thought it was probably Biville-sur-Mer, which, despite its name, was not really on sea but a mile inland, cut off from the beach by the high cliff. But then again, the name was not much more dishonest than Southend-on-Sea, which at low tide needed a mile-long pier to get anywhere near the briny.

There were trees ahead, and low buildings. No light anywhere, except faint moonlight from behind the clouds.

Margaux pressed her mouth to his ear.

'Quiet. Pond.'

He wondered what this meant until they were creeping past the small circle of water, and a loud honk broke the silence. A swan.

Oh come on, bird, Lemming thought, show some loyalty, all your English cousins belong to the King. Margaux urged him forward more quickly. The honking was not repeated.

A few minutes later, Margaux's mouth was by his ear again.

'This is the house.'

Across the lane, silhouetted against the sky, was a long, single-storey building, set back a few yards behind a small front yard. A farmhouse. They stared at it, straining to sense human presence. There was no smoke from the chimney. Not a hint of light from within. No motion in the garden.

Lemming remembered what Sylvia Trench had said about the lady occupant getting up at dawn.

'Do we wait till first light?' he asked, his mouth nuzzling Margaux's hair.

'No.'

They listened for signs of life along the lane, then crossed it, stooping low. The garden wall was rough, made mostly of flints. They crept around the boundary of the farmyard, moving away from the lane. The sharp edges of the wall's facade scuffed at their clothes.

They were lucky. The house had no closed courtyard, so they could see right round it. At the back, there was no one. No sentries. Just a vegetable garden that smelled of leeks or onions and, a few yards further away, what looked and reeked like a cowshed. Its double doors were closed.

'I'm going in,' Margaux said. 'You hide.' She looked around, clearly wondering where he could secrete himself.

'Not in the cowshed,' he said. 'They'll start mooing to be milked.'

'There.' Margaux was pointing to a smaller building near the lane, on one corner of the property. 'If you hear a struggle, don't try to save me,' she told him. 'Either I come and fetch you, or it's all gone to hell and you'll have to escape. Somehow.'

They were crouching by the garden wall, their faces pressed together. Lemming would have liked to kiss her, if only to wish her luck. But she was probably still angry at him for doubting her loyalty. And they were on a military mission, after all.

'Good luck,' he said.

Without reply, she slid nimbly over the brick-lined top of the wall, and he moved away towards his hideout.

It was a miniature version of the house, a building made of flints interspersed with lines of brick. It had a single bolted door that was not padlocked. All very promising, except that when he reached up to muffle the bolt with his sleeve, prior to sliding it open, he was hit by a familiar smell, unmistakeable to anyone who had been near a country house. It was pig muck. Which presumably meant pigs. He couldn't go in there without waking up any inhabitants. But then again, he couldn't go anywhere else, either, because this was where Margaux was coming to fetch him. He would just have to crouch down outside. If he stayed motionless behind the garden wall, he ought to be invisible from the lane.

He pressed his back snug against the wall, crouching with knees bent so that his backside stayed off the damp earth. The flints dug uncomfortably into his spine, but his feet were nearly dry, he noted. The walk and his body heat had got rid of most of the seawater. He was very thirsty, though, and dying for a cigarette. To keep his mind off both cravings, he picked a thick blade of grass and began chewing.

It was just after he had noted the alarming loudness of a snapping grass stem at night that he heard footsteps. They were confident, not afraid of the dark. With a curfew certainly in force, there was little chance of them being French.

He poked his nose over the top of the wall and saw a light waving back and forth, like a torch being swept in front of a walking man. A patrol. About fifty yards along the lane, coming this way.

Oh God, he thought, this is it. If one of them so much as peeped into his garden, he would be seen.

There was only one thing he could do.

Gritting his teeth and edging the bolt back as smoothly as possible, he opened the pigsty door, silently blessing whoever had kept its hinges decently oiled. The stench of pig and dung was overpowering, but this was no time for faint heart or nostril. He pulled the door shut behind him, and with his fingers, knees and toes digging deep into the bed of filth, began to crawl forward. He could hear a warm, gently snoring presence. Just one pig, it seemed. And so far the animal had not been disturbed from its unwarlike dreams.

Outside, Lemming heard that the men had stopped.

'Hier ist das Haus,' one of them said. So the address was known to the neighbourhood's newest residents.

'Sollen wir umschauen?' Thanks to his time in the Austrian Alps, Lemming knew that this meant they were thinking of taking a look around.

He could not take that risk. And he needed to warn Margaux. He decided to act.

With all his might, he took a bite at the nearest area of pig. It felt like an ear. As he had intended, the pig awoke and gave a deafening squeal. Then, switching to a loud, plaintive snuffling, it struggled to its feet.

Immediately, torchlight probed through the crevices in and around the pigsty door.

From the sound of their voices, the Germans were suddenly afraid. He thought he heard a gun being cocked.

'Mach auf,' one of them said. Open up. Lemming guessed that it was one German commanding another.

He reached upwards and his knuckles knocked against wooden rafters. Swinging himself as if on a trapeze, he was relieved to meet another beam within kicking range. He looped his leg over it and tautened his biceps and stomach muscles to pull himself as high and horizontal as possible. His head throbbed with the effort, but he held fast.

There was a clunk outside and the door was wrenched open. The pig squealed again, bounding towards the intruder and knocking the torch to the ground. The response was very military – a swipe from a rifle butt that sent the pig reeling backwards, complaining bitterly about Nazi brutality.

A helmeted head poked around the door, and angrily but accurately swore at the animal for being a 'Schwein'.

Lemming held his breath and closed his eyes. If he was going to be captured by a Nazi, it was now.

Or perhaps he would fight. He had the element of surprise and two well-trained fists. He opened his eyes and tensed himself for action in case he was seen.

The next thing he heard was the door being slammed shut.

There was a relieved German laugh from outside, and a voice said, 'die Bauerin hatte einen Wachschwein' – the lady farmer had a guard pig.

'Ein Schweinhund,' another voice replied.

The men – it sounded as though there were just the two of them – seemed to think this was hilarious. As Lemming hung on, praying that the object of their mirth would not take an interest in its remaining visitor, he listened to the Germans' whispered conversation about whether to kidnap the animal and supplement their rations. Finally, though, they rejected the idea, apparently because their sergeant already had his sights set on extra rations of pork at some time in the near future.

The soldiers went away, and Lemming was able to swing down from the rafters, almost giggling with relief. He had survived his first head-to-head encounter with the enemy.

The pig was either stunned or sleepy, because it was lying down again, snorting but no longer protesting. He went to stroke its head and thank it for playing such a perfect role in his diversion.

However, when he tried to open the pig sty door again, he found that he was stuck with his new friend. The German had slid the bolt home. Not daring to force the door and make a noise, there was nothing for it but to wait until Margaux came to free him. He was sure that she would have heard the commotion and worked out what was happening.

He squatted against one wall, keeping his trousers as far out of the mire as was possible in this porcine dormitory cum lavatory, and ruing the fact that there would almost certainly be no way to bathe or change his clothes tonight.

He forced his mind to turn away from the painful subject of cleanliness and on to more pressing matters. The lady farmer must have been arrested some time ago, he thought, otherwise the floor of the pigsty would have been clean, and no doubt covered in fresh hay. She would have shovelled the muck all over her vegetable patch or on to a field. Pig muck was far too valuable a commodity to be left for pigs to lie in. It was not the most valuable sort of animal excrement, though, he mused. When he had been out in the Caribbean the previous year, an old colonial had told him that there were adventurers risking storms and U-boat attacks to hunt out a treasure even more valuable than Blackbeard's hidden doubloons – this was guano, the most nitrogen-, phosphate- and potassium-rich natural fertilizer on the planet. There were whole islands of the stuff out there, just waiting to be mined. Or harvested, rather, because the birds never stopped producing it. And thanks to the wartime economy, these islands could be bought for a song. Lemming thought that perhaps he would look into it after the war. If there was an 'after' for him.

His get-rich plans were interrupted by a faint knocking.
'Ian?'
'Yes. Let me out, please, before my girlfriend wakes up.'
About ten minutes later, they were hiding in an apple orchard outside the village, on the fringe furthest from the sea. It was still a couple of hours before dawn. Margaux was whispering in Lemming's ear again.

The farmhouse had been unoccupied, she told him, but it had been searched – torn apart. Fitted cupboards pulled away from the walls, floorboards ripped up, mirrors shattered, the floors littered with pans, smashed crockery, clothes and upturned furniture. If the woman had had a radio, it was gone.

The only fortunate aspect to all the destruction was that amongst the clothes strewn across the floor were some men's garments, approximately in Lemming's size. Margaux had rescued a pair of trousers, a shirt, a pullover, a raincoat, even a flat cap made of almost colourless French tweed. She reasoned that if anyone came to the house to examine the chaos, they would never notice some missing clothes. Either that or they would blame looters.

Lemming ducked behind an apple tree and changed into his disguise. He returned to Margaux dressed as a baggily-attired Frenchman, thinking she would laugh, but she merely looked him over and asked what he had in his pockets.

He showed her his cigarette case.

'You should throw it away,' she whispered.

'It's silver.'

'And I expect it's engraved, too. "To my darling Ian, assistant to the head of British naval intelligence, with love from Lady Churchill, address care of ..." '

'It's not engraved,' he said, stuffing it back in his pocket and thinking how lucky it was that he had not brought along his prized 00 Commando knife. In a fit of pride, he had had his name carved on the blade. He would have had to abandon it in this orchard.

'I've got this, too,' he added, pulling out his gold propelling pencil. 'It's a toy I had made in London. Pull on this little lever and it will squirt tear gas.'

'Are you joking?'

'No, I've tried it out. It works.'

He heard Margaux puff, either in laughter or mild disdain, he could not tell. He put the pencil away.

'Anything else?' she asked.

'Apart from a lighter and some English money, only my identity card.'

'Show me the lighter.'

'Damn!' He had forgotten. It was a present from a woman, and she had had it engraved 'To I Love L'. An in-joke. Her name did not begin with L. The letter stood for 'elle'. It was an excellent lighter. Silver, too.

'You'll have to bury that, your money, uniform and ID card here,' Margaux told him. 'You can come back for the lighter and the money after the war. And take this, too.'

She removed her oilskin jacket and gave it to him.

Using a kitchen knife that Margaux had taken from the house, Lemming dug a hole at his feet, then moved away to another tree to do the same for his ripped-up ID photograph. As for his uniform, he cut off its insignia and did his best to cover it with clods of earth and turf, before stomping the heap down flat. He did the same with Margaux's oilskin.

It would take a very inquisitive apple farmer to dig it all up, he thought, and a treacherous one to reveal its existence.

Once Lemming's mining operations were finished, they shared a pot of plum jam that Margaux had found in the kitchen, taking alternate hungry mouthfuls with a spoon that she had also liberated.

'That pig nearly got us caught,' Margaux whispered. 'We should have used the knife to slice off some bacon.'

'No, she saved ours,' Lemming said, and described how he had bitten an ear to alert Margaux to the Germans' presence.

She was impressed.

'We'll make a secret agent of you yet,' she said. 'Well, the Nazis would say you are one, anyway. In civilian clothes, you'd be shot as a spy.'

'Makes no difference,' he replied. 'In uniform, I was a commando, and Hitler has said they should all be shot on sight. So I'm no worse off, except that I look as though my tailor is a drunk and my hatter genuinely mad.'

'We need a hiding place.' She nodded towards a building at the end of the orchard. 'One barn is probably as good as any other.'

They crept around the orchard wall and listened at the barn door. Silence. Again, it was bolted but not padlocked. These Normans were very trusting. Or resigned.

Inside, it was dry and relatively warm. They felt their way through the darkness to a pile of hay bales and climbed on top. The stack was five or six bales high, above head height. It felt safe. They lay down.

'If the farmer sees his door unbolted, he'll know someone's in here,' Lemming said, nuzzling his face into Margaux's hair yet again. The intimate gesture felt natural now.

'It's a chance we'll have to take,' she replied.

In the distance, they could hear a busier road. The occasional vehicle growled past, but it all sounded a long way off. A dog barked somewhere, but went unanswered.

Lemming closed his eyes and fell asleep, dreaming that a submarine was out there, impatiently waiting for him.

III

He awoke and instinctively threw out an arm to grab his cigarettes from the bedside table. Instead, he embraced a body. Breathing in a shocked mouthful of hay, he remembered where he was.

Margaux sighed and shifted in her sleep.

He opened his eyes and looked at her peaceful face, surprised to find himself thinking that this might well be the first time in his life that he had slept with a woman without trying to sleep with her.

The glow of daylight was shafting through the gap between the barn doors and a few small holes in the roof. There were sounds of activity outside. A distant engine, some hammering, hooves on a road surface. Plenty of bird song, the tiny creatures twittering away, blissfully unaware of the war that was rumbling all around them.

He was tempted to play the hunter-gatherer and go off in search of breakfast, but decided that it was better to wake Margaux first. He did this by whispering in her ear, something he had only ever done to a woman previously when he wanted to enjoy some sunrise entertainment. Which was out of the question this morning. And to think they called it a roll in the hay.

'Margaux. It's morning.' He permitted himself the slightest slap on her cheek, remembering her less delicate touch the previous night.

Her eyes shot open. She took in Lemming and the barn in an instant.

'Right, yes. Bonjour,' she said, sitting up.

'I was going to search the barn in case there's any food,' he whispered. 'Or drink. I'm dying of thirst.'

She nodded, and he climbed softly down, checking carefully that he was not going to tread on anything easily snapped or upended. Creeping around the barn, rummaging silently below tools and behind a woodheap, he drew a blank until, beneath a rusty, upturned bucket, he found a bottle. It was relatively clean, corked, and contained a golden liquid. Normally he would have wished that it could be Normandy's native apple brandy, calvados, but now he was relieved to find something less potent. It was cider, presumably home-made.

Encouraged, he searched on, and between two hay bales, just in arm's reach, he came up trumps. Or rather carrots. A secret stash of vegetables, presumably to keep them safe from the soldiers. They were small but fairly hard. He pulled out a fistful and went back to Margaux.

It was not the most spectacular cuisine he had ever tasted in Normandy, but it felt like a godsend. Gritty raw *carottes (sans moutarde)*, washed in spit and rubbed on clothing, accompanied by a blessedly weak cider, drunk straight from the bottle.

After breakfast, they took it in turns to have a few moments' privacy in separate corners of the barn, then regrouped on top of the haystack for a strategy conference. It was Margaux who did all the talking.

'You stay here,' she whispered. And that was the full extent of her strategy, it seemed. When pressed, she explained that she would go and make contact at a nearby address, where there was someone who ought to take them in and hide them in more decent living conditions. She refused to say where it was, and when Lemming protested, she simply told him, 'you'll have to trust me.'

'What if the farmer finds me?' Lemming asked, quite reasonably, he thought.

'Tell him you're English, that he should bring you some food and water, but otherwise leave you alone. You speak French, I'm sure you'll be able to improvise.'

With that and a promise to return as soon as possible, she was gone.

For the next few minutes, Lemming listened at the barn door for sounds of her capture. If he heard any, he would leap out and intervene with his kitchen knife. But there was nothing, and he resigned himself to a long wait.

He was determined, however, to make himself useful, and undertook a more detailed search of the barn. It turned out to be a treasure trove. Hidden in the most inaccessible corners of the building, he found bottles of cider, some onions, a sack of potatoes, a row of apples neatly lined up on top of a rafter, and – oh joy – a long, hard sausage. All he needed was a saucepan and he could have made *pot au feu* for Margaux's return.

He requisitioned a share of the booty – he didn't want to starve the farmer and his family – and, chomping on an apple to rid himself of cigarette cravings, lay back to wait.

He wondered again about Margaux's loyalties. He still felt offended that she had not entrusted him with the truth about her mission. But he had to admit that it was perfectly reasonable of her to keep her secrets. Telling everyone that she was going into Dieppe was a sound way of sending any pursuers in the wrong direction if one or all of the commandos were caught and tortured into talking. In her position, she was literally risking her life every time she trusted anyone. And if he had to be honest, his being here was doubling the risk of her capture.

He was, he realized, like an alarm clock in her luggage, liable to go off at any moment and advertise her presence. It was a tough responsibility to bear.

He had never knowingly been anyone's luggage in his life. In the past, as soon as he felt that he was not entirely welcome with someone, for whatever reason, he had moved on. No hard feelings, *c'est la vie*. Perhaps he ought to go now, he thought, and leave Margaux unburdened. That might be the honourable thing to do, like that chap in Captain Scott's tent at the Antarctic. Perhaps he should walk out of the barn and accept his inevitable fate.

But now he was just being childish, he told himself. If Margaux had brought him along, it meant that she trusted him to some extent. That she needed him, even.

And after all, he thought, the worst thing from his, and Britain's, point of view that Margaux was likely to do was share her secrets with De Gaulle's people. And the Free French were trying to liberate France just as much as anyone. Just a bit less efficiently.

All in all, he was duty bound to stay on and do his bit. He allowed himself a hunk of sausage as a reward for this noble thought.

He was dozing when he heard sounds at the barn door. It was opening softly. And – the hairs stood up on the back of his neck – was that the snuffling of a dog? A Nazi Alsatian, come to sniff him out? He gripped his knife and the neck of a cider bottle, preparing for a fight.

Yes, there was definitely a dog in the barn now, whining slightly, impatient, sniffing the air. Lemming swapped the bottle in his hand for the sausage. Either he would use it as a club, or distract the animal with the promise of a meal.

But had he made too much noise, rustling around up there? It sounded as though the dog, accompanied by human steps, was coming towards the haystack. He tensed his muscles and gritted his teeth, just as he had always done in the seconds before a boxing match.

'Come down,' a voice hissed at him. 'Quickly.' The dog whined again and was silenced with a slap.

But it was a female voice, speaking English. It was Margaux. With a dog?

It turned out that she had stolen it and tied a rope around its neck as an improvised lead. While the ugly mongrel, apparently a mix of labrador, sheepdog and pig, chewed happily on a chunk of sausage, she brought Lemming up to date.

It looked as though her second contact had also been arrested. The situation was even worse than she thought. The house was being guarded by a *gendarme*, who was, as everyone who had ever been undercover in France knew, not to be trusted. The French police had routinely carried out arrests for the Nazis and had been known to hand over airmen and commandos, even Resistance workers, to the occupiers. There were rumours that they had committed much worse crimes, escorting convoys of hostages to trains heading east into Germany and the unknown.

Somehow, Margaux and Lemming had to get into this second house and look for a document, she said. To do this, they needed to distract the *gendarme*.

'That will be my job,' Margaux announced. Lemming, meanwhile, would sneak inside, go into the *salon* – living room – and retrieve a book, a novel called *Nana* by Emile Zola. According to the pre-arranged protocol, it should be on the bottom shelf of a small bookcase, tucked into the right-hand corner. She made him repeat all this until she was sure he had memorized it.

'You'll only have a couple of minutes,' she said. 'I'll tell the policeman I found this dog wandering about, and ask if he knows whose it is, let him flirt a little.'

'Is that safe?' Lemming asked.

'You think I might give in to his charms?'

He laughed, relieved that they were now on good enough terms for a joke.

'Your accent,' he said. 'I'm sure you speak French beautifully, but you know, we English are all a little "où est la plume de ma tante?" Even I am, and my mother was Swiss.'

'Don't worry,' she said. 'I've been training with Parisians.' That sounded rather risqué, but Lemming didn't like to say so. 'The house is about a kilometre away,' Margaux added. She described exactly where, and Lemming thought he could picture the road on his mental map of the region. He was pleased how well he recalled a document that he had studied for only a few hours. 'It'll be safer if we move separately,' she said. 'You go through the fields. The *chien* and I will take the lane. We'll rendez-vous in the trees opposite the house.'

With no further ado, Margaux opened the barn door, and Lemming felt as though he was about to perform his first parachute jump.

IV

There were, predictably, people about when Lemming and Margaux emerged from the barn. A mother and daughter were hurrying along the lane hand in hand. The daughter, just older than a toddler, stared at the strangers, but the mother knew better and strode on blankly.

Lemming ducked behind the barn into the orchard, and made his way across it, trying his best to look like some kind of tree inspector who was making a very brief check for pests. An old man in the next field, digging with a long-handled spade, did not look up from his work. Lemming got across the lane unseen and went to a small gate, swearing at it in his best French when it refused to open straight away. 'Merde,' he told it, 'con.'[3] Shocked perhaps by this obscene onslaught, it finally opened.

He saw Margaux ambling along the lane with her dog, a young Norman *mademoiselle* going about her business. She was walking towards a woman who was hitching a small chestnut-brown horse to a cart. Lemming did not have time to wait and see whether the two women would begin a conversation. He had to skirt his field, following a low wall, and would need to do the first fifty yards or so on all fours if he did not want to stand out like a duck in a shooting gallery.

At the end of this section of wall, alongside which he had waddled like a toad in an overcoat, he was able to stand up, hidden by the corner of another brick-and-flint barn. He stuck his head out to reconnoitre, and almost fell over backwards.

---

[3] 'Shit ... idiot' (though 'con' is also a vulgar word for the vagina).

Parked in the lane, about a hundred yards away in the direction that Margaux was still ambling, was an open-backed military vehicle. It was a camouflaged lorry, its rear wheels replaced by long caterpillar tracks. And it was carrying a small Nazi army. From the swift glance he got, Lemming estimated that there were a dozen of them. He had seen the horrifically familiar square-looking helmets, and a thicket of rifles pointing at the sky, ready to turn on him if he showed himself. The strangest thing, though, was that they were in colour. He had only ever seen these people in black-and-white newsreels. And here they were, dressed in a curiously unnatural grey-green, their black shoulder straps joining in a V on their back, like some perverse kind of women's underwear. He thought he had seen the flashes on the side of their grey helmets – SS. But at this distance, that might have been an hallucination.

The soldiers were apparently waiting for something. And Margaux had to walk straight past them. Lemming knew that if she failed an identity check, he would not be able to leap to the rescue with his knife. Even the cider bottle in his coat pocket would be of no use.

The worst thing was, though, that he had no time to hide until they left. He had to get to the end of the field.

Mercifully, he was covered by a large hedge and the long side of a Norman farmhouse. He took a chance and ran so that he would be in position sooner to monitor what was happening in the lane.

Peeping out from the edge of the field, he saw Margaux drawing level with the Nazi patrol. The soldiers in the lorry were all looking at her. Not, he was relieved to see, in a military way. Their rifles were still aimed upwards, even though their eyes were fixed on the female target passing at point-blank range.

He wondered what she would do. Smile and say hello, to allay their suspicions? But no, she looked away, pulling the dog closer to her on its leash, as if for protection. Oh no, Lemming thought, she's giving herself away. But then he saw one or two of the soldiers laughing and exchanging a comment. And he realized that she had played the scene perfectly. She had been exactly as fearful as any girl, whatever her nationality, would be when walking past a truckload of armed Nazi invaders.

A few minutes later, she wandered into the trees where he was crouching. He clicked his fingers to attract her attention, and she moved a few feet closer to him.

'That's the house,' she said quietly, nodding towards a two-storey construction. It was larger and wider than most of the buildings around it, with tall brick chimneys at either end of a newish slate roof. A wealthier family, perhaps.

'The window on the left should open if you give it a push in the very centre, between the two vertical panes. It's something we arranged. The salon is at the front of the house. The shutters are open, so stay low. Good luck.'

With that, she was gone. Lemming had no time to prepare himself, to picture what could go wrong. It was now or never, action or failure. This secret agent business was all go.

Lemming walked swiftly and unfurtively out of the trees and up to the back of the house.

With the flat of his hand, he pushed at the wide strip of wood between the two panes of glass, where a clasp would usually lock a typical French double window. With only a minor squeak, it opened. Lemming stepped over the thigh-high wall into the room beyond, and closed the window behind him.

At once, he realized that his visit might be pointless. This place was exactly as Margaux had described the other house. The floor was ankle-deep in debris. He was in a small rectangular room that had obviously been used for storage. There was not much light, but he could see a stack of framed pictures that had been tipped over, a desk drawer that had been smashed, a box of candles emptied out.

Treading carefully across the broken glass of a mirror – the Nazis were heading for at least seven years' bad luck, he told himself – he made his way to the closed door. Listening at it, he thought he heard Margaux's voice beyond.

The door opened on to a corridor, and opposite there was another doorway. That had to be the *salon*. Putting his ear to the wood, Margaux's voice became frighteningly clear. The front window must be open, he thought. Unless she was actually in there with the policeman.

Taking the bottle out of his pocket as a potential cosh – something in his upbringing told him that he would not be able to use the knife to stab a policeman in cold blood, even if the uniform was French – he pressed down on the embossed bronze door handle and pulled at the door.

It would not budge.

Swearing at it softly in French, which had done the trick with the gate, he pulled again. No movement. He felt a sweat of panic run down his spine. What was he going to do if he couldn't even get into the room?

You have to *think*, he told himself. Fast.

He did so, and pushed. The door opened. He swore at himself, in English this time.

Poking his nose into the room, a few inches off the floor, he saw that the lounge was devoid of human contents. Half the front window had been smashed in, maybe by one of those Nazi rifles he had seen in the lane.

He could hear conversation outside.

'I'm so glad I came across you and not a criminal,' Margaux was saying, in apparently perfect French. 'One doesn't feel safe walking alone these days.'

The *gendarme* made suitably heroic noises, and Lemming crept into the *salon* on his hands and knees, keeping a close lookout for broken glass. This room had suffered the same fate as the first. The stuffing had been ripped out of a rather elegant Louis XVI sofa, the embroidered material of its back and cushions cut as cleanly as that same king's neck 150-odd years earlier. Two wooden armchairs were upside down and tipped forward as if at prayer. Even the chandelier had been torn from the ceiling, its thick glass bowl smashed into curved pink shards.

'You don't know whose dog this is?' Margaux was now asking the *gendarme*. It sounded as though the conversation might be coming to an end. No time to waste.

The bookshelf was still standing, but it had been emptied of all but a few volumes. The books, mainly unbound paper editions, were heaped on the floor. Lemming began to examine the pile furthest on the right.

He was a book collector, the owner of one of Britain's finest collections of scientific first editions, and he shuddered instinctively at the evidence of disrespect for the printed word that he saw before him. Even so, he half-hoped to find a hidden jewel – a forgotten family copy of Montgolfier's treatise on the expansion of gases, perhaps? But no, it was all banal stuff.

He picked up a bible, its title pages blasphemously torn, a badly creased Proust, which he didn't mind so much – he had never had the patience to read that dull man's procrastinations – and a picture book of treasures from the Louvre, all the paintings absurdly colourless, of course.

'Where should I try looking for the dog's master?' he heard Margaux say outside. She was putting up a valiant show.

Lemming finally found his Zola. It had suffered little damage during the bookcase abuse. It was a yellowing paperback edition with a plain, text-only cover. '*Nana*, Emile Zola,' it read, with a long subtitle, '*Les Rougon-Macquart, histoire naturelle et sociale d'une famille sous le second empire*'. The second empire was, Lemming knew, the reign in the mid-1800s of Bonaparte's racy nephew, Napoleon III. But 'a natural and social family history'? It sounded very boring.

'Unless *you* want to keep the animal?' Margaux was suggesting.

The policeman chuckled. She was doing splendidly.

Lemming opened the Zola and got a shock – he had come nose-to-buttock with a full-page illustration of an attractively-shaped young lady who was admiring every single one of her physical attractions in a full-length mirror. The only garments protecting her virtue were a pair of stockings that stopped just above the knee.

Even more shocking was the man sitting behind her, fully dressed in evening wear and looking up from his newspaper as though the naked girl had just interrupted him in his reading of that day's racing results, to ask him whether he thought her breasts were reposing at the right angle.

And this was the book that Margaux had chosen to use on her mission?

'Very well, thank you, I will try,' Margaux said, loudly. It sounded very much like Lemming's signal to get moving.

He crawled back across the floor and out of the room. A few seconds later, he was in the back garden and running for the woods, fully expecting to hear a shouted French order to stop.

It did not come, and as soon as he was behind a tree, he sank to the ground, breathing hard. He looked back. Nothing.

Staying low and moving fast, he jogged through the trees, hardly caring about the twigs that snapped beneath his feet, or the blackbird that he sent clucking up into the branches.

Soon he was back at the tree where Margaux had met him with the dog. He crouched behind it and waited. He thought he could hear the Nazi vehicle roaring to life. Yes, there was the crunch of its tracks on the road. He prayed that it would not come his way. For a minute or so, he could not tell where it was heading. Then the sound began to fade.

That's right, he thought, scuttle off to your barracks for some beer and sausage. Enjoy it before our lads come and boot you back to Berlin, or to hell.

Margaux suddenly landed in the grass beside him. She looked calm. She was dogless, but he didn't think it was worth asking why.

'Did you get the book?' she asked.

He could not resist a laugh.

'Some book,' he said. 'Decidedly racy. Naked illustrations. Did you know that?'

'Of course, I chose the edition we'd use.'

'Did you now?'

She held her hand out impatiently for the book.

He gave her the bible.

'I thought this might be more suitable reading for a young lady,' he told her.

Margaux looked as though she had been shot by one of those Nazi rifles. She blanched visibly, staring at Lemming as if he had been the man to pull the trigger.

'You idiot,' she hissed, 'you brainless, snobbish, frivolous, presumptuous –'

He gave her the Zola.

Now she looked as if she was about to weep. With her eyes clenched shut, she rocked silently back and forth.

When she finally looked up, she was grinning.

'You really are the worst kind of fool,' she told him.

But this time she said it the way a man likes to hear a woman say it.

V

Margaux flicked through the Zola, clearly looking for a certain page number. When she found it, she took a small phial of liquid from her bag and poured its contents on to the paper.

'What's that?' Lemming whispered.

'The ink is baking soda solution,' she answered.

'And what are you pouring on it?'

'A semi-acidic liquid. Of physiological origin.'

Lemming could not help cringing.

Although Margaux was holding the book close to her chest, Lemming could see that a few words had appeared between the lines of Zola's text. Margaux read them intently, then tore off that small section of the page, popped it in her mouth and chewed it up.

Lemming cringed even more. Had she just swallowed her own ...? Or someone else's ...? Surely not. What was the world coming to when well-bred young ladies had to sully their lips in the name of freedom?

Margaux now ripped out two or three whole pages, including the one she had already torn, and crumpled them. She wiped them on the ground until a smear of mud was clearly showing. She then lobbed the paper ball into a bush a few yards away. The book she stuffed into base of the bush by her side.

Lemming was looking puzzled, and she whispered, 'If anyone finds those scrunched-up pages, smeared with muck, what do you suppose they'll think it is?'

He could hardly believe his ears. The cream of England's womanhood had been taught scatological camouflage. And he had been embarrassed just escorting her to the lavatory.

Margaux, meanwhile, was thinking hard, staring into the middle distance.

'What did the message say?' he asked.

'I can't tell you that.'

He was suddenly angry.

'Listen Margaux. Like it or not, I'm part of your mission now. I went in the house to get that book. Yesterday I bit a pig. You *have* to trust me.'

She was unperturbed by his show of manly indignation.

'I don't have to trust anyone,' she said.

'No, you don't *have* to,' he conceded. 'But it would be sporting of you if you did. And it might even help you. Your contacts are all blown, or so I gather. And I have been known to come up with a few ideas in the line of espionage.'

Margaux looked him in the eye.

'And if you're caught, you'll hold out long enough under torture to allow me to escape?' she asked.

'Who knows? I've never been tortured. Except when I arrived at Eton, of course, but the prefects weren't trying to get information out of me. That was purely for pleasure. Theirs, I should add. But I'll tell the Jerries you've gone into Dieppe. That was your cover story. If any of the commandos have been captured – God forbid – that's what they'll tell the Gestapo. It will all fit. And as far as I can gather, you have to find out as urgently as possible who's dismantling your network. You need every brain cell you can recruit.'

Margaux thought about this, then nodded resignedly.

'It wasn't in code,' she said. 'It was only cryptic.'

'You mean it was written in a hurry?' Lemming asked.

'Probably. By someone who could feel the net closing in on them. The note said "Chez Tante Agathe, elle est toquée". At Aunt Agathe's place, she's crazy.'

Lemming considered this. Agathe had to be the code name for an agent. If she was 'crazy', did that imply it was an anagram?

'I know where we're going,' Margaux added, 'but not how to get us both there. Any ideas on how to get you across country without attracting the attention of Hitler's Atlantic army?'

Lemming didn't answer. His brain was racing, spurred by the challenge of an enigma. Then, with an almost literal flash of inspiration, it hit him.

'I think I've just worked out where we're going,' he said.

'Oh really?' she asked with a dose of her withering irony.

'Yes. You made a slip,' he said, smiling triumphantly. 'When we were on the train to Brighton. You're not as watertight as you think.'

'Tell me where we're going, then,' she said.

'Very well. Aunt Agatha. The aunt of Bertram Rooster, employer of the literary butler, Peeves.'

'Damn you,' she said.

'And "toquée" gives us the place. I'm right, aren't I?' Margaux neither confirmed nor denied it, so Lemming went on. 'Le Touquet. That's where PG Brickhouse was living before the war. You mentioned his house when we were on the train. It was a slip of the subconscious. You must have known you might be going up to Le Touquet.'

'You're right,' Margaux said, looking genuinely appalled. 'Talk about careless talk.'

'It's not your fault,' Lemming said, wanting to reassure her. 'Without sounding arrogant, I am very well known in London for getting women to do things they don't really want to. Or rather, what they didn't *realize* they wanted to do. There's a very big difference.'

Margaux shook her head.

'Do stop wittering, Ian. We don't have time. Now, if you want to help out, you can tell me how you think we can cover the fifty or so miles along the Atlantic Wall with you looking exactly like an English sailor dressed up in a stolen French peasant's costume.'

VI

Their only chance, they eventually decided, was to steal, or preferably buy, some bicycles. Walking was much too slow, and there was no public transport to speak of. The only other motor vehicles going along the coast would be full of Nazis. Lemming's suggestion that he somehow appropriate a German officer's uniform and a staff car was quickly dismissed – by Margaux, anyway.

'Staying as far away as possible from the troops is our primary objective,' she said. 'Our best hope is to cycle along small roads, parallel to the coast but well inland. With a bit – or a lot – of luck, we might cover the distance in 24 hours. Even then, the chances of stumbling across an army roadblock or an over-curious gendarme are high. So prepare yourself for the worst, Ian. I won't hold it against you if you say you'd prefer to opt out and try to find your way home straight away.'

'And leave you here alone?' Lemming replied indignantly. 'I wouldn't abandon a girl on her own in the middle of Trafalgar Square, never mind occupied Normandy.'

And so they set out, across country, towards the centre of the small town of Biville-sur-Mer.

It was broad daylight, a clear but cloudy day, relatively warm for early spring. The birds and hares were enjoying the weather, and there were people in their fields and gardens, others walking into town. Margaux and Lemming were bound to be seen, but she did not want to wait until dark. And it would look suspicious to be trekking across country, so Margaux suggested they walk in the lane, keeping an eye out for uniforms approaching.

'Adopt a limp,' she told Lemming, 'or better still, paralysis of one whole side of your body. Your excuse for not being away working in a German factory.'

He decided to drag the right side, and put his hand in his coat pocket, his fingers clamped around his knife. Even so, he managed to maintain a steady pace, and loped along beside Margaux, keeping watch over the hedges for approaching helmets or *képis*.

Soon they were approaching the edge of town.

'Bonjour.'

The voice came from behind them. The only thing that stopped Lemming instantly drawing his knife was the voice's high-pitched tone. He and Margaux turned to see a boy, aged about nine or ten, on a small bicycle. It was harnessed to a home-made cart made out of what looked like two pram wheels and a collection of cupboard doors. The cart was full of onions.

The boy was eyeing them, not suspiciously but curiously. He was quite a specimen, Lemming thought. Wearing long grey shorts, a black hand-me-down jacket with the sleeves rolled up half a dozen times to make them short enough, and an oversized beret, he looked just like a miniature Frenchman. Well, of course, that was what he was. His face had a pinched, underfed look. Too many onions and not enough meat.

'Vous voulez des oignons?' the boy asked them.

'Non, merci,' Margaux told him.

'Qui ne veut pas d'oignons?' he said – who doesn't want onions? He put on a salesman's expression of pantomime disbelief. He had done all this before.

'Nous,' Lemming said, and fished into his trouser pocket for some small change, his usual method of getting rid of a bothersome boy in the street. Then he remembered – he had no change, no money at all.

'Merci, mais on a déjà beaucoup d'oignons,' Margaux told him.

'Vous voulez du cidre, alors?' The boy told them he could go and get some cider from his mother.

'Merci, mais j'ai du cidre,' Lemming said, producing the bottle from his coat pocket.

The boy laughed at this magic trick.

'Are you lost?' he asked. 'I can direct you.'

'Non. Merci,' Margaux said, impatient now. She pulled on Lemming's arm to get him moving and waved the boy onward.

'Go into town,' Lemming told the boy. 'You'll find plenty of customers there.'

'You don't think that's where I'm going? I just wanted to give you a chance before everyone else buys my onions. Everyone wants onions.'

He cycled on ahead, looking back once or twice at the two strange walkers.

'He knows,' Margaux said.

'You think he'd sell us to the Nazis for the price of a pound of onions?'

Margaux just grunted in reply, and they walked on.

In Biville, it seemed to be market day. This meant that there were people in the streets. Not a crowd exactly, but enough bodies to make two strangers less noticeable.

They stopped beneath a willow tree, on the bank of the pond that they had passed in the night. A swan was gliding slowly around, no doubt unaware that it might one day end up on the market stall nearby.

Away to their right was a curiously-shaped church. It looked as though three brick barns had been joined together side by side, and a small steeple added on top. Around its walls stood the graves of those who had left the town in spirit, but opted to remain there in body.

In front of the church grounds, in a single line along the road, were four stalls that made up the market. Though 'stall' was a flattering description. In fact they were simple tables.

The market must have been much livelier in peacetime. Now there was only a straggle of customers sizing up the meagre displays of produce. A fruit and vegetable seller had laid out her few apples like chess pieces, next to an iron washtub full of small potatoes and some piles of root vegetables – turnips, beetroot, radishes and tiny white tubers that Lemming did not recognize[4]. It was still morning, but compared to the French markets that Lemming had seen in the past, the contents of this stall looked like the dregs left at the end of a winter's day.

A meat stall had only skinned rabbits on offer, hanging in a row like pink stockings on a washing line. Though they might have been cats or poodles.

An old man had set up a minor exhibition of household goods – sieves, buckets, brooms, various baskets. He had no customers and sat sucking on a smokeless pipe.

A woman, swathed in a bright-red overcoat, her hair wrapped in a scarf of the same colour, was trying to sell clothes, calling out to reluctant women: 'Venez, Madame, regardez'. But it was an odd selection of coats, dresses and blouses – single models of each one. Second-hand, no doubt.

There were no fish or cheese stalls – the trawlers were probably confined to harbour, and families were keeping their camembert for themselves or having it requisitioned by the troops.

The rest of the scene was even less typically Norman.

On the opposite side of the road, next to the board of 'Notices Municipales', stood a white totem pole of German military signs, with arrows pointing in different directions towards the 'Heereskraftfahrpark', the 'Rüstungsstab', 'Feldkommandatur' and 'Ortslazarett'[5]. The black gothic

---

[4] These were probably Jerusalem artichokes, a vegetable that the French had fed to their animals before the war, but were now forced to eat themselves.

[5] 'HQ transport park', 'Weapons staff', 'Military command HQ', 'Local hospital.'

lettering was stark. The double 't' at the end of 'Ortslazarett' looked like a pair of gravestones.

Beyond the line of market tables, side on to the small square, was a tiny *boulangerie-patisserie* in a building that was leaning a few degrees aslant. Outside its low doorway was a queue of women, old men and children, waiting patiently, baskets and shopping bags in their arms. A young soldier, a Nazi infantryman, walked into the shop without waiting. He emerged seconds later with a round loaf, pulling at the crust to eat the first fresh mouthful. It was a simple human gesture of enjoyment that did not sit well with the uniform.

Lemming wondered where the soldier had come from, then gripped Margaux's arm in warning. Across the top of the few market stalls, he now spotted a line of square helmets and rifle barrels. It was another patrol truck, probably not there in case the traders overcharged for radishes.

'We'd better get out of sight,' Margaux whispered.

They turned, to find the onion-selling boy behind them, both hands clamped on his handlebars. He was staring directly at them, weighing them up. And he seemed to be holding one thumb on his bicycle bell.

Surely not, Lemming thought. He's not going to sound the alarm on us? He hoped he wasn't going to have to brain the lad with his cider bottle.

'Venez avec moi,' the boy said.

'Où?' Where? Margaux reasonably asked.

Lemming gripped the neck of the bottle.

The boy repeated that they should follow him. They couldn't stay in the street. Someone would see them.

Jerking his head over his shoulder, he began to pedal back the way he had come.

'Venez!' he said, more urgently.

Abandoning his limp, Lemming set off, pulling Margaux with him. She resisted, but Lemming just tugged harder.

'Sometimes you have to trust people,' he said.

The boy led them through the streets of Biville, pedalling slowly a few yards ahead of them. He stopped at every corner to check that the coast was clear. Once, he held back, but only to let a donkey cart pass. He waved a greeting to the woman at the reins.

Another time, the boy turned around from the corner and waved Margaux and Lemming into an alley. He joined them, whispering 'flic!' (cop).

After this detour, he made his way to a crossroads, and this time he beckoned them over. Pointing to a stocky, white-painted house opposite, he told them,

'Go into the garden behind the house. There's a hut. Wait in there. I'll talk to granddad and grandma.' He called them 'pépé et mémé'.

This time, Margaux did not hesitate. They were riding their luck and had to see where the chance encounter took them. She and Lemming went around the side of the house, climbed over the low wall, and ducked into a wooden hut standing beside a tall, mature apple tree.

The inside of the hut stank almost as much as Lemming's pig sty from the previous day. Along one end of it was a wire enclosure containing half a dozen unoccupied nests. The chickens were presumably outside, foraging.

'Now we really are cooped up,' Lemming said.

'Save the jokes for the gendarmes.' Margaux pressed her face to the wall nearest the house, to look out of a knothole.

'I trust the kid,' Lemming said.

'Lucky you.'

A few tense minutes later, with the chicken smell getting less bearable every second, a door opened in the house, and an old man came out into the garden. He looked alarmingly like Marshal Pétain, the Frenchman who had told his army to surrender in 1940, handing his country to the Nazis without a fight. This old man had white hair and a moustache of the same colour, and was wearing a sky-blue sleeveless jumper and grey trousers that could almost have been part of a French army uniform. Surely this couldn't be Pétain's holiday home,

Lemming thought. It would be quite something, getting captured by the head man of Vichy himself.

The door of the chicken coop opened, and a worried face gaped in at Margaux and Lemming. It looked as though the man had not wanted to believe his young grandson's crazy story, but now it was confirmed.

'Spick Frensh?' he asked.

'Oui,' Margaux said.

'Une bonne nouvelle, au moins,' the man said – that was one piece of good news.

VII

It was comforting to be in a Norman house that had not been ransacked. Furniture stood upright, a varnished dresser still had china bowls and plates on its shelves, a clock hung on the wall, defiantly ticking the time, and an oval mirror was in one piece above the intact brick fireplace.

A small, slender old lady was standing beside a blackened stove. Her fingers fidgeted with the buttons of a flowery overall, and she stared at her two visitors as though they were giraffes or Apaches. She also shot a panicky look at her husband, the man who had invited these strange creatures into her home. The boy stood behind her, smiling nervously. Here was the proof that that he had been telling the truth.

'Des Anglais,' the old man said.

'Des Anglais?' his wife repeated.

'Bonjour, madame, enchanté,' Lemming said, and came forward to kiss her hand. He knew that it was an absurdly flamboyant gesture, but he thought it might reassure the poor dear. It didn't. Now she looked even more haunted than before.

'Vous avez soif? Faim?' the old man asked. Were they thirsty or hungry?

'Nous avons de la tisane,' the lady said, shaking herself out of her daze. She was offering them herbal tea. Verbena and mint, from the garden, she explained.

Lemming would have preferred a whisky and soda, but accepted with thanks.

'Parfait, madame,' Margaux said.

It was warm in the long kitchen-dining room, and Lemming took off his coat. Margaux did the same.

'Go and sell your onions,' the old man told his grandson.

'But I want to stay.'

'Your mother needs the money,' his grandmother said. 'Go. Now.'

Convinced by the old lady's sudden sternness, the boy agreed, but told Margaux and Lemming, 'I'll sell them in no time at all. Wait till I come back.'

He dashed out of the kitchen towards the front of the house, and they heard the door open and slam.

The four adults sat at the table, drinking from bowls of hot herbal tea, which was actually tasty, defying Lemming's prejudices against drinking stewed weeds.

'It's best that he's out of the house,' the old man said. 'He took an immense risk. The Boches shoot children as well.'

'Yes, we're sorry to put you in danger,' Lemming said. 'We won't stay long.'

'Are you part of a network?' Margaux asked.

'No, no,' the old couple chorused, as it if were a German asking.

'The lad hears me complaining about the Boches,' the old man said. 'He knows how we feel. And I should tell you that we don't blame you English for Dunkirk. I know you got lots of our boys out as well. I've always blamed the maréchal. Did we surrender in fourteen, when the Boches were at the Marne? No, we went and stopped them. It cost us dear – my own two brothers died in the trenches, I spent four years there – but we booted them out in the end.'

'My brother died at Dunkirk,' Lemming said, simplifying history somewhat, but wanting to stress his sympathy.

The old couple looked deeply moved.

'So you know what I mean,' the old man said.

'When are you coming to invade?' the woman asked.

'We don't know,' Margaux answered quickly. 'No one knows.'

'Are you here to plan the invasion?' she asked.

'No,' Margaux said. 'We were flying over Paris. Our plane was shot down near there.'

'Oh là là,' the woman said.

'You came on foot?' the man asked.

'Yes, on foot,' Margaux said.

'How many days?'

'Four,' Lemming improvised.

'Do you want to take a bath? I can heat some water,' the woman offered.

'Oh oui,' Lemming said.

'Non merci,' Margaux said. 'We must leave. We need bicycles. And my colleague needs papers.'

Lemming nodded. Sitting in this cosy home, he had become acutely conscious of wandering about France like a homeless vagabond.

'Papers?' The old woman shook her head.

'Papers.' The man reached across and took his wife's hand. He had a questioning look in his eye. She breathed deeply, then nodded.

The man left the kitchen, and returned a minute later carrying something before him. He put it on the table. It was a French identity card, with the photograph of a man a few years younger than Lemming. Dark-haired, with a moustache. He was called Peletier, Henri.

'Our son, Henri,' the man said. 'He was killed at Dunkirk, too.'

The woman took another deep breath, apparently trying to avoid sobbing.

'Perhaps he died fighting alongside my brother,' Lemming said. He felt suddenly closer to Mark than he had since he first heard the news. But then he was, physically, much closer. Mark's body might be buried just a hundred miles up the coast. If the Nazis buried prisoners' bodies.

'Together, they saved the British army,' Margaux said, giving the old lady's hand a squeeze. 'You have to know that everyone in England has felt grateful every day since then to those who fell at Dunkirk. When we win the war, it will be thanks to men like your Henri.'

The old man placed his own hand on those of Margaux and his wife.

Lemming felt a tear prick one of his eyes. He could hardly believe it. Such lack of self-control in a naval officer.

He picked up the identity card and put it in his jacket pocket.

'Merci,' he said. 'And I will die before this card gets into the hands of a Boche. I promise you that.'

'Or the gendarmes,' the man said. 'You can't trust them, either. And we've had some Milice around here too, the bastards.' He looked as if he wanted to spit on the floor at the very mention of these black-uniformed French fascists.

'We should go, in case anyone comes,' Margaux said. 'Do you know where we can get some bicycles?'

'The Boches came round requisitioning them all,' the old man said. 'But we gave them our old rusted ones. I have some newer ones in the cellar. They haven't been on the road for a year or more, but if the tyres haven't rotted ... I'll go and look.'

'I'll come with you,' Lemming said, but the old man refused, telling them to get a meal and a quick wash.

The old woman sat watching the two *Anglais* as they emptied bowls of a tepid stew, mainly consisting of onions and potatoes, with a few scraps of meat that had been stripped off a bone. Lemming got out his cider bottle, but the women gestured that he should put it away, and produced a jug from a cupboard.

Spooning up the stew, sipping cloudy cider, Lemming caught Margaux's eye and smiled. He wondered if she too was thinking back just a couple of days to their dinner in Mayfair, when aproned Frenchmen had been falling over themselves to serve them sophisticated food and wine, while Lemming was trying out his most urbane conversation.

Now, there was virtual silence around this humble country table, but there was a hundred times more mutual understanding. He realized how much of his past life had been play-acting. This simple meal in a Norman kitchen was real, intense, urgent. It was living life to the full.

The old man returned with good news. The tyres were not rotten, he said, and he had pumped them up. Lemming and Margaux only had to wheel the *vélos* up the cellar steps.

He was also carrying a pair of off-white cotton shorts, like abbreviated pyjama bottoms. They looked freshly washed.

'I didn't dare help myself in the ladies' lingerie cupboard,' he said, and his wife got up, beckoning Margaux to follow her.

In the laundry room, a grateful Lemming got changed, wondering if he had ever put clean underwear on to a dirty body before. It was intolerable. He didn't even have any cologne.

Then he heard the front door open. He listened, gripping the knife in his pocket. There were voices. But it was only the boy being scolded or contradicted by his grandparents.

When Lemming emerged into the kitchen, Margaux was already there, watching an argument that consisted mainly of the boy being told to obey his elders' instructions.

'He wants to cycle ahead of us, opening the way,' Margaux explained to Lemming. 'We've told him it's too dangerous, but he won't listen. You talk to him. Be the RAF pilot at him.'

Lemming went and gripped the boy's shoulder.

'Comment t'appelles-tu?' he asked the boy.

'Jean,' he answered. 'Comme pépé.'

'Listen to me, and to your pépé and mémé,' Lemming told him gravely, in his best French. 'It is very courageous of you to want to act as our guide. And you have already shown great courage in the face of the enemy, bringing us here. But it is much too dangerous for you to escort us through the town. So I am ordering you to stay here. You understand? This is a military order from a captain in His Majesty's Air Force.' He let his hand weigh even heavier on the boy's shoulders. 'Besides,' Lemming went on, 'I have a vital mission for you. It is of critical importance to us that there be no sign that we have ever been in this house. You must search the hut and this kitchen, and all the rooms where we have been, to make sure that we have left nothing behind. If you find anything, destroy it. Perhaps you should even do the washing up, so that our bowls bear no fingerprints.' Lemming winked at the grandmother. 'But your most vital mission of all is secrecy. No one must know we were here. Not even your mother.' He stabbed a finger at the boy's chest to press his point. 'You understand?'

'Oui.'

'You know, in England,' Lemming went on in his most fluent French, 'we have a special medal, the Médaille des Secrets. So when we have won the war, and when we come back here to Biville to say thank you, if we find that no one except your grandparents knows our secret, I will write to the King of England and tell him that you deserve this Medal of Secrets. And if you're very, very lucky, Princess Elizabeth will come and present it to you. Have you seen photos of Princess Elizabeth?'

The boy shook his head.

'Well, she is very beautiful. She looks like my colleague here.'

The boy gave Margaux an appraising look, and nodded, apparently very satisfied.

'Well, if the Princess doesn't mind, I think I'd prefer mademoiselle to come and present it to me,' the boy said, beaming at Margaux.

Lemming punched him softly on the shoulder. 'You will go far, my boy,' he told him. 'You're already a typical Frenchman.'

The grandmother put her arm around the lad, pulling him close, as if to rule out any chance that her grandson would disobey.

'When we've gone, break the lock on your cellar,' Margaux told the grandfather. 'If anyone asks you, tell them your bicycles were stolen.'

'Take some apples, too, then,' the woman said. 'A thief would not leave them.'

Margaux and Lemming thanked their saviours, slipped out of the back door and into the cellar, and extricated the bicycles. 'Bright idea, the medal,' Margaux told Lemming. 'You're good with kids.'

'It's because I've always been one,' he said, meaning it as a joke but realizing that it was painfully true.

VIII

They headed a few miles inland, adding time to their journey but avoiding the town of Criel-sur-Mer. It had a harbour and a beach, and was therefore a possible invasion site. Lemming had seen from aerial reconnaissance that it was heavily armed and manned.

The countryside was generally flat, with narrow lanes running between muddied fields of root crops. Visibility was excellent – or disastrously dangerous, depending on how you looked at it. A Nazi guard post hidden in one of the rare coppices would see them coming for a kilometre or more. And if they spotted an army vehicle, it would definitely see them. Their only option was to ride and hope.

Margaux had a small compass hidden in the heel of her shoe, and she used it to keep their front wheels pointing generally north. Cycling was hard for both of them, despite a light supporting wind. The bicycles were heavy, their chains un-oiled. Lemming realized how tired he was, and out of condition. Even though he had hardly smoked for 48 hours, his lungs were rasping. All those years of sixty a day had apparently taken their toll. Margaux kept up with him easily, outstripped him occasionally.

When they met other travellers, mostly women on foot, they greeted them with a workaday 'bonjour'. On the few occasions when they saw people in the fields – an old farmer leading his huge workhorse, a group of women digging up roots, a boy hacking at a tree with an axe – they acknowledged them in passing, as any ordinary French person would do. No one gave them a suspicious look. In wartime France it was apparently best to keep your head down.

At one point, they caught sight of the top of a lorry, its roof moving behind a hedgerow. They turned off quickly into a lane and ducked behind the nearest bushes. They found themselves beside a stream that was crawling sluggishly through a thicket of high reeds and grasses. There would be wild irises here come summer, Lemming thought. If summer ever came.

They heard the lorry passing on the road above, but did not peep out to see whether it was possible friend or definite foe.

Crouching by the stream, Margaux pulled a tiny square of silk out of her blouse collar, where it had been concealed. She unfolded it and laid it on a dry patch of ground. It was a map. Judging by the fonts used in the place names, it was a copy of a captured Nazi document.

'You'll be delighted to know,' she told Lemming, 'that we shall be passing through the village of La Pipe, which, rather incompatibly, is next to La Vièrge.'

This was a bawdy joke – 'pipe' being the slang word for fellatio, and 'vièrge' a virgin.

'I'm shocked you should even make the connection,' Lemming replied, thinking yet again that Margaux showed a promising lack of prudery. He wondered whether she had ever done her bit as a Mata Hari. A girl like her could work marvels for De Gaulle. Give her one night at the Admiralty, and she could even seduce old Rashbrooke into revealing all the navy's plans. Mind you, Lemming thought, if she wanted to seduce the rear admiral, she would probably have to dress up as an aircraft carrier.

'I'm also very impressed by your pronunciation of such key French words as "pipe" and "vièrge",' he told her. 'Not a trace of auntie's plume. How is that? I'm sure a finishing school doesn't make you *that* fluent.'

'Honestly, Ian,' she tutted. 'Do you really think I'd tell you? But talking of accents, you were right about yourself. You've got to tighten your vowels if you want to sound a bit less like a Sussex parson on a tour of the Norman châteaux.' She pronounced the last word with perfect Frenchness.

'I'm not *that* bad, surely,' Lemming said.

'You speak wonderful French, Ian, but you'll have to make much more of an effort if you don't want to sound English. When we English speak French, we usually get the conjunctions and genders right to prove we learnt them at school, but the pronunciation is just too much bother for us. We think that pursing the lips and making guttural noises is too vulgar. Too foreign. It didn't matter in Biville, when we were among friends, but if we have to talk our way out of a trickier situation, perhaps it's better to leave the talking to me. If someone asks you a question, try mumbling. Maybe that wound of yours has affected your brain as well as your body. Either that, or ham up your accent as if you were playing it for laughs on the stage at Eton. Get your spittle moving. Then it might become almost authentic.'

'Touché,' Lemming said. 'Or should I say tooo-shaaay?' He made his accent pantomime English.

'Sorry if I've hurt your feelings,' she said, folding up her map, 'but this is like the French Revolution, when one slip of the accent could get you guillotined.'

'I take your point. Honestly. And one day I really am going to get you to explain how you mastered all that French tongue work.'

'Keep your mind on the job, please,' she said, but she was smiling.

It was not until their first river crossing that they hit a roadblock. It loomed suddenly at them, as a good roadblock ought to, when they rounded a bend at the foot of a small incline. They were travelling quickly, and it was lucky that their sudden braking could have been interpreted by the men at the roadblock as a desire not to crash into a hedgerow.

'Oh well, it's been fun,' Margaux whispered, riding slowly towards the waiting men. 'Don't forget your limp.'

The roadblock was set up at a small bridge. A Nazi lorry was parked at the side of the road, in front of one of the area's typical barns, with its stripes of orange brickwork colouring low whitish walls. There were a couple of Nazis sitting under the lorry's tarpaulin, apparently relaxing.

Leaning against the cab were two soldiers, one with a rifle over his shoulder, the other cradling a machine pistol. They were smoking cigarettes. When they saw Lemming and Margaux appear, they stopped talking and stood up straight.

On the opposite side of the road to the truck stood a French policeman, in classic *gendarme* uniform, with a flat-topped *képi*, and a wide blue-black cape covering his jacket. He was not smoking. So it was collaboration, but without excessive fraternization.

The road was blocked by a white pole set on two white Xs of wood or metal. It looked like a show jump, and for an instant Lemming pictured himself sailing over it on his bicycle.

Margaux, taking the lead, went up to the policeman. She did not even look at the soldiers. Lemming did the same, keeping his head high, like a defeated yet proud warrior, while feeling his heart beating like the most terrified coward. The water flowing under the bridge was roaring, but only just louder than the blood in Lemming's ears.

He kept his wits about him. When he stopped his bicycle in front of the policeman, he made sure that he landed awkwardly on his left foot, and let his right arm dangle by his side, half-paralysed. He allowed his jaw to slacken, too. It struck Lemming that he had spent his whole life trying to look the fittest, ablest man in sight, and now he was getting adept at doing the opposite.

'Bonjour, monsieur l'agent,' Margaux said.

'Papiers, s'il vous plaît.' The *gendarme* held out his hand.

'My friend has a little difficulty,' she said, and reached into Lemming's coat pocket.

Lemming did his best to look frustrated by his physical condition, and allowed himself a gruff, slurred 'B'jour', hoping that he sounded like a wounded Norman peasant.

Margaux handed over Lemming's identity card and her own, which Lemming had never seen before. He realized that she had not even told him her cover name. That was taking secrecy to an absurd level, surely.

The policeman looked from cards to faces. When he compared Lemming's flat-capped head with the moustachioed portrait of the dead Henri, he seemed to flinch slightly.

Lemming's heart rate doubled, and he felt a surge of helplessness, as though he really were paralysed. Their amateurish attempt at subterfuge was going to fail at the first hurdle. And he had broken his promise – the identity card was already in the hands of the enemy. He wanted to yell with fury.

'Where are you going?' the *gendarme* asked, above the roaring of the stream.

'Valéry-sur-Mer, to my sister's,' Margaux answered, more quietly.

'Where have you come from?'

'From Dieppe. We were seeking work for my fiancé. It is difficult, you understand, in his condition.'

The *gendarme* looked Lemming in the eye. Lemming met his gaze steadily, and saw suspicion. Something was not right, and the policeman was wondering how to deal with it. All this in the space of a single glance.

The *gendarme* licked his lips once, nervously, then nodded.

'Wait here,' he said, turning towards the soldiers.

Lemming wondered if he would be able to grab and swallow the identity card before he was beaten unconscious. He steeled himself for the pain to come.

But now the *gendarme* was lifting the white pole out of its X, pulling it aside, and holding out the identity cards to Margaux.

'Très bien,' he said loudly, as Margaux took them. And then gave a swift, and almost inaudible, 'vite'.

So he was helping them.

Despite his desire to shout with relief and give the Nazis the V for victory sign, Lemming made a great show of being a partially disabled man setting off awkwardly on his bicycle, only one strong leg on the pedals, one fully fit arm on the handlebars. He followed Margaux along the lane, away from the bridge, and heard the pole fall back into place.

When they were well out of sight, they stopped by a tree and Lemming produced his bottle of cider. He was sweating and, ignoring his natural gallantry, he took a hard swig before handing the bottle to Margaux.

'So they're not *all* collaborators,' he said, as she drank.

'A year ago, six months ago, he might well have handed us over,' she said. 'These policemen aren't stupid. They know the wind is turning, and their coats are turning with it.'

'Lucky for us.'

'Damned lucky. Let's get away before he changes his mind.'

'You played the scene very well, mademoiselle Chevalier, Irène,' Lemming said.

Margaux did not look pleased that he had seen her French name.

'Thank you, but forget it,' she said. 'And well done to you, too. Your "bonjour" sounded just right.'

'Merci, m'dame,' he replied, attempting the same slurred accent.

Margaux climbed back into the saddle and started up a gentle rise out of the valley. Lemming puffed after her.

IX

They spotted the tanks from half a mile away, a line of four Panzers driving straight towards them along a narrow lane. A few seconds later, they heard the noise of growling engines. It

117

was an almost unreal sight, these four hideous monsters in the idyllic rural scene. The hedgerow along the roadside was just coming into leaf. The farmhouse down in the valley to their left was snug, protected by bare but vigorous-looking fruit trees. The large piebald horse in the pasture to their right was much more interested in grass shoots than tank manoeuvres. And the two cyclists on their rural day out were riding straight down the barrels of four of the deadliest machines on the planet, capable of unleashing instant death on everything in that scene.

The men behind the metal shields were just as deadly, Lemming thought. The Panzer divisions were known to be amongst the most fanatical of Hitler's troops. Get in the way of their grinding tracks and you would be mercilessly squashed to pulp.

He could now see heads above turrets, the tank commanders surveying the view. He felt certain that at least one of them would be observing the two approaching cyclists through binoculars.

The road was sloping downwards, sending the bicycles ever closer to the tanks, which were growing more gigantic with every yard. The two riders could even smell the diesel fumes pumping out above the four turrets.

'I doubt if they'll stop to interrogate a couple of cyclists,' Margaux said, though she did not seem entirely convinced.

'Unless they need to ask directions.'

The joke did not go down well. Margaux ignored him and braked hard. She stopped by a gate that led into a field bordered by high chestnut trees. There, she dismounted and stood with both hands on the handlebars. Lemming did the same, remembering to feign disability.

'Try to look scared,' Margaux said.

'Thanks for reminding me.'

When the first tank was almost on top of them, it slowed down, ominously, its tracks clattering even more loudly on the road surface.

The machine was enormous. Its muddied tracks came up to shoulder height. Its armour, painted green with earth-coloured smudges and inscribed with the sinister black cross, looked as thick as a Norman farm gate. Its gun barrel, pointing straight ahead, was a veritable tree trunk.

The head poking out of the first turret, a very white face topped by a dark grey forage cap and earphones, was saying something above the engine noise.

Margaux shouted 'Comment?', meaning 'what?'

Lemming decided to squint stupidly.

The head rose higher and grew a pair of shoulders covered in an alarming black leather jacket. The shouting grew louder. This seemed to be one irritated Panzer commander. A large pair of binoculars was hanging around his neck. He must have seen the cyclists from afar and grown curious, Lemming thought. Oh well, if you were going to lose a fight, this was about as one-sided as it could get. One knife, a cider bottle and a tear-gas propelling pencil were not much use against four tanks. Casually, he put a hand into his pocket to clasp the identity card. One thing was for sure – those old folks in Biville were not going to get a visit from a herd of Panzers.

The second tank commander was shouting, too. The man in the leading tank hauled himself even further up, until he was more than waist-high out of the turret. This revealed the bulbous pistol holster on his belt. Even that, Lemming thought, the smallest weapon in the tank, was more than enough to terminate their mission.

Margaux put up her hands in surrender. Lemming raised his 'good' arm, too, and began to struggle with the other, which was clutching the folded identity card. Almost time to start chewing on paper, he decided.

The tank commander was laughing at them. That was a bit much, Lemming thought. The Nazis at their arrogant worst.

But the man was also waving an arm, as if swatting away a finger that might be pointing in his face. He did it again, and now Lemming thought he could make out the words he was shouting.

'Eh car tay foo!' he was saying. 'Ow sem vek!'

Lemming translated the sounds into words: 'Ecartez-vous. Aus dem Weg.' The man wanted them to get out of the way in two languages.

'Oui, oui,' he shouted back, nodding furiously. He bent low towards Margaux's ear.

'Ecarter, écarter,' he said, pulling at her arm with his good hand.

As quickly as possible, given the need for Lemming to maintain his mime of partial paralysis, they moved their bicycles a few yards along the line of trees, out of the way of the gate.

The leading tank commander yelled something down into his tank, and the metal beast swivelled on its access, its engine howling, its gun barrel swishing through the air where Margaux's head had been. The tank then drove straight over the wooden gate, effortlessly splintering it to pieces, and was followed in quick succession by the other three tanks. None of the commanders gave the cyclists a second look. The two civilians had ceased to exist, exactly like the gate. Never in his life had Lemming felt so glad to be irrelevant, invisible, as inoffensive as one of the birds squawking away from the clanking machines that were now taking up residence in the field.

Lemming and Margaux began freewheeling down the hill, away from the engine noise.

Even after this let-off, there was no time to indulge in relief. They were on the outskirts of the town of Eu, a strategic place despite its microscopic name. Lemming knew from his history books that this was where Queen Victoria had met France's King Louis Philippe sometime in the mid-19th century[6], to begin the long healing process that would culminate in the Entente Cordiale. Now, though, it was not a place for English people to be seen. Just a few miles inland from the harbour of Tréport, Eu's impressive *château* was known to be occupied by a

---

[6] Lemming ought perhaps to have known that *two* meetings took place in Eu between the British and French monarchs, in September 1843 and September 1845.

large Nazi garrison. The whole town would be teeming with soldiers.

Stopping briefly in a patch of dense woodland, they consulted Margaux's map. They were at its very edge now.

'If we can get across the river,' she said, pointing at the silk square that she had laid on the damp grass, 'it's a straight run up to the Somme.'

To Lemming, it was strange to hear Margaux sounding optimistic about entering that particular zone of France. Lemming's father had been killed on the Somme in 1917, about a hundred miles east of where he was now sitting. His brother had been mortally wounded not far north of here. In short, almost half his immediate family had died in the region, and now here he was, cycling through the war zone, unarmed.

Even so, he had fond, vivid memories of the area. Driving too fast along these rural roads, flashing past these same farms, woods and rivers as he impressed some girl with his skill at the wheel, had been one of his greatest pleasures of the interwar years.

His memories of that time were also brightened by oysters, champagne and sparkling company at the casinos along this coast. He wondered if gambling still went on there now. If so, the whiteness of starched shirts and sheer gowns had almost certainly been replaced by the grey of Nazi uniforms.

In the distance, they could hear loud engines, the noise rising and falling as though vehicles were entering and emerging from tunnels. Or being tested, perhaps.

'Let's try and stay away from that, whatever it is,' Margaux said.

Lemming tried to think what might produce such a sound. Nothing very friendly, that was for sure.

X

It was an airfield. The worst possible news for anyone hoping to cycle through the area unmolested. There would be guards, patrols, fences, dogs, and a general state of high alert.

Coming out of the woodland and getting a view across the valley, they could see the planes clearly, and hear the engines every time a gust of wind blew in their direction. Two fighters and a larger double-engined aircraft were taxiing slowly across the horizon, looking menacing but clumsy. They seemed to be heading towards low, rounded hangars on one side of the field.

Margaux and Lemming stopped abruptly as soon as they saw the planes.

'That's a passenger Heinkel,' Margaux said. 'Some top brass arriving, perhaps.'

'Or a consignment of caviar for Goering. Either way, we'll have to cross the river somewhere else.'

'Yes, further inland, damn it.'

Not dwelling on the annoyance, she turned and began riding southeast.

They explored two river crossings, but each was heavily populated by unfriendly-looking types in square helmets. Both times, they had to climb the hill again, to the edge of the valley, pumping their legs to the brink of exhaustion.

An hour or so later, they crouched beside a hedge, both of them breathless – Lemming a lot more than Margaux. She still seemed fresh, whereas Lemming felt as though his lungs had been churned to pulp and were siphoning up into his throat.

They looked down into the town of Inchville.

Below a low ceiling of cloud, the view was clear right into the wide town square, which was also a crossroads. On opposite corners stood a white-walled church with a stubby steeple, and a *château*-like brick building, no doubt the town hall. The space between the two was crammed full of grey vehicles, of all them bearing the black-and-white cross. There were lorries carrying men and supplies, half-tracks armed with spindly machine guns, staff cars with red swastika pennants, motorbikes, with and without sidecars. Some of these vehicles were moving, others stationary. And all around them, like passengers waiting their turn to board, were soldiers.

'Looks as though they think the invasion will come through here,' Lemming said. 'Do you think it will?'

Margaux looked incredulously at him.

'Honestly, Ian, if I did, would I tell you?'

'Of course not, I was only …' She had a knack for making him feel foolish that he hadn't encountered in decades.

'Let's go,' Margaux said. And she was off again, heading back northwest.

'Where?' He would have preferred to rest for a few minutes. Or hours.

She pointed down at a troop of men marching northwards out of town.

'We've got to get across the river before that column of soldiers takes up guard posts or whatever they'll be doing.'

It was a hard slog along the valley's edge, and it was half an hour of lung-searing effort before they reached the next turning towards the river. Here, though, there were no soldiers in sight.

It was a joyous freewheel all the way down, and two or three minutes later they were recovering, hidden from the main road by a low whitewashed wall. They were crouching in the entrance to a field that bordered a sawmill yard on one side, a house on the other. A ten-foot-high stack of logs hid them from the sawmill itself, but they could hear voices there. French voices, by the sound of it.

Lemming was just about to say this to Margaux when she gripped his wrist and goggled her eyes in the direction of the field behind him. He turned and saw a uniformed man ambling away towards the sawmill fence, just a dozen yards or so away. He had his back to them, and they could see the machine pistol hanging lazily by his side. He didn't seem to be on the alert, though. No, he was fiddling with his trousers, and stopped by a fencepost. Adopting the typical feet apart, one hand on hip, stance of the carefree open-air urinator, he began to whistle as he watered the fencepost and took in the pleasant Norman countryside beyond.

They just had to hope that their bicycles, parked against the white wall, would not attract attention.

Holding their breath, staying immobile, they heard the whistling stop. When Lemming estimated that the coast ought to be clear, he took a quick look, and gave Margaux the thumbs up.

'He's gone into the sawmill.'

No sooner had he said it than they heard the whine of an engine. Or engines, coming down the hill from the main road.

Peeping around the corner of the wall, Lemming pulled his head back sharply.

'Two lorries. Nazi.'

'Down flat,' Margaux said, pulling her bicycle over and lying beside it. Lemming did the same, pressing his face into wet grass, and praying that its young stalks were long enough to hide him if one of the lorries' drivers or passengers looked towards the field.

Ten, fifteen long seconds passed. The lorries braked as they reached the foot of the hill, their gears crashing. They seemed to be about to stop completely. Lemming could not help himself seeking out and gripping Margaux's hand. She squeezed back.

Sure enough, the lorries were coming to a halt by the side of the road. Without looking up, it was impossible to tell how close they were, or whether the drivers had pulled over because they had seen what looked like two unconscious cyclists lying in the grass.

A lorry door opened and closed, then another. There was a brief exchange in German that Lemming could not make out.

Then nothing.

Margaux was the first to move. She lifted her head, then placed her mouth against Lemming's ear.

'Over the wall into the garden,' she said. 'And lie down. Leave the bikes here.'

In one fluid motion, she lifted herself to her hands and knees and flopped over the garden wall. Lemming followed, landing on top of her.

She grunted with pain. 'Get off me and crawl to the back of the house. Must be an outbuilding where we can hide.'

Dragging themselves on their elbows, commando-style, they covered the twenty or so yards into the back yard with a speed that surprised Lemming.

Behind the house there was, as Margaux had predicted, an outbuilding. Like the wall, it was whitewashed, and topped with ochre tiles. It had a half-size wooden door. An animal pen of some sort. Oh no, Lemming thought, not another pig.

But if there had been a pig in there, it had long since been carved up and eaten. The small building was empty, dead and musty. It contained only an orderly stack of tiles, a clutch of fence-posts and a ploughshare wrapped in sacking. The floor of the hut was bare earth, so Lemming unwound the sacking for them to sit on.

For the first couple of minutes, they sat in reflective silence. Lemming wanted to ask what they were going to do, but instead he started working out a plan.

'We'll have to wait till dark,' he said.

'No. We'll play it by ear,' Margaux said. 'Take the occasional peek to see what they're up to, and move on as soon as they've gone.'

So much for his plan, he thought.

Hungry, thirsty, tired and discouraged, neither felt much need for conversation. Lemming would have liked to say something chirpy, but all he could think of was that he would do anything for a cigarette. Put me up against the wall, he found himself musing, tell the firing squad to wait a minute, and give me one last gasper. One of my own, the ones I have made for me personally by Morland's of Grosvenor Street. It's my own blend of tobaccos, don't you know, Herr Hauptmann.

'If you're going to fidget like that, have a cigarette,' Margaux said.

Lemming felt an almost sexual rush of gratitude.

'You don't think it'll give us away?'

'There's no chimney, there are no windows.'

'God bless you,' Lemming said, and pulled out his cigarette case.

It was only when he had opened it that he remembered that he had buried his lighter.

The torture of frustration was almost too much to bear. He wanted to go and bomb Berlin to rubble just to punish the Nazis for imposing this abstinence on him. Usually, sleep was the only thing that kept his fingers away from his cigarette case. He had not spent so many daylight hours without a smoke since he was at school.

'Surely there's some way of lighting them,' he said.

'Rub two fence-posts together?' Margaux suggested. 'Or bash a tile against the plough, and attract the whole Nazi army?'

Lemming took a deep sniff of his sparsely populated cigarette case, inhaling a few microns of nicotine. Only nine smokes left. Under normal circumstances, he never let supplies get that low. Nine would not normally have lasted him more than a couple of hours in the office.

'A smoke, a smoke, my kingdom for a smoke,' he groaned.

'I think there be six Woodbines in the field. Five have I smoked today,' Margaux replied.

Lemming stopped sniffing tobacco.

'Oh Lord,' he said, 'don't tell me you're one of those people who are so well educated that they can quote the whole of Shakespeare and the bible?'

'We put on an all-girl production of Richard III at school. I played the lead.'

'Well, I'm sure you would never have allowed the lack of a horse to stop you escaping from the battlefield. You'd just have stolen the nearest bicycle.'

Margaux laughed softly.

'You're rather good at compliments,' she said.

'Yes, but usually they're said with a specific motive,' he confessed. 'That one was as pure as the driven snow.'

'Good. You wouldn't want to do the right deed for the wrong reason.'

'What?'

'TS Eliot,' she said. 'We did Murder in the Cathedral, too.'

'Well, I hope you were the one who got murdered.'

Lemming immediately regretted his joke.

'Sorry,' he said. 'I wasn't thinking. Completely the wrong time for a stupid quip like that.'

'Don't worry. Eliot has that effect on most people.'

God, he thought, what a woman. He was suddenly seized with a desire to crush her with a kiss and make love to her on this dirty sacking, in this sordid hut.

With any other woman, if they had been sheltering from a storm, he would have done so. Or suggested doing so. But now something stopped him. And it came as a shock to realize that it was respect. Plain respect. He felt that this woman was his equal in every way. Superior, even, in some of them. He had never felt that about a woman before. Leaving aside the question of physical strength, he had always felt, or been allowed to feel, dominant. Even if the women were partially play-acting for his sake, he had always been ready to fulfil the role of the decider, the inciter, the alpha male. Even after an evening of sophisticated conversation, on an equal footing, women became mere objects of his desire.

Margaux was desirable, certainly, but she was different. Usually he would have propositioned her despite her rejection in London, and not cared if his advances had been rejected again. But now he found that he did not want to offend her in any way. If something was going to happen between them, it had to come from her.

It was a startlingly new sensation.

127

XI

Lemming awoke terrified that he was trapped beneath a heavy weight. He was on his stomach, his face pressed into rough sacking. The sensations became clearer. There were knees on his back. Or elbows. Margaux's?

A voice whispered in his ear. But it was not hers. It was French. And male.

'Bouge pas.' A man, who had not used toothpaste recently, or soap, was ordering him not to move.

Lemming could see nothing. It was dark and his face was jammed against the sacking. He struggled but could not free himself. His hands were behind his back, and apparently tied.

He received a sharp jab in the spine.

'J'ai dit, ne bouge pas.' The voice was angrier now.

'Qui –' Lemming began, and the jab came again, crunching against his vertebrae. It felt like a gun barrel.

'Ta gueule,' the voice hissed, a crude way of telling him to shut his trap.

Lemming did what he was told, and listened. There was rustling, more whispering. No sound of Margaux's voice. He wondered if she was in the same predicament as him, or had escaped.

'Lève-toi,' the voice told him. Get up.

He was pulled to his knees, and immediately a blindfold of some sort was wrapped around his head and knotted tightly.

Lemming was scared, but to some extent reassured. These sounded like real Frenchmen. So there was a chance that they were allies. Unless, of course, they were the notorious *Milice*, the fanatical pro-Nazi French militia. Now he really was scared.

He was shoved out the door of the hut, and felt the shock of cold air on his face and hands.

'Debout,' he was told. Stand up. Then a strong hand gripped him at the elbow and led him away. He remembered to limp, causing his captor to yank impatiently on his arm. Undeterred, he continued to drag his right side. It was, he knew, his only cover.

They walked a few yards before a door was opened and he was bundled down some stone steps into a warmer place that smelled musky and slightly sweet. A wine cellar, he thought, or cider cellar, perhaps. He heard several sets of footsteps coming down the stairs behind him, and tried to work out whether one of them was female.

The door closed, and the voice in his ear grew slightly louder and more relaxed.

'Assied-toi.' Sit down.

Lemming bent his legs and reached out with his tied hands. He felt a curved wooden structure behind him, and eased himself downwards. He came to rest perching uncomfortably on a wooden chair. It had obviously been condemned to the cellar because it needed repair. It was cane-seated, and its woven strands had broken. He had to struggle to stop himself sinking right through the ring of wood like a child on its potty.

Despite his blindfold, he saw that a light had been turned on.

'Qui es-tu?' the same voice asked him. It was male, mature, slightly rasping. Its owner had been smoking as heavily as Lemming, but lower-quality tobacco. Even so, right now Lemming envied the voice its smokiness.

'Et toi?' he asked, putting as much French phlegm into the question as possible.

The voice told someone to empty Lemming's pockets, and a hand was soon tugging at the material of his coat.

The voice grunted with apparent surprise.

'Très chic.'

Lemming guessed they had found his cigarette case. The realization that they might smoke all his cigarettes made him even more aware of the discomfort of his situation. Blindfolded, jammed into a broken chair, and no chance of a gasper. This really was torture.

'Peletier, Henri, Biville-sur-Mer,' the voice said, and Lemming's whole body tensed. He wanted to issue a threat, but did not trust his accent. 'Qu'est-ce que tu fous ici?' he was asked. What the hell are you doing here?

'Et toi?' he repeated.

'*Qu'est-ce* que tu *fous* ici?' A hard object, presumably the gun barrel, was used to stress key words against his chest. It occurred to him that this was probably the first gun that ever had been pointed at him personally. The other day on the submarine, the Nazis had been firing in his general direction. He had trained with guns, of course, but they had always been pointed elsewhere. It was alarming to feel himself just one finger twitch from death. But something made him defiant.

'Tu es de la Milice, toi?' Lemming asked. 'Tu aides les Boches?' Was the man helping the Germans?

This question caused voices in the room to consult in inaudible murmurs. Three people, he thought, one of them young, or maybe even female.

'On va demander à ta copine,' the gruff voice said. They were going to ask his girlfriend. So Margaux had been captured, too. 'Et si elle nous dit pas, on va la convaincre.' If she didn't talk, they would 'convince' her. It was the sleaziest of threats.

'Laisse-la!' Lemming growled. Then he had a brainwave. 'Si vous voulez, je vais vous l'écrire,' he said. He would write it down for them. Again, he put all his half-paralysed, saliva-driven Frenchness into the accent.

'Ecrire quoi?'

'Il veut son stylo,' another voice said. He wants his pen.

It was a propelling pencil, but Lemming was not going to quibble. With his blindfold off and his little tear-gas spray in his hands, he would have a chance.

'Pourquoi il veut son stylo?' the first voice said. Then a few seconds later, Lemming heard a short squirt, and the voice spluttered. 'Putain!' This meant whore, but Lemming knew it was also an obscene exclamation. The man must have sprayed himself with tear gas. He was coughing and swearing. It was satisfying in a way, but infuriating, too. Lemming's trump card had been played too soon.

'Oh bugger,' he murmured to himself.

'Qu'est-ce qu'il a dit?' the spluttering voice said. The man was recovering. He had clearly not received a crippling dose of gas. The design of the spray would evidently have to be improved. Or the potency of the gas.

'Un truc allemand,' the second voice said. They thought he had spoken German.

Lemming lost his temper at the absurdity of it all.

'No it was not German, you bloody clowns. It was English. I said bugger, from the verb to bugger, meaning sodomize, which I hear from certain ladies that you Frenchmen are inordinately fond of. I can only assume that it's because your members are so small that you can't get satisfaction from less constrictive orifices.'

There was silence, except for a cough or two from the gas victim.

'Alors là,' one of them said, an expression of amazement. A woman's voice.

'On dirait qu'il est bien Anglais,' the other man agreed. He meant that Lemming really did sound English.

'Yes, I am English, so why don't you Milice bastards either shoot me or hand me over to your Boche bosses so they can torture me. At least they might give me a cigarette.'

He doubted whether the French would understand, but he was actually enjoying himself. Anger was an excellent, if temporary, remedy for hopelessness.

'On n'est pas la Milice, nous,' the first voice said, rasping even more since its dose of tear gas. 'On est la Résistance, nous.'

'Nous sommes sur le même côté, alors,' Lemming said – we're on the same side. His outrageously English accent proved that he had abandoned all pretence of being French. 'Détachez-moi.'

'Bah, non. Justement,' the voice now said, implying that his Englishness was precisely the problem.

'Pourquoi, justement?' Lemming asked.

But then he heard scuffing shoes, a door opening and closing, muffled voices. Some of them had left the room. Not all of them, though. He still heard breathing.

Sitting ever more painfully, his buttocks sinking lower and lower into the broken cane seat, his hands beginning to throb because of the tight bindings, Lemming tried to think. Why, if they really were Resistance, would his Englishness be a problem? The indignation with which the man had denied being in the *Milice* had been real. And no *Milice* man would bother to deny it. By all accounts they strutted about in black uniforms, like junior members of the Gestapo.

'Pourquoi est-ce qu'il y a un problème entre les Anglais et la Résistance?' Lemming asked. The only explanation he could think of was the conflict between the SOE and De Gaulle's private army. But could things have got so out of hand that they had become real enemies?

'Ta gueule,' a male voice ordered. Shut your muzzle.

Then the bombing started. It began with a faint tremor and a distant boom, then grew steadily more volcanic. After less than a minute, Lemming found himself bouncing half an inch off the floor, and he heard the creaking of wood and metal as the building around and above him complained about the violence of the attack. Bottles chinked. His French companion swore a few times, and then said, 'Voilà des Anglais.'

Was that it? Were these Resistance fighters angry that the allies were bombing France? But the planes were aiming at airfields, fortifications, railway supply lines, troop formations. Surely no Frenchman could object to that?

A deafening roar and a minor earthquake signalled that a bomb had fallen very close. Lemming began to sweat. Even so, he found himself feeling surprisingly calm.

'Vous n'aimez pas les bombardements?' he asked. 'Mais c'est contre les Boches.' He was challenging the man. If he didn't like the Nazis being bombed, what did that make him?

'La Luftwaffe va l'avoir dans le cul,' the man said, a metaphorical reference to the buggery that Lemming had mentioned earlier. 'Et c'est nous qui leur avons indiqué la cible,' the man added. He was indignantly pointing out that his group had told the bombers where to aim.

Curiouser and curiouser.

About twenty minutes later, the air raid was over. The atmosphere in the cellar was dustier, sweatier, but the building seemed to be intact.

A door opened, and Lemming heard someone sit down. 'Voilà le problème.' It was the smoky voice again.

'What have you done to Mar–?' Lemming just stopped himself in time. 'Ma fiancée,' he corrected himself.

'Ecoute-moi.' The voice was telling him to listen. It went on to explain in clear, slow French why the *Anglais* were causing concern.

It was nothing to do with the bombing. It seemed that several Resistance workers had been arrested recently – Lemming knew this, of course, but did not say so. And each time, the Nazi arrests had come while the victims were harbouring an Englishman. By all accounts, the same Englishman.

The Frenchman let the accusation hang in the air.

'Ce n'est pas moi,' Lemming said.

'Tu es sûr?'

'Oui.'

Lemming heard the man get up and walk towards him. He braced himself for a punch. He tried to tighten his stomach muscles without making it too obvious, and he made sure that his tongue was not between his teeth. Let them do their worst. He had boxed at Eton.

But now the man was behind him.

'Si on pense que tu es le traître,' he said, threateningly – if we think you're the traitor – 'même si on ne peut pas le prouver' – even if we can't prove it – 'on te marquera' – we will leave our mark on you.

Lemming felt a tickling on the back of one of his hands.

'Ton couteau laissera un joli tatouage.' Your knife will leave a pretty tattoo. 'Un grand T pour traître.' A big T for traitor.

The man pricked Lemming's right hand, presumably with the kitchen knife.

'Je ne suis pas traître, moi,' Lemming said.

'C'est ce que prétend ta copine,' the Frenchman replied – that's what your girlfriend claims, too. He sounded open to debate. The only solution is for you to convince us, the Frenchman added.

'Comment?' Lemming asked. How?

'Explique-nous tout ce que tu as fait en France.' Tell us everything you've done in France.

'Jamais,' Lemming answered. Never. He could not do that without betraying his friends in Biville. And without breaking every rule of secrecy.

'Pas de noms,' the man agreed. No names. He said that he wanted to know only the bare details of Lemming's landing, and where he had been hiding – in houses or barns.

'Je ne peux pas,' Lemming said.

'Fais-nous confiance,' the Frenchman said. Trust us.

Lemming laughed in his face.

'Va chercher la fille,' the man said. Go and fetch the girl.

'If you touch one hair on her head, I'll –' Lemming did not know what to threaten. Tied and blindfolded, it was hard to imagine what he could do.

Lemming heard steps, then Margaux's voice.

'Are you OK?' she asked.

'Yes, you?'

'Fine.'

'Tied up and blindfolded?' she asked.

'Yes, you too?'

'Like Christmas turkey. But I don't think they want to eat us.'

'Parlez français,' the leading French voice ordered.

'D'accord,' Margaux said. She then explained to Lemming that the men had given her a couple of code words to identify themselves as part of a network. 'I really think they might be genuine,' she went on, in French. 'We just need to convince them that *we* are. So can you tell them, in the vaguest terms possible, what we've been up to so far? No place names, no people, just the type of places we hid and searched. If our stories tally, they might believe us. Understood?'

Lemming thought about this. It was a test. If only he could work out what exactly it was testing. Did Margaux's intervention here mean that her loyalties were in any way skewed, that she might be in with the Gaullists against the SOE?

'Je veux l'embrasser,' he said. He was demanding to kiss her.

'Quoi?' the gruff voice asked.

'L'embrasser.'

'Vous voulez lui souffler quelque chose.' The accusation was that Lemming wanted to whisper something to her.

'Non, juste l'embrasser, sur le front.' No, just a kiss on the forehead.

Surprised by his demand for a show of affection, the French agreed, and Lemming heard Margaux move towards him.

'I'm not sure that this is the right time or place,' Margaux said, in French, 'but I'm very flattered.'

He smelled her presence. If she had been wearing perfume, it had faded, but her hair and face smelled of femininity. There was no other way of describing it. He lifted his face, bent forward, and found what he was looking for. First her forehead, then just below it, the roughness on his lips of some kind of scarf or napkin. So she was blindfolded, too. That was what he needed to know. If her eyes had been uncovered, it might have been proof that she was in cahoots with the Frenchmen.

'D'accord,' he said, and described in the vaguest possible terms his adventures of the past day or so. The pig sty next to the house that had been searched. The second house with the *gendarme* and the dog. He did not mention the book, of course, so as not to reveal anything about Margaux's methods. Then the orchard and the barn. The house where they had 'stolen' the bicycles and an identity card. The roadblock and the tanks. Then the sawmill and the lorries.

At the end of it all, the French voice told him to wait.

There were retreating footsteps again, a door opening and closing.

'Are you still there?' It was Margaux.

'Yes. You too, I gather?'

This time, no French voice told them to shut up.

135

'Good storytelling,' she said. 'I think you convinced them.'

'What's going to happen?' he asked.

'No idea. Maybe they'll untie us and disappear. Maybe they'll take no chances and shoot us. Who knows.'

'What was all that stuff about an English traitor?' Lemming asked.

'Yes. Strange. I don't know,' Margaux said.

Was that hesitation? Was she telling the truth?

The captors came back into the room. There was a tug at Lemming's wrists, and his hands were free. He shook them to restore the circulation, then reached up to remove his blindfold. He had to blink at the sudden brightness.

Margaux was sitting beside him, rubbing her wrists.

They were in a basement with a low wooden ceiling, earthen floor, and metal wall-racks that had probably held wine bottles at one point. Now they were all empty.

The other occupants of the room were two men and a woman, all of them with woollen balaclavas over their heads. Only their eyes were visible.

One of the men was stocky. He was dressed in a grey suit, but tieless. He was sitting in an old armchair, a British Sten machine gun on his lap. Beside him stood a thinner, perhaps younger, man in a dark brown coat. He was holding a pistol. It looked like a German Luger. Standing slightly to one side was a woman in a light-green flowery dress. She was the only one without a coat. So she was probably the owner or tenant of the house. She was unarmed.

'Vous êtes Gaullistes?' Lemming asked.

'On est communistes.' It was the younger man who answered, defiantly.

'La Résistance active, pas passive,' the older man said. His was the gruff voice.

So there clearly was strong rivalry between the two outfits, Lemming thought.

'Ce n'est pas important,' Margaux interrupted, a little too quickly for Lemming's liking. She demanded that they explain in more detail why this Englishman they had mentioned was thought to be a traitor.

The two men took it in turns to tell the story. From what they had heard, an English pilot had parachuted out while on a raid. This was not uncommon. There were air raids practically every day, with airmen of all nationalities crash-landing or jumping out of damaged planes, most of them bomber crews downed by anti-aircraft flak. Some of the men were taken in by brave citizens and then smuggled out of France through tried and trusted escape routes. Many, inevitably, were captured. And here was the strange thing: people had seen the Englishman being marched through the streets of Dieppe by Nazi troops, but then he seemed to have escaped and re-appeared. Definitely the same man, according to locals. After his escape, he was taken in by a woman, who was arrested almost immediately, and he was re-captured. Then the same thing happened again. A *pilote anglais*, wandering through the area, was hidden by sympathisers and then re-captured, along with the people who were hiding him. It looked as though the Englishman had been used as a lure.

This Resistance group had been waiting for him to re-appear yet again when Lemming had popped up, along with Margaux.

'Je croyais que vous alliez me balancer aux Boches,' the woman added. She thought they were going to betray her.

'Non, non,' Margaux said. She told them that she and Lemming had come from England precisely because of this problem. And now they had to continue their mission.

'Où?' the older man asked. He wanted to know where they were going.

Margaux shook her head. She could not say.

'On peut vous emmener en camion,' the young man added. They could take them by lorry. The Nazi guards had left, he said.

Margaux still did not react.

'I think we have to trust them,' Lemming told her. 'They could have handed us over, tortured us, anything they wanted. And I don't think we're going to get very far on our bikes. Have you seen these troop concentrations?'

Margaux was staring at the three balaclava-covered heads, obviously sizing them up.

'Quel genre de camion?' she asked. What kind of lorry?

'Pour le bois,' the older man said. For wood. He explained that he made regular trips all over the region, fetching freshly-cut timber from the large forests near Boulogne-sur-Mer and the Somme estuary, and delivering planks and poles to Nazi construction sites. They could call him a collaborator if they wanted, he said, but his work meant that he could learn plenty of things.

'La preuve – le bombardement de ce soir,' he said. The proof was tonight's air raid.

Lemming nodded to Margaux. He thought it all sounded credible. And Le Touquet was directly between the Somme estuary and Boulogne-sur-Mer.

He whispered in her ear.

'We get him to drive towards Boulogne, and we tell him to drop us off when we want. No need to mention Brickhouse.'

Margaux nodded.

'Très bien,' she announced. 'On y va tout de suite.' She wanted to leave straight away.

The older man nudged Lemming.

'C'est elle la patronne?' he asked. Was Margaux the boss?

'Oui.'

'Ah, ces Anglais,' the man said, shaking his head.

XII

Lemming was getting used to confined spaces – the submarine, the pig sty – but the spaces were getting more and more confined. Now he felt like a medieval knight, laid out below his tombstone. His one consolation was that a lady was laid out beside him. He only hoped that it would not be for all eternity.

They were concealed in a compartment on the bed of the lorry. A false bottom had been constructed by leaving a single-bed-sized gap in a framework of planks that had been covered over with boards and a tarpaulin. Air was let in through holes punched in the new floor, and from one side – the hiding place was in the top left-hand corner of the lorry bed.

Now Lemming and Margaux were lying side-by-side in the darkness, their hips more than touching, their noses a few inches from a ceiling of rough wood, on to which they could hear logs being dumped. The lorry was going to take a small load of firewood up the coast.

Lemming was breathing fast and deeply, as if his body was afraid that Margaux might get too much of the available air. He could not help himself testing the ceiling, to see if it would budge. He was more used to the wide-open spaces of hotel lounges, casinos and country-house dining rooms. His attempt to lift the board earned him a rap of protest from above.

This, he realized, was real trust – when you let someone shut you in your coffin.

The lorry belched into action. The whole chassis began to shake. The ride was going to be even rougher than necessary because this was a gas-powered vehicle, fitted with two bulbous tanks, like a boxer's cauliflower ears, one each side of the cab. The gas was charcoal-based, the driver had explained, and just like a human being, the lorry coughed at having to breathe in all that smoke.

Lemming had wanted to ask for more technical details, but Margaux interrupted the conversation, saying there was no time. For Lemming, there was always time for mechanical details, especially if they postponed the moment when he would be sealed into a wooden tomb.

Now Lemming was already thinking that he would have preferred to take his chances on foot or bicycle, dodging tanks and soldiers.

'It's just for an hour,' Margaux said.

So his nerves were showing.

There was an uncomfortable bump, then the lorry was out of the sawmill yard and the ride became smoother, if barely less noisy. Lemming smelled coal-like exhaust fumes. What a fate, he thought, asphyxiated in the back of a French lorry while chugging along the very road where he used to race in an open-top Bentley.

He swore and tried to will himself to stay calm.

'Talk to me,' he said to Margaux. 'Tell me something to take my mind off this hell. Where did you train in spy craft, for example?'

'Why don't you tell me what you got up to when you came to France in 1940,' she replied. 'From what I read about you, it sounded fun. And it was a great success.'

Another well-deflected question, he thought. But he found that he wanted to talk about it. Those had been innocent times, exciting times, when he had had a purpose that he understood, one that he had chosen for himself. Not like now.

'It was June,' he said, turning his face towards Margaux's right ear, 'and the Nazis were already crossing the Low Countries. I was sent into France to convince the French admiral, Darlan, to bring his fleet to Blighty and join up with the British navy. The trip was my idea, actually. So I grabbed a wireless operator and flew to Paris, and then we drove down to the Château d'Artigny, near Tours. Do you know it?'

In his usual circles, there was always someone who knew the French *château* that was being discussed.

'No, go on.'

'Well, Darlan was sure that France would repel any invasion, by land or sea, so he didn't want to listen to a messenger from London. Besides, he was very proud of the fact that his great-grandfather was killed at Trafalgar. We English were still the enemy. We still are to some Frenchmen, don't you think?'

'Some,' Margaux said non-committally.

The lorry was slowing down. They heard, and felt, the change of gears. The lorry stopped, and the driver began a conversation. A roadblock perhaps. The engine was still juddering enough to make hearing individual words impossible.

Then the engine growled to life again, and they set off. One less obstacle on the road north.

'So what did you say to Darlan?' Margaux asked, once the engine had settled back to a constant note.

'Nothing much. A few days later, dive-bombers started attacking the château – even then, the French must have been betraying each other. We offered to give Darlan the whole of the Isle of Wight as a French outpost, but he preferred to head south in the hope of rallying his men there.'

'He went down to North Africa, didn't he?'

'Yes, and when it looked like the Nazis were going to seize the French fleet, Churchill gave the order to our lads to scuttle the lot at Mers-el-Kébir in Algeria. The French have never forgiven us for that. De Gaulle certainly hasn't.'

Again, Lemming let this idea hang in the woody, smoky air – which was now more breathable thanks to the inrush of cold wind from the side of the lorry.

'Darlan eventually got bumped off by a French patriot,' he said.

'And to think he could have had the Isle of Wight.'

'Can't blame him for refusing, really, can you? Who wants to live there? But that was no excuse for becoming a collaborator. After Mers-el-Kébir, Darlan announced that he wanted the remaining French navy to join forces with Hitler, you know. It goes to show, even today, 130 years after Napoleon, there's no love lost between Britain and France.'

He wondered whether he was being too heavy-handed with the subject of Anglo-French, Gaullist-Churchillian rivalry.

'Well I hope our driver has forgiven us for Waterloo,' Margaux replied.

The lorry was slowing down again, but this time to negotiate a rise of some sort. The engine whined loudly as the vehicle struggled to get up the slope. They slid backwards until their feet were jammed against the end of their hiding place.

'Perhaps we should get out and push,' Margaux suggested.

'I wish I could get out and smoke.' Lemming had cadged some matches and smoked one cigarette in the cellar, but it had only renewed his cravings.

When they were back on the flat and travelling smoothly, Margaux prompted Lemming again.

'Then you were in Bordeaux?' she asked.

'Yes, it was chaos. Worse than Henley during the regatta.'

'That bad?'

He let the irony pass. He was picturing the scene that had met him when he arrived on the southwest coast of France in June 1940.

'Ships all over the place, French and British, queuing up to dock, launches chugging back and forth to fill up the ships with refugees, retreating servicemen, consulate officials and supplies that no one wanted to fall into the hands of the enemy.'

'Wine and suchlike?'

'Exactly. Cognac, foie gras, military secrets. All the essentials. I made sure that a consignment of aircraft engines were loaded up, bound for Portsmouth. And a few cases of Château Margaux '32. Couldn't let the Nazis have that.'

'Of course not. And you were helping the refugees, too?'

'Yes, the harbour front was teeming with them. Children crying, women pleading, men crying, too. Offering me and anyone nautical-looking a small fortune for a passage. From the simplest people to the crème de la crème.'

'Who didn't want to end up brûlée.'

'Bravo. Yes, though we let the poorest ones on board for free, of course. The harbourside was like the car park at Ascot. Bentleys, Rollers, Daimlers, Mercedes, even a couple of Cadillacs. The chicest people in western Europe were trying to bribe the crane operators into winching their limousines aboard. I had to persuade them that they would be lucky to get on ship with their hand luggage. I was drying their tears as I talked them up the gangplank cuddling their furs and jewel boxes.'

'And that was the men.'

'Exactly. And then, just as the last ship was about to sail, came the most beautiful 1930 Rolls Royce Phantom I've ever seen. A perfect butter yellow, smooth and silent as a stalking lion. It was followed by a herd of smaller cars, all madly tooting their horns. And out of the Phantom climbed none other than King Zog of Albania, looking strangely like Hitler with his little black moustache. He had brought along his family and his whole staff. As well as the crown jewels of Albania. Not many of them left, just a few tiaras and chains, but enough to pay for a comfortable exile. Zog begged me to let him take the Rolls on board. I sympathized – it was a spectacular motor car – but I told him he could always get another one. He was almost on his knees. He promised me a dukedom on the Bosnian border if I could get it on board.'

'So are you Duke Ian of Herzegovina?'

'No, we had to leave his Phantom on the docks. I swear he was weeping as we sailed.'

'Perhaps it had sentimental value,' Margaux suggested.

'You mean, King Zog and Queen Geraldine had enjoyed unforgettable journeys in the love seat? Perhaps. But I suspected it had hidden compartments stuffed with cash. Or that the whole chassis or bodywork was made of gold.'

'It would weigh a ton.'

'Yes.' Lemming had already considered the technical practicalities. 'He'd have had to bolster the suspension. Double springs on the rear axle. He'd have needed a bigger engine, too, of course. More than the standard fifty horsepower. But it would be the perfect way to ship your money from one place to another without import duty or bank charges.'

He found his mind turning the idea over yet again, this time in relation to the war effort. If he had been back in Room 7 at the Admiralty, he would have sketched out a short working paper: The usefulness of hiding valuable or experimental metals by moulding them into the bodywork of a car. The vehicle could be stopped at a border post and pulled to pieces, and nothing suspicious would be found, unless the customs men scraped off the paint and analysed the metal below.

The lorry suddenly bumped and jerked, slamming Lemming's head against the wooden floor. He cursed the driver, who seemed to have driven too fast over a railway crossing or some similar hurdle. Lemming hoped it was a Nazi sentry.

They stopped, and again the engine idled while a conversation went on outside. This time, someone got up into the back of the lorry and walked around. Footsteps made the floor tremble and bend. Logs seemed to shuffle just above their noses. Shafts of light pinpricked into their coffin, illuminating floating dust. A torch, perhaps, accompanied by a rifle. But then the light went away, as did the footsteps. The lorry lurched back up to speed.

They breathed a simultaneous sigh. They had probably never been nearer a jackboot.

'You like to drive, don't you?' Lemming asked Margaux. He remembered her threatening to do a hundred on the Brighton road.

'I love to,' she answered immediately. 'The faster the better. Patrick has a nippy little Riley MPH ...'

At the mention of her brother, Margaux's enthusiasm died suddenly, like a faulty motor.

'He'll be driving it again soon, I'm sure,' Lemming told her. 'The Nazis don't mistreat RAF officers, even in their Stalags. The POWs receive Red Cross parcels and letters. He'll be fine there.'

Margaux did not respond.

'Tell me about the Riley. Please, I'm interested,' Lemming went on. 'The MPH is meant to be a superb little motor. Does he have the seventeen HP model?'

'I don't know.'

'The bodywork is made of aluminium, though, isn't it? It flies like a bird, so I'm told. Up to ninety.'

'It's fast,' she conceded.

'When all this is over, I'd love to drive it. Or have Patrick take me for a spin. Only a few of them were made, you know, back in '34. It's probably worth a bit of money. Not that you'll be selling it, I'm sure.'

Damn, he thought. He was treading as carefully as a Nazi tank in a field of potatoes.

'I hope our friend stops at the right turning,' Margaux said. Given the fact that they had no view of the road, they had been forced to tell the man, their male captor with the smoky vocal cords, where exactly to drop them.

'Even if he gets it slightly wrong, I can find my way to the house,' Lemming said. 'That is where we're going, isn't it?'

'I'll show you when we get there,' she said.

This continuing furtiveness, combined with the fact that his spine and skull were being vibrated to jelly, his bones chilled by the forty-or-so-miles per hour wind being jetted through the airholes, and his lungs filled with wood chips, made Lemming grind his teeth. But he knew he had to put up with it. If he were back in London, he would no doubt be asleep between his soft hotel sheets, or rucking those same sheets in the company of a sweet-smelling female. But he was also aware that there were, at that very instant, people getting bombed, shot and tortured, people trapped in sinking ships and submarines, people trying desperately to bale out of a flaming tank or aircraft, or wondering which one of the bullets, shells and grenades flying at them would find its target. By comparison, he was not so badly off. He was not, he realized, even bored. It was pitch-dark, the background noise was mind-numbingly repetitive, the conversation had died, but he was not feeling even a twinge of his usual *ennui*.

He was even looking forward to tramping through the dark, damp woods of Le Touquet that might be infested with Nazis – without being allowed to smoke a cigarette on the way.

Well, on second thoughts, there were *some* things he could not so easily put up with.

XIII

At last they saw their French captor's face. He had worn his balaclava even while he was sealing them up in the lorry. Now, in the pale glow from the shrouded headlights, they saw a reddish countenance below a wide-brimmed hat that was cocked at an angle. He had lively hazel eyes, and a pipe held jauntily between his lips. He was the type of man who, freed from the constraints of war, would probably have been sitting at a bar over a Pastis, making worldly jokes and teasing the *serveuse*.

He had parked just off the road, and he made a quick, efficient job of freeing them. While they found their sea legs, he walked round to the front of the lorry and was now standing up against a tree, looking like a driver who had stopped merely to relieve himself. He was speaking over his shoulder, without turning to face them.

'Le centre est à quatre-vingt-dix degrés d'ici,' he said. The way to the centre of Le Touquet was perpendicular to the road.

'Oui, merci,' Lemming said, blinking into the dark woodland opposite. Tall sand pines were rocking in a freshening breeze, protecting smaller, stubbier trees and shrubbery beneath. The scene was swathed in shadow, but he could remember it vividly in the bright, heady sunlight of pre-war summers.

'Attention aux Boches,' the man said.

He told them that he had passed a huge column of soldiers in the Somme valley, and that in a way it had been lucky because the roadblocks were so busy with troop traffic that they had only given the lorry a cursory search. There might, he said, be a regiment of soldiers camping in the woods around Le Touquet.

'Vous pouvez dire tout ça à Londres?' Lemming asked him if he had the means to let London know about the troop build-up.

'Oui, oui,' he replied, and asked whether they had any more messages to transmit.

'Non,' Margaux answered firmly.

Lemming was surprised. It might have been useful to let London know that he and Margaux were alive and at large. But he figured that his was not to reason why.

'Merci, et bonne route,' he told the man, who was still facing the tree.

'Bon courage,' the man replied. Lemming did not know exactly what this meant, but thanked him anyway.[7]

Margaux and Lemming sprinted across the road, which was empty in both directions, and stopped at the fringe of the woods to listen. Not a sound except the faint overhead swishing of the sand pines. The darkness spread deep into the distance.

They set off in a straight line towards the coast. The undergrowth was thick and tangled. It had rained here recently, and their feet were soon soaking. It was slow going, too, and hard to maintain a steady course.

Lemming grabbed Margaux's sleeve.

'Let's take the road,' he whispered.

'Dangerous.'

'I'll find the place sooner. It's about a mile. That's where we're going? His house?'

'All right. Yes. Any sound, just lie down flat. Carry your knife.'

He pulled the kitchen knife out of his pocket and led Margaux to the right, where he thought there was a road leading into the suburb of Le Touquet where PG Brickhouse had made his French home before the war.

Sure enough, they found the solid surface of a lane, and turned left, seawards. Now they took long, silent strides, flinching whenever one of them trod on a twig, a pine cone or a crunchy snail.

---

[7] 'Bon courage' is a French way of wishing a person the fortitude to deal with the challenges ahead. It is more optimistic than a mere 'bonne chance', which would imply that the person also needs the help of luck.

They saw large gates marking the openings to driveways. The houses here were mostly mansion-like versions of Norman villas, and they were all set in spacious grounds. This was not an area where anyone ought to be abroad on foot at night, unless they were a sentry, a spy, or the owner of an insomniac dog.

The gates were mostly open, suggesting that the driveways were in constant use – no doubt by billeted troops. Lemming and Margaux stopped at each gate to listen for the tread of boots or the murmur of German conversation. But the area seemed blessedly sleepy.

Lemming was looking for a long villa that would be facing the road behind a low hedge, a building with Tudoresque beams and a facade made up almost entirely of windows. Many of the houses were in a similar faux-English style, but Brickhouse's was distinguished by a sign at the gate, 'Low Water'. Lemming had always suspected that the name had been a joke – the name sounded like *'les waters'*, a quaint French term for the lavatory – but he had never dared to ask the famous author. It would have lowered the tone of the conversation, and the genial but shy Brickhouse said little enough anyway.

The darkness began to echo to the low sound of an engine. They listened hard. It was too deep and constant to be a car or lorry. And it was coming closer. They ducked behind a thick growth of hawthorn on the verge. But as the sound grew louder, it also lifted higher. It was in the air. The low hum swelled into a deeper, multi-layered drone that seemed to fill the whole neighbourhood. If it was an aeroplane, it was flying very low. Then they saw it, a small glow in the sky just to their north, moving slowly on its way towards the sea. When it was almost overhead, they recognized it.

'Doodlebug,' Lemming whispered.

It was a V1 flying bomb en route to cause random destruction in the south of England. Instinctively, they both listened for the moment when the engine would cut out – this was always what happened on the other side of the Channel. You would hear the deep throb of its motor, and then silence, and you knew it was time to hit the deck because the fuel had run out and the bomb was coming down. On houses, hospitals, schools, anywhere. It was one of the worst symptoms of total war.

'It's very low,' Margaux whispered back. 'Maybe a launch site around here.'

'Should we look for it later?' Lemming asked. It deserved a visit from the RAF.

'First things first.'

'Of course.'

They walked on, the sound of their movement covered by the overhead drone of two or three more doodlebugs.

Only about half an hour after leaving the lorry, Lemming found the 'Low Water' sign. It was as much luck as judgement, but he pointed to it as though he had zeroed in unerringly. Margaux nodded her approval.

The house was dark, and there were no vehicles in view. It was difficult to see clearly, but the front looked shuttered up.

Lemming gestured as though to ask whether they should hop over the hedge into the grounds. Margaux shook her head. She waved him towards the far corner of the grounds, where a large pine tree cast an even darker shadow.

When they were standing against its trunk, hidden from the road, she pulled Lemming's head down towards her mouth, and whispered.

'Far left wall of the house. In the middle, on the ground, walnut shell.'

'What?'

'A walnut shell. We take it. Then out, same route.'

Lemming nodded. Clutching his knife, he climbed through rather than over the hedge, and then bent low to keep his head beneath the line of a wooden fence that bordered the grounds of Brickhouse's neighbours. It was only about thirty yards to the end wall of the house.

Everything was as dead as a country churchyard.

In the centre of the whitewashed side of the house there was a small square window. A bathroom, perhaps. It was unlit.

Margaux got to her knees and began scrabbling with her hands at the base of a low ornamental hedge. Lemming put away his knife and did the same, right under the square window.

It was impossible to see. Their fingers were their only guides. There were plenty of small stones down there, what felt like the occasional snail, something soft that Lemming did not want to think about. Then he found something round and crenulated. There was a ridge around the centre, culminating in a tiny point at one end of it. It had to be a walnut shell.

'Got it,' he said, a little too loudly.

'Levez-vous,' said another voice, even more loudly. Get up.

A torch came on behind them, throwing their stark shadows against the white wall of the house.

'Levez-vous!' The voice sounded more urgent.

Lemming obeyed, but did not stop when he was vertical. He swung his arm above and beyond the torch, in as powerful a right hook as he had thrown since his schooldays. It landed on hard flesh with a painful crack, so he followed it up with an equally windmilling left, which hurt his fist just as much, but had the satisfying result of stopping any repeat of the order to 'levez-vous'.

The torch toppled, as did the man who had been holding it. The swinging light revealed a Nazi who had been wearing a forage cap, but who was now hatless and stretched out on the lawn.

'Go,' was all Margaux said. She picked up the soldier's machine pistol and his torch, and dived headfirst over the five-feet-high wooden fence, as if she expected to land in a swimming pool on the other side.

'Halt!'

The shout from a few yards away shocked Lemming into action. Summoning up his *victor ludorum* agility, he sprang over the fence feet first as a shot rang out behind him.

The torch flew into the air – presumably Margaux had thrown it as a distraction. The whirling beam lit the scene in flashes. He saw Margaux raising the barrel of the machine pistol as if to fire, and he dived to one side as the air was rent with sound, light, and the swish of flying bullets. Then he saw Margaux running in a crouch along the fence, back towards the road. He followed her as fast as he could. There was a single shot from Brickhouse's garden, then another, and a third, but the bullets did not whistle close. The guard must have been firing blind.

They jumped over a wall into the road, and ran, not caring about snapping twigs or crunching snail shells. Behind them, there were flashes of torchlight, shouts and more shots.

At the first crossroads, after the fastest two hundred yards Lemming had managed since Eton, they stopped to catch their breath and listen. Both were puffing hard, Margaux for once, as hard as Lemming.

Despite the darkness, Lemming could make out the incongruous figure of a modestly dressed *mademoiselle* armed with a Nazi machine gun.

'Got the walnut?' she asked, wheezing.

It sounded like an absurd code question, as if Lemming was meant to respond, 'In spring, hazelnuts are sweeter' or something equally surreal.

'Yes. In my pocket.'

'Well done, let's go.'

And she was off again, running along the empty road. Lemming followed, and heard the sound of an engine starting up. A motorbike. The soldiers were coming after them. He got his knife out of his pocket, noticing as he did so that his right knuckles were throbbing. He must have broken a jaw, he thought, or at the very least dented a cheekbone. His first actual fight with the enemy. Hand-to-hand combat, just like a commando.

The motorbike engine was growing louder, so Lemming pulled Margaux off the road and into the driveway of another large house. It was risky – the commotion behind them would have woken up every billeted soldier within a square mile, but at least they could run across a lawn out of sight from the lane.

They saw and heard the vehicle sweep past, its searchlight swinging about, as though out of control. It was a motorbike with a torpedo-like sidecar that was empty. Lemming hoped that its usual passenger was still snoozing on Brickhouse's lawn.

They kept running, crossing gardens, jumping fences, listening to the motorbike speeding ahead of them. It stopped now and again to illuminate the scene with a sweep of its light. Then it seemed to be coming back towards them, while another engine was approaching from the direction of the coast. A second patrol, perhaps.

Lemming realized that they were running towards the main road, though he had no idea what they would do when they got there. Jump one of the motorbikes? Try to clamber on to a doodlebug as it took off towards England?

Then suddenly Margaux stopped right in front of him, and they collided, sprawling headlong.

'My God,' he heard her say just before he flattened her.

XIV

Margaux was not even angry about being rugby-tackled by a knife-wielding naval officer. Pausing only to uproot her sleeve from the ground, where it had been pinned by Lemming's blade, she sprang to her feet and ran diagonally across the main road, swerving to her right.

Rolling slowly towards them were the two dimmed headlights of a lorry.

Margaux ran towards it, waving her free arm, the one not holding a machine gun. The lorry stopped in the middle of the road. So would I, Lemming thought, if a Schmeisser-toting woman leapt out of the woods in the middle of the night. Either that or run her over.

He expected to hear the motor roar up again, and to see a frightened driver aiming for Margaux or trying to head back home.

But the lorry began edging forward. So it was going to be the run-her-over option, but in slow motion.

Then he understood. It was the same lorry, the wood delivery truck that had dropped them off. A familiar head appeared out of the driver's window, followed by a frantically beckoning arm.

'Derrière!' he called. 'Et jète la flingue!' He was telling Margaux to throw away the gun. She removed the magazine from the machine pistol, before lobbing both parts into separate areas of the woods.

They arrived together at the back of the lorry, and Lemming unceremoniously swept her into his arms and up over the tailgate. He clambered in, and the lorry accelerated away.

They skidded forward on their hands and knees until they found the heap of logs that was the driver's excuse for his trip. Climbing over it, they lay down against the wall of the cab, and pulled logs on top of them, like so many tiny blankets. It was poor camouflage, but the best they could do.

Lying back, almost enjoying the pain in his burning lungs and the throb in his knuckles, Lemming felt exhilarated. He reached out, pushing aside logs until he felt Margaux's coat. He patted it several times, and her hand slid down to meet his. Wordlessly, they congratulated each other for being alive and free.

'I didn't stab you, did I?' Lemming finally asked. 'When we fell?'

'Were you trying to?' But he could tell that she was joking.

'This Frenchman is someone you can trust,' Lemming said. 'He must have waited just in case.'

But the time was sentiment was clearly over.

'Have you got the walnut?' Margaux asked.

Lemming felt in his pocket, and found half a walnut. The shell had obviously fallen in two at some point. And the half shell in his hand felt empty.

He gave it to Margaux, who swore even more virulently than she had done that first day he met her, when she had been fighting with her umbrella.

After ten minutes or so, the lorry shuddered to a halt. If this is a roadblock, Lemming thought, we've almost certainly come to the end of the road.

But it was the driver who came to order them out of the woodpile.

'Vite,' he said, and began throwing the logs to one side of the lorry. Lemming and Margaux followed suit, then the man was able to lift the false floor, opening up the hiding place.

So they were going back into the coffin.

Lemming recoiled.

'Get in,' Margaux hissed at him, lying down in the opening.

The driver assured them that it was for only twenty minutes. 'Allez,' he said.

Lemming complied, saying a quick 'merci, mon ami', as the man lowered the coffin lid. The logs were flung back over them in a thunder of impacts just above their faces, and then the lorry set off with its familiar crunch of gears.

Once the engine had reached its steady note, Lemming asked the key question.

'What was in the walnut shell?'

'A message. Rolled up. Are you sure the other half is not in your pocket?'

Lemming did his best to explore every seam of the large side pocket of his coat. It was old, and the pocket was worn. It had been roughly mended by the feel of it, so that the edges were uneven. There might even be a hole big enough for half a walnut shell to fall through.

His fingers met the cool flatness of his cigarette case, and this awoke his addictive craving for tobacco. Just one deep breath of smoke was all he wanted. If that Nazi motorbike rider had been calling out 'give yourself up, and you can have a Gauloise,' he would have handed himself in without hesitation.

He was stroking the metal almost erotically when his fingertip met an unexpected obstacle. Something was caught in the tiny flap of metal that covered one of the hinges.

He lifted the cigarette case carefully out of his pocket and felt more closely with his other hand. Yes, it was a fold of stiff paper.

He unfolded it in the darkness, until it felt about the size of a small matchbox top.

'I think I've got it,' he said. 'Give me your hand.'

Margaux reached out and he placed the paper in the centre of her palm.

'Oh God, yes,' Margaux gasped. Lemming had often heard women make similar sounds, and this time was as pleasing as ever. 'Good work, Ian.' That was not something the women usually said afterwards, though.

'Now we just have to read it,' he said. 'Do we need more of your magic potion to make it legible?'

'I expect so, though we'll have to wait until we have enough light.'

'Maybe not.'

Lemming rummaged in his other pocket, and for just a moment their coffin was brilliantly floodlit.

'Thought it might come in useful,' he said. He had grabbed the German's torch after Margaux threw it away.

Margaux laughed. 'Genius.'

She was able to extract her tube from a pocket, and drip some of its contents over the message. It took a few minutes because of the danger of dropping either paper or tube as the lorry jolted along. Lemming had to grimace at the idea of splashing that particular liquid around in such an enclosed space.

Finally she announced that it was done, and read the words on the wet slip of paper.

'I don't understand it,' she said.

'Well what does it say?'

She did not answer.

'Come on Margaux, if you don't understand it, maybe I will.'

There was no sound except for the rumble and clatter of lorry on road.

'Margaux? Trust me, please.'

Again, she was infuriatingly mute. Then she spoke.

'I give up,' she said. 'It doesn't make any sense.'

'But what does it say?'

'It's cryptic again, rather than encoded. And it says "prune au lolo hotel" followed by the figures ten and four.'

'Oh.'

'Prune is obvious,' Margaux said.

'Is it?'

'Plum, of course. PG Brickhouse's nickname. But lolo? It's a children's word for milk. Plum in milk? Are they whitewashing him, or cooking him?'

'Lolo is also something else as well, isn't it?' Lemming said. 'The slang word for a lady's breast. But you knew that, of course.'

'Think, Ian,' was all she replied.

The minutes passed with no more conversation than the occasional shared gasp of pain as the lorry jolted over a bump.

Despite the fact that he was caught in a rattling trap in the back of a lorry, Lemming could not help himself running fondly through the different French slang words for parts of a lady's anatomy. There were some very picturesque ones. *'Abricot'*, or apricot, was a colloquial term for the vagina, which was bizarre until you ripped one in half. An apricot, that is. His favourite French term for that same part of the body was *'moule'*, or mussel, though he had always considered that *'huître'*, oyster, would be more appropriate.

In any case, the French seemed determined to combine food and sex in their *argot*. A *'poireau'*, or leek, was a penis, and *'miche'*, or circular loaf, was slang for the buttock. Then there was *'maquereau'*, mackerel, for a pimp, and *'morue'*, or cod, for a whore – an aggressive use of such a passive fish.

'Lolo', on the other hand, was an affectionate term, capturing the milkiness of the skin on a fine breast as well as its potential contents. Much more attractive than some of the common English terms, which sounded just plain vulgar. Tit, boob, knocker ...

'That's it!' he said. 'I know where we have to go.'

'Where?' Margaux sounded gratifyingly curious.

Now it was Lemming's turn not to answer a direct question.

'I'm also pretty sure the message was written by an Englishman who can speak French argot,' he said.

'Tell me,' Margaux said. It sounded like an order.

But Lemming wanted his moment of triumph.

'If I tell you, do I get a kiss?' he asked.

'Don't be so trivial, man,' she snapped, like a furious sergeant to a new recruit.

But Lemming was too pleased with himself to bow down.

'Oh come on,' he said, 'Just one congratulatory kiss. Or do you value your virtue more than the mission?'

'If you think a girl's virtue hangs on a single kiss, you understand absolutely nothing about women,' Margaux said. 'Now tell me the bloody message.'

'I'm pretty sure we have to go to that most unvirtuous of cities, Paris.'

'Why?'

'The Nazis have interned Plum in the Hotel Bristol in Paris. You knew that, surely?'

She answered his question with one of her own. 'But how does the message imply the Bristol?'

'Lolo. Don't you see? Boob, knocker, bristol. Only an Englishman would have called it that. It looks as though our treacherous pilot is sending us to see PG Brickhouse in Paris.'

Margaux thought about this.

'I can't think of any other explanation,' she finally said. 'Unless Brickhouse himself wrote it. And the number must be the date. Tenth of April. Tomorrow. But it feels like a trap. Just like the message telling us to go to Le Touquet. We walked into that one.'

'I thought that if you knew something was a trap, you could avoid getting caught in it.'

'It depends. Just because you know you're in a minefield, it doesn't mean you won't get blown to smithereens.'

'Even so, we have to go there, don't we?' Lemming said. 'Brickhouse might be in mortal danger.'

'Or he might be part of the mortal danger.'

'You think he could be as treacherous as that?'

'I don't know, but you're right, we have to go to the Bristol tomorrow. Hundreds of lives might be at stake.'

'Really? Why?'

'Oh Ian, if I told you ...'

XV

The driver had said they would be travelling for only twenty minutes, but it had been much longer. Of course, there might be good reasons for this. The man was not going to stop and let them out if he was sharing a parking space with a Nazi tank.

But they needed to get out urgently, for a whole list of reasons: hunger, thirst, aching hands and limbs, for a start. Lemming also felt a need to empty his bladder that was being made more excruciating with every lurch of the lorry. It took superhuman determination on his part to resist the temptation to bang on the wall behind his head and shout above the noise of the engine.

At last the lorry slowed and stopped, and the engine was turned off. A door slammed shut, and they felt the weight of the driver stepping towards them. The logs began to scuff and tumble across the false floor above. Then the wooden surface was lifted away, and cold, fresh air flooded in.

It was dark, but Lemming could see that the shape standing over them was not their driver. The silhouette was slimmer, taller. He felt a jolt of fear. What if this was a soldier?

Margaux had not noticed the change of personnel. She was pushing herself up into a sitting position, groaning slightly as she loosened her shoulders. This gave Lemming the cover to grasp his torch in his left hand, and then, with a single thrust of his right arm, to launch himself up, simultaneously smashing his elbow into the man's midriff and shining a blinding torch into his face. They fell headlong into the woodpile, and Lemming grabbed one of the logs, ready to hammer it down blind on to the body trapped below his.

'Non, non, mister!'

A hand gripped Lemming's arm and pulled the log away. It then confiscated the torch and turned it off.

'Il est un ami,' a smoky voice told him. 'Calmez-vous.'

Lemming was pushed and pulled to his feet. The man squashed underneath him was reciting a glossary of French insults. 'Enculé, tête de nœud, enfoiré ...'[8]

It turned out that they had arrived at a roadside camp occupied by lorry drivers. This consisted of a large circular tent at the centre of a clearing in the woods. There was a bonfire, too, giving off enough light to reveal three lorries and two vans parked in a row.

The man who had climbed into the lorry to help Margaux and Lemming's driver was a trustworthy friend, they were told. After Lemming's unprovoked attack, he had gone sulking back into the tent, where the other drivers were asleep. It was nearly dawn, though, and the men would soon be waking up.

There was a flame-blackened cooking pot by the fire, and Margaux and Lemming were given enamel bowls of weak but restoring *bouillon* broth. The hot bowls scalded the fingertips, and not for the first time, Lemming wondered why the French had never thought of putting handles on the larger receptacles they drank from. Apart from small coffee cups, they always drank steaming liquids from handle-less bowls. Absurd, and painful.

Their driver escorted them to the dark fringe of the clearing, so that they would not be visible to inquisitive passers-by.

It was a wise precaution. This road seemed to be busy, even at night, no doubt because they had now travelled to where the English Channel was at its narrowest, and the occupiers at their most apprehensive. In just a few minutes, three Nazi vehicles passed – a speeding staff car accompanied by its motorbike

---

[8] Literally: bugger, dickhead, (shitty) idiot.

escort, and a half-track full of soldiers. None of them stopped or even slowed down.

'Un flic est censé nous contrôler,' their driver said – a policeman was meant to keep a check on them. 'Mais il vient plus jamais.' He never came any more.

Margaux was sitting on a tree stump, while Lemming and their driver squatted on the ground. Lemming felt the dampness seeping through the seat of his trousers, and thought that until this unplanned trip to France, his had been an existence founded upon picnic blankets, beach towels and car rugs. Even in the Alps, he had usually found a clean, dry rock to sit on. But now he was getting used to the fact that one's backside did not always need to be warm, dry and comfortable. Insulation, he now realized, was one of the buttocks' natural functions.

Margaux asked the driver where they were, exactly.

'Hardelot,' the man said, or 'ard-lo' as he pronounced the name.

Lemming knew the place. It was famous amongst the many golfers who visited this part of the French coast. The Golf des Pins course had been designed by an Englishman called Tom Simpson in 1934, and was an intriguing place to play. Its greens were hidden amongst the pine trees, and its long, deceptively narrow fairways were for crack shots only. Pull or slice your drive and you were digging around in the woods to find your ball.

'Vous jouez au golf?' he asked the driver.

'Golf? Moi? Non.' The man frowned at Lemming as if he had asked him whether he liked to dress up as a chorus girl and dance the Charleston.

People don't understand the excitement of a game of golf, Lemming thought. In PG Brickhouse's stories, a golf club was usually the realm of idiots – more of a goof club. But the course itself could be a place of suspense and almost brutal rivalry. It was a shame, he thought, that no one had written a novel that captured the thrill of an 18-hole game where the players were battling for high-stake bets.

160

'Je viens ici pour le bois,' the man said. He came here for the wood. He explained that these forests had been amongst Napoleon's favourite places for sourcing timber. The *empereur* had used Hardelot tree trunks to build the fleet of barges that were supposed to invade England in 1805. Now the *Boches* wanted the wood, not for barges but to repair bridges and railways blown up by allied aeroplanes – or by the Resistance. With metal in short supply, wood had become as vital a resource as in medieval times.

Margaux explained in urgent whispers that she and Lemming needed to get to Paris, fast.

The driver agreed that that was every *Anglais* should be trying to do, especially the military.

'Mais c'est difficile,' he said. 'C'est essentiel pour vous de monter à Paris?' the man asked. Was their trip vital?

'Oui, primordial.' Margaux added that in Paris, they hoped to end the vicious circle of betrayals that had closed down the Resistance networks in this area of France. And if they didn't get to Paris in time, a whole network there was at risk.

As if to add weight to her words, an aeroplane whined overhead. Whose it was, they could not tell. But it was a stark reminder of the war that was going on all around them.

'Peut-être que je peux vous emmener.' Maybe the driver could take them.

The man said that he could go to the Hardelot depot and pick up a load of wood, then falsify the order sheet to give a Paris address. He might even be lucky and find that there was a real order waiting to be transported.

Lemming wanted to know how long it would take.

'Sept, huit heures,' the driver said.

'Impossible.' Lemming could not imagine himself surviving that long in their mobile coffin.

The man reminded Lemming that if the *Boches* caught him, it would be a more permanent coffin. But it was true, he added, that if they shot Lemming straight away, the initial discomfort would be shorter-lasting.

'Merde,' Lemming concluded. Then he had an idea. 'Je peux fumer ici?' Could he smoke here, in the camp?

'Oui.'

Suddenly eight hours of torture seemed more bearable.

As dawn approached, the sky filled with aeroplanes. Again, Margaux and Lemming did not know whose they were, or whether they were about to unleash bombs.

They were riding in the back of the lorry, mercifully on top of the logs rather than under them, because the driver had promised them a reprieve before the long haul to Paris.

He dropped them off at a nearby *auberge* while he went to his depot. The inn was a two-storey brick house with a paved front yard, no doubt full of tables in summer. Behind its warmly-lit front window, a shadow was moving. The shape looked reassuringly female. The driver parked by the side of the house and ushered his two passengers into the back yard, where there was a stable, a low outhouse and a vegetable patch. Sweet wood smoke hung in the chill, silent air.

He left them standing in the pre-dawn light, and returned a few minutes later with a large metal tray. On it was a plate of bread in thick crusty slices, a dish of yellow jam, a spoon and two steaming china bowls. He set it down on a bench.

'Voilà, le petit déjeuner à la chambre,' he said. Breakfast in the bedroom.

As Margaux smeared jam on bread, he told them that he would be away for an hour or so. The outhouse, he said, was primitive, but there was water in there, if they needed it.

This, thought Lemming, was an understatement. He had never been so many days without shaving since his chin had first sprouted hairs.

If there was any kind of problem, the man said, they should lock themselves in the outhouse. There were two *Boches* billeted upstairs, but they usually went out through the café's front entrance.

The knowledge that they would be sharing the plumbing with the Nazi army came as something of a shock to Margaux

162

and Lemming, but they thanked the man, anyway. He went out the back gate and drove away.

The bread was fresh, the jam tangy but not very sweet – quince, they decided. The hot liquid was chicory, which made Lemming swear to himself that at the first opportunity he would pay a month's wages for a scalding pot of strong, black coffee made from real roasted, freshly-ground beans. And that after the war, he would start every single day with the same treat. Cold-pressed or not, he didn't care.

Margaux took first turn in the outhouse, while Lemming stayed in the yard and smoked as if his bloodstream needed to reload every corpuscle with nicotine. He was down to only six now – at the roadside camp he had been obliged to offer one to their driver, and to Lemming's horror the bastard had accepted.

He looked around and thought he might have visited this *auberge* once. It was very close to the local *château*, which was a 19th-century folly, a miniature Windsor Castle imposed on the French countryside by an eccentric Englishman. The *château* was surrounded by marshland, and Lemming had often imagined it as the house of a gothic madman who tempted travellers in, to watch them sink into the bog, consumed there by eels and poisonous frogs.

Dickens had come here, it was said, and had set up his English mistress in the village, so that he could visit her without being spotted by his adoring Victorian readers, to whom the author was famous as a model husband and father. A true under-the-covers secret agent, that Dickens.

From the direction of the palely rising sun there came a low booming like distant thunder. An air raid on Calais, perhaps. Whether or not the allies landed there later in the year, the RAF and USAF were determined to reduce its defences to dust.

Almost directly above, Lemming again heard the coughing whine, like a badly-tuned motorbike, of a doodlebug. There had to be a launch site near here. He would ask their driver to take a look sometime, and radio in its location. The launch sites had to be destroyed.   There was something inhuman about this faceless, robotic addition to the war. Bombing from planes was savage, certainly, but at least there were men up there, who had accepted the wager of war – risk your life to take a life. Doodlebugs, on the other hand, were cowardly, like bullets fired blindly into a civilian crowd. But maybe that was the future of war.

Margaux emerged from the outhouse, pink-faced.

'There's no soap, and the water is pumped up from the Antarctic, but who cares,' she said.

In the darkness of the concrete-floored outhouse, Lemming stripped off and doused his whole body with ice-cold water. It was something he liked to do of a morning, especially after a late night of gambling and drinking. But usually he preceded the ice bath with a few minutes soaking in almost unbearably hot water.

As in many other aspects of life, extremes were all that interested him. His philosophy was: drink either no alcohol or too much. And either ignore a woman or proposition her. So far, this trip had afforded him only the disappointing side of each equation.

He was standing naked on the wet concrete floor, regretting that he had no razor, and wondering how to dry himself off, when the outhouse door opened. Daylight came in, followed by Margaux.

So the time has come, he thought. The inevitable – two bodies welded together by the heat of war. He turned towards her, making no attempt to cover himself up.

'Come on in, the water's lovely,' he said.

'Sshh,' she replied.

All right, he thought. No need for words.

She moved towards him, her face seeking his. He waited, letting her take the initiative.

Then he noticed that she was carrying their breakfast tray. Which was strange.

Her mouth against his ear, she whispered, 'soldiers.'

So that was it. She had come in here to hide. He felt more foolish than afraid. He could hear them now. The back door to the café had opened, and there were heavy footfalls and voices just inches away on the other side of the thin outhouse wall. Two of them by the sound of it, no doubt the men billeted at the inn. They were talking about Calais. 'Scheissbomben,' one of them said. One soldier was more authoritative than the other, telling him to hurry up: 'Mach schnell!' The other answered, 'Aber ich muss pissen.' He needed to piss. Lemming tensed, gripping Margaux's arm in case she had not understood. The man was going to come in and find them.

There was one consolation, Lemming thought – if a Nazi opened the outhouse door, he was going to get a rude shock when he saw an attractive girl apparently serving breakfast to a wet, naked man. It might give Lemming the time to get in one of his knockout punches.

Clenching his fist, he stared at the door, preparing to unleash a right hook at face height.

Outside, someone grasped the door handle, and pressed down.

'Wir haben keine Zeit,' the voice of authority said, and the handle was released. Apparently there wasn't enough time, and the Nazi in need of relief was going to have to exercise his fabled Teutonic discipline.

Footsteps receded, the gate opened and clicked shut, and Lemming lowered his fist.

It took him a few seconds to realize that he was still naked and in Margaux's presence. He looked down into her face, and in the semi-darkness of the outhouse he thought he saw her smiling. Maybe it was not too late after all.

'Close thing,' she said.

Surely she realized the double meaning?

'Very close,' he replied.

'Sorry, Ian. False alarm.' She left the outhouse.

She had been mocking him. But he did not mind. And surely accepting rejection with good grace meant that he was in with a second chance?

All in all, things were looking up. Not only had they had survived yet another brush with Nazidom, but Margaux had been with him while he was naked, without showing the slightest embarrassment.

He dried himself off on the lining of his coat, and felt truly alive, ready to face anything, even eight hours shut in a glorified cigar box.

XVI

The lorry returned. The driver had two sets of good news. First, he had a genuine order for the Paris area. Second, they would not have to hide under the false floor of the truck, because the load he was carrying was too heavy to lift. He was transporting a consignment of fence posts – to protect the entrance to a factory.

He had brought more bread and a bottle each of wine and water. Though it would be better not to drink too much before getting in the lorry, he added, with a pained expression.

The load consisted of rough wooden poles, about ten feet long and pointed at one end. The driver told Margaux and Lemming that they could climb over the tightly-packed stack of wood to a small space that had been left just behind the cab. He had jammed a pair of crates there, like props in a mineshaft, to keep the gap open.

Of course, if he crashed, he said, the load would probably shift forward like a glacier and crush them, but this was war.

Further good news was that there should not be any searches, because his load and his destination marked him out as '*un vrai collabo*', a true collaborator.

But he assured them that he was not a traitor to France. And he wanted them to tell London that he was only working for the *Boches* so that he could get vital information for the Allies. Sometimes at the depot, he added, he and his friends soaked the wood to weaken it. Occasionally he cracked a few planks in a consignment so that they would collapse. But sabotage was punishable by instant death, so usually they all just collaborated and spied.

'Nous le dirons,' Margaux promised him. She asked him how he presented himself when he communicated by radio.

'René,' he said, 'ou Matisse, comme l'artiste.' He explained that his friends called him the 'Matisse of the map' because of his skill at drawing the locations of Nazi installations quickly and clearly. Neither René nor Matisse was anything like his real name, of course, but someone in London would be able to match the code names to his true identity.

Not one of De Gaulle's men, though, René stressed. He explained that he didn't trust the man's operation, or his politics. If *le général* came back to govern France, he would be much too right-wing for René.

'Vous n'êtes pas gaullistes, vous?' he asked them.

'Oh non,' Lemming replied. He looked to Margaux for a reaction.

'Pas Française,' she said, which could have meant anything.

'Moi, je suis churchilliste,' Lemming added.

'Ah oui,' René agreed, holding up two fingers in a way that was meant to signify 'Victory' but would have earned him a punch on the nose from your average Londoner.

'Qui Churchill trouve,' Margaux said, and René laughed and congratulated her. Lemming did not quite get the joke.[9]

'C'est le problème,' René added, more seriously. He said that he knew there were other Resistance groups in the area but did not want to link up with them. The safest way to operate was with just a few trusted friends. Nothing too organized. He had heard that with De Gaulle's outfit, there was a hierarchy, with too many high-ups in the know about other members. That seemed to be the reason behind this string of arrests in the region.

Throughout this short speech, Lemming watched Margaux. Predictably, though, she did not give anything away. She did not

---

[9] Margaux was making a pun on the French proverb 'Qui cherche, trouve' – who seeks, finds.

even reveal how irritating it must have been to have Lemming staring at her.

They climbed over the load and into their hiding place. The engine chugged to life, and the lorry moved off. As it did so, rain began to fall. Soon, heavy drops were spitting on the tarpaulin roof and into the lorry. Lemming arranged his coat as an umbrella above their heads. To stay dry, they had to squeeze together side-by-side, which suited Lemming fine. What suited him less was that Margaux insisted he should not smoke inside their improvised tepee. But then he was running seriously low on cigarettes, anyway.

To forget his craving, he asked Margaux what she thought of this René alias Matisse.

'No complaints so far,' she said. 'It will be interesting to check up on him in London. We'll see how long he's been sharing information about his work. Collaborators are like the gendarmes. Lots of collabos have decided only recently that it might be better to take out insurance. If you've been working with the Nazis since 1940, now's the time to rat on a Milice officer so that you can claim to be in the Underground. I hope our René isn't one of those.'

Lemming did, too. He liked the man and his fearless, matter-of-fact way of ferrying them around France. Now, for instance, they were sitting in the back of his lorry while he drove past any number of nervous Nazis. A single lapse of concentration on his part over the next seven or eight hours, and he would be blindfolded and up against a wall before the day was out.

'Do you think René's trying to make up for a sordid past?' he asked as the lorry grumbled its way up a long, steep hill.

'With a past like yours,' Margaux replied, 'I can understand why you believe in the need for redemption.'

He did not know whether to take her barb as a compliment.

'I see we're back on the thorny question of obtaining forgiveness for our sins,' he said. 'But personally, I don't think I've ever done anything I'm truly ashamed of.'

'Then either you're shameless or you've led a very sheltered life.'

Lemming had to admit that both might be true.

'Well, if I were a deity,' he said, 'which I'm not –'

'No? I rather thought you saw yourself as a kind of Apollo.'

'Touché,' he said, 'but if I were a deity, I think I could pardon most acts that we commonly call the seven sins. What are they? You probably know the list.'

He was joking, but she immediately began to check them off.

'Lust,' she said.

'The healthiest and most natural of emotions.'

'Gluttony.'

'Perfectly fine, in moderation.'

'I'm not sure you can sin in moderation.'

'True. Sometimes moderation is a sin in itself. Unforgivable, too.'

'What about greed?' she asked.

'Potentially an excellent motivation.'

'Sloth.'

'Something we all enjoy now and again, especially after a good lunch.'

'Wrath.'

'Have you never heard of righteous anger?'

'Envy.'

'Another excellent motivator.'

'Pride.'

'If you can't be proud of your achievements, what's the point of achieving?'

'Then, Ian, I can confirm that you are a sinner who is ironically without sin. Or maybe you just forgive all of us our trespasses.'

'But even as the most forgiving of gods, there is one sin I could never excuse,' he said.

'Chastity?'

'I'm being deadly serious. There is one moral line I could never cross, and that is working for the Nazis. I sincerely hope our friend René has not crossed it. There may be other great

169

moral divides in the future, but for the moment this is the one. Either you're for the Nazis or you're against them. And if you've ever been for them, it's inexcusable. It's like cheating at cards.'

Margaux laughed.

'Cards? Oh, Ian, you really have led a sheltered life.'

'I'm not comparing Nazis and card cheats, of course, though I'd be willing to bet that all of Hitler's cronies cheat at games. I'm just saying that there are some things a chap can do that make me want to avoid frequenting him forever.'

Margaux was silent for a moment, listening. The lorry was slowing down. But it regained speed, and everything was back to normal.

'Yes. You're right,' she finally said. 'Collaborating with the Nazis is a stain on the character that can never be erased.'

Conversation petered out, and they leaned back, almost enjoying the vibrations of engine and chassis that both mugged and massaged their tired spines.

XVII

Lemming and Margaux had been dozing. A metallic tapping woke them up.

Margaux was alert, listening. The tapping resumed on the metal wall behind them. The lorry had stopped. Everything else was total silence. This was certainly not Paris. It was still light outside, so they could not have travelled for the full eight hours.

They felt the suspension give a jerk, then, a few seconds later, another. Someone was climbing on to the back of the lorry.

'Eh-o. Eh-o.' A soft voice was calling from beyond the load of wood.

Margaux shook her head at Lemming – don't respond.

'C'est moi,' the voice said. 'Vous m'entendez?' Whoever *moi* was, they wanted to know if they could be heard. 'Il faut sortir.' If it really was René, he wanted them to get out.

Margaux and Lemming held their breath. Lemming pointed to his own chest, then in the direction of the voice. He would go. Margaux nodded.

Taking the knife out of his coat pocket, he crawled up on to the load.

'Eh-o!' the voice was as soft as before, but more urgent.

Lemming edged forward as silently as possible, scraping his stomach and elbows on the rough surface of the fence posts. He was getting skilled at these commando tactics, he thought. Raising himself on his elbows and knees, ready to jump down with knife in fist, he peeped over the edge of the load.

'Eh-o!'

'Ah, c'est vous,' Lemming said, making René jump.

'Venez vite,' René said.

'Où sommes-nous?' was Margaux's first question, and a reasonable one. They were at a crossroads in what looked like a small village. The lorry was parked alongside a head-high stone wall. Above it poked the branches of a fruit tree of some kind. No fruit, unfortunately, Lemming thought. On the other side of the road was a church that looked vaguely familiar. It was a sort of stumpy, poor man's gothic, constructed out of the same grey stone as the wall.

'Au verre,' René said. Which made no sense to Lemming. By the glass? A way of selling wine. Though a glass of anything alcoholic would be very welcome.

'C'est trop loin de Paris,' Margaux told René. It was too far from Paris. So she knew what he was talking about.

René was looking nervous. There was no one else in sight, but he was glancing right and left, as if frightened that they would be seen. He told Margaux that she and Lemming would have to hide here while he delivered his load.

She did not agree. She wanted him to drop them off in Paris first. But René was worried that the *Boches* might ask him why he had taken so long, and why he had done so many kilometres between Hardelot and the factory. Tell them you got lost, Margaux suggested. René shook his head.

171

It was essential to leave them here, he explained, still glancing anxiously around. And if he got a look inside the factory, he could report back to Margaux and Lemming. If this place was manufacturing something secret, then the secret needed to get to London as quickly as possible. He would radio it over there as soon as he got home, but he wanted to make double sure the information got through. And this would also allow Margaux and Lemming to confirm that René, alias Matisse, was a true *Résistant*, and a reliable source of information.

'Non, nous allons directement à Paris,' Margaux insisted.

'Non,' René replied.

'Si.'

'Non.'

It was like one of the childish arguments Lemming used to have with his Swiss mother.

'Let's do as he says,' he interrupted after yet another exchange of yes and no. Margaux stared at him furiously, but he asked René how long he would be away, and where they should hide.

'Une heure, dans ce jardin,' René said. 'La maison est abandonnée.' He added that they were only just across the river from the site of the Nazis' new factory, which was in Méry. If all went well it would take less than an hour.

'We have to get to Paris as quickly as possible,' Margaux told Lemming.

'But he's not going to take us now, believe me.' Lemming knew a stubborn Frenchman when he saw one. 'And we're wasting time, and taking risks, arguing about it.'

Margaux gritted her teeth. This was clearly not the first time during the war that she had suffered similar confrontations with masculine stubbornness. She considered for a few seconds whether it was worth holding out.

'Une heure,' she finally told René.

'Merci,' he said, relieved.

As a reward for their co-operation, René gave them a fresh bottle of water and half a loaf. Before Lemming had even helped

Margaux over the wall, the lorry had driven away, downhill towards the river.

It had rained here too, and the ground was sodden. Even so, they stayed away from the house. It was shuttered up, its chimney was lifeless, and its roof was mottled with moss, but it might not be completely empty. They crouched under yet another tree, amidst a lumpy carpet of fallen and rotting plums, and began to eat their meagre meal.

'Where are we?' Lemming asked.

'Auvers-sur-Oise. You know, Van Gogh's village.'

'Of course. I thought I recognized that church. Though it's much bluer on paper than in real life.'

'Like your memoirs will be,' Margaux said.

Lemming laughed.

'I don't think I'll be writing my memoirs,' he said, imagining the string of lawsuits and cancelled social invitations that would inevitably ensue.

'Not your true ones, anyway. But you'll write an embroidered version. I've read some of your reports and memos. Imaginative stuff.'

'Well, merci beaucoup.'

'You know this is where Van Gogh shot himself?' she said, matter-of-factly.

'This very garden?'

'No, in the fields just above. He borrowed a pistol, saying he wanted to shoot crows, and plugged himself in the stomach.'

'Absurd. If you're going to kill yourself, put a bullet in your brain. A stomach wound is hellishly painful and can take an eternity to kill.'

'He lasted two or three days.'

'Insane. And all very un-Dutch of him, don't you think? Cutting his ear off, shooting himself in the belly. We don't generally imagine the Dutch being capable of such melodrama.'

'France can make a drama queen out of anyone.'

'True,' Lemming said. 'I've heard that De Gaulle is capable of such tantrums that Churchill calls him a "female llama".

Though how Winston knows the difference between males and females of that particular species, we shall probably never know.'

'And didn't Churchill once offer to appease De Gaulle by offering to kiss him on the cheeks – "all four if necessary"?'

Lemming had heard the story before, but laughed wholeheartedly. As far as he could recall, it was the first time Margaux had said anything against the *général*. A good sign, surely.

The bread was finished. Lemming lit a cigarette, offering to share it with Margaux. She declined, very sportingly, he thought. He was down to his last five.

René returned almost exactly on the hour and summoned them back over the garden wall. He was in a rush to tell them what he had seen in nearby Méry. They were 'absolutely obliged' to radio the information to London. He joined them in the back of the lorry to explain in full. The words gushed out of him like the smoke from his lorry's exhaust.

He told them that the wooden posts he had delivered were for a barbed wire fence to protect a new branch of the railway. It led to a huge underground tunnel. The workers above ground were mainly French, and he had been able to speak to one of them, even though they were heavily guarded by soldiers. There was apparently a small army of *Boches* living in the woods, posted there to guard the site. They were so entrenched, they even had a small pig farm.

Pigsties were of limited interest to her bosses, Margaux told him.

'Oui, oui, pardon.' René regained his wits. One of the Frenchmen helping him to unload had said that the tunnel was being prepared to receive a new kind of Nazi weapon. Details were thin, but the rumour amongst the electricians was that the underground quarry was going to stock enormous bombs. Not ordinary bombs, to be dropped by planes, but self-propelling shells.

'Les V un?' Lemming prompted him.

'Non, plus grand, plus dangereux.'

Margaux asked René if he had seen anything that looked like a launch site – a ramp, a tower, something similar.

'Non, juste le tunnel.'

She asked him whether any missiles had been delivered there, to his knowledge.

René shrugged his ignorance.

'Merci.' Margaux promised to relay the information to London, along with his aliases.

Satisfied, René climbed out of the back of the lorry, almost landing on the toes of an old man in a black trilby hat. Margaux and Lemming could see his head clearly. He was cleanly shaven and wore a sky-blue scarf that looked soft and expensive. Even as René landed beside him, the man was staring into the lorry at the two seated passengers.

'We might have to take him with us,' Margaux whispered.

Lemming's heart sank. Violence against the aged was not part of his idea of war, unless of course those old men were uniformed Nazis, or cheated at cards.

'Mais qu'est-ce que vous foutez là?' the old man demanded, a mildly impolite way of asking what they were up to.

'Il y a une auberge ou un hôtel par ici?' René asked him. Was there an inn or hotel nearby?

The old man ignored the question. He stared René in the face for a few seconds, then looked back inside at Lemming and Margaux.

'Ce qu'il y a par ici,' he said, his eyes firmly fixed on Margaux, 'ce qu'il y a par ici,' – what there is nearby – 'c'est plein de Boches' – is a whole load of Nazis. And they didn't want any trouble in the village, so would the strangers please leave?

It was not collaboration, but neither was it resistance. It was a common French attitude to the Occupation: keep *stumm* and carry on.

René said nothing more. He jumped in his cab and coaxed the engine back to life. As the lorry rolled downhill, the old man was walking towards the church, his head down.

Lemming and Margaux were lying flat in the back of the lorry, hidden only by the wooden crates that René had used to prop open their cubby hole. He had left the rear flap of his tarpaulin rolled up, as if to prove to the world that the vehicle was empty. From the prone position, they could see very little except clouds and the occasional smoking chimney, but could now hear a much busier world outside.

There were other vehicles on the road, including loudly growling motorbikes and the clattering tracks of tanks that made the lorry tremble as it passed. Impatient drivers sounded horns or accelerated to overtake. René had to stop at a whole series of crossroads, where they heard an occasional shout in French or German. A church bell was ringing. Once, a child laughed.

The laugh made Lemming think of his fellow Londoners, old and young. The weapon that René had described would give them all nightmares. From what he had heard, these new Nazi bombs were radio-guided missiles that would make the V1s look like firecrackers. If you could direct a bomb to fall on a precise target, it would theoretically make destroying strategic installations simpler and cleaner, with less collateral damage to the civilian population.

On the other hand, if you were a Nazi, you could send destruction to the most densely populated areas of London, purely for the hell of it. You could land a bomb in Winston Churchill's ashtray – providing you knew which one of his many ashtrays he was using at the time. Parliament would have to meet in secret, or in a bunker deep enough to resist a direct hit. The royal family would be forced to take refuge in the Australian outback. Nothing and nobody would be safe.

The idea was dizzying. With enough of these weapons, one man could hold the entire world to ransom: 'hand over the crown jewels, or London will be reduced to rubble and ashes. Give me the keys to Fort Knox, or I scrub New York and Washington off the map.' The prospects were truly terrifying.

If – no, *when* – Lemming got back to London, his first act would be to order aerial reconnaissance flights over Méry-sur-Oise.[10]

Well, his first act after a bath, a shave, a quadruple gin and tonic, and at least ten cigarettes. Saving the world could wait that long.

---

[10] In July and August 1944, British and American planes bombed Méry-sur-Oise, putting an end to all attempts to turn the quarry into a V2 storage site. However, the first V2s hit Britain in September of that year. In response, British counter-intelligence leaked the false information that V2s aimed at London were overshooting. The Nazis duly adjusted their targeting, with the result that most of the remaining missiles fell on less-populated Kent. Not pleasant for Kent, of course, but less deadly for the general population.

PART THREE

I

Parting with René was brief. He parked in the access road to a small brick-built factory that was belching out damp, dark smoke. He did not even turn off his engine. Lemming shook his hand and said 'merci, mon ami.' Margaux seemed even more grateful − she clasped both of René's hands, then hugged him quickly, whispering her thanks in his right ear. She was getting very good at mouth-to-ear contact.

They were close to 'la porte de la Villette', René told them. Lemming understood the words but not the location. Being near this 'Villette door' meant nothing to him. His knowledge of Paris was restricted to the area around the Ritz, the antiquarian bookshops of Saint-Germain des Prés, and one or two classy establishments near Opéra where the girls were either genuinely well-bred, or quick-witted enough to be convincing about it. He had visited the famous monuments, of course, but once each. Now he was lost. The only way he could have found their destination, the Hotel Bristol, was to hail a taxi.

'Let's go,' Margaux said, walking off confidently. Lemming followed her.

The landscape did not look Parisian at all. There were piles of stone rubble everywhere, but no bomb craters, as though buildings had been painstakingly demolished. A grimy six-storey tenement stood alone, its side walls still bearing the traces of wallpaper from the neighbouring buildings that had deserted it. The assorted industrial yards around them looked poor − one contained only broken barrels, in another a teenaged boy was shovelling at a heap of bones and hooves.

The people, too, looked poor. An old woman wearing a high-collared overcoat and a cloche hat that would have been fashionable twenty years earlier was pushing a child's perambulator loaded with empty bottles of all sizes and shapes. Other women were carrying half-empty shopping bags. There were plenty of men around, of all ages, so Lemming did not feel out of place, except for his burgeoning beard. But most of the men were walking with eyes down, as if avoiding eye contact.

Lemming soon understood why. Turning a corner, they came to an army barricade. A wall of sandbags had been erected across the wide boulevard. It was ten feet high and as thick as a house. At either end, leaving space for one vehicle to pass, there were barriers manned by Nazi soldiers. The poles blocking the roads were painted red, white and black, as if to specify their national origin.

If the poles were designed to stop vehicles passing through, they were underemployed. There were no vehicles in sight, except the parked motorcycles and sidecars of the guards. This was what struck Lemming the most. The Paris he knew had always been awash with cars, taxis, buses and the delivery lorries that kept the city stocked up with everything that made it Paris. Now the streets were empty of motor vehicles, and eerily silent. The loudest noise was coming from a train that was puffing up to speed, out of sight to their right.

The soldiers at the barricade did not seem to be stopping pedestrians, or even the occasional person pushing a cart or a bicycle. They were keeping an eye on proceedings, perhaps hoping to spot a stray British uniform – or an unshaven fugitive. Lemming made sure that his limp was accompanied by a suitably depressed facial expression. His body language informed everyone around that he was a useless nobody, too lethargic even to lift a razor.

Taking Margaux's arm, Lemming hobbled along the pavement, keeping his eyes resolutely down. As he passed a pair of jackboots, he was sorely tempted to spit, but his mouth was too dry with nerves.

Then they were through, and he heard Margaux exhale with relief. He raised his eyes slightly and saw a café terrace occupied by a dozen civilians, men and women. All of them were sitting watching the barricade as if it were just a vaguely interesting market stall. That was true lethargy, he thought. He envied them their drinks, though. It was now approaching evening, and the glasses were red or golden.

Not for the first time, he was shocked by the sight of men of military age doing nothing except sit and watch the war. In London, it felt as though only ancient and infirm males were out of uniform – apart from French waiters, of course. Perhaps he was already romanticizing his home town, he thought, but all the men he saw in London, and most of the women, seemed to be involved in the war effort in some way, even if it was only clipping the train tickets of travelling soldiers. Here in Paris, they might call it the Occupation, but the men seemed to be unoccupied.

Even so, for today, it suited Lemming's purposes to be in possibly the only city in northern Europe where a man of military age out of uniform was *not* suspect.

Margaux was speeding up.

'Drop the limp unless you see soldiers,' she told him. 'We need to get to the Bristol as quickly as possible.'

'You know the way?'

'This isn't my first walking tour of the city,' she said, and sped up even more.

They strode for a good half an hour through a Paris that Lemming had never seen before. Some of this was because they were in a northern, working-class area of the city. They crossed a whole neighbourhood of butcher's shops. These were apparently wholesale places, because there were no queues of shoppers, only men and women in bloodied overalls moving a meagre supply of carcasses from hook to cart or vice-versa.

They did see one long line outside a shop marked 'Œufs Beurre Fromage'. However, things did not look hopeful for the waiting women – unlike all the Parisian *crèmeries* that Lemming remembered, this shop window was bare. On the pavement outside, there stood a huddle of aluminium milk churns, a couple of them tipped over, empty.

They passed a small park where the lawn had been dug up and planted with what looked like leeks.

Heading further towards the centre of the city, the streets became slightly busier, but with unusual vehicles. A chic-looking man, a blanket over his knees, was being pulled along in a home-made cycle taxi. The bicycle, pedalled by a teenage boy, was pulling a small armchair mounted on wheels.

They saw a horse and carriage, too, straight out of the 19th century – and the horse looked as though it had not eaten since then. Presumably the animal was too useful, and too stringy, to be eaten.

There were signs of the occupiers, of course.

At a large junction, they saw a restaurant that had been taken over, and was now decorated with an enormous black-and-white sign renaming it a 'Wehrmachtspeiselokal' – an army eating place. The building looked as if it had previously been a traditional Parisian *brasserie*. Its wide, glass-fronted facade suggested that it might once have been reasonably classy. Now men in Nazi uniform, most of them unarmed, many of them bordering on shabby, were entering in small groups. Lemming wondered whether the waiters inside were the same as before the war – Frenchmen in aprons huffing when Nazis took too long to order, or fawning over them, telling them 'excellent choix, mein Sturmbannführer'.

Similarly, they saw a modest-looking hotel taken over as a 'Soldatenheim'. Lemming thought 'soldiers' home' was probably a euphemism. He had heard that many Parisian brothels had been reserved for the occupiers.

All these requisitioned buildings were decorated with an alarming variety of Nazi flags – some were simple swastikas on a red background, others bore the old iron cross, or complex combinations of the two emblems. The flag industry was clearly one of the healthiest in Germany.

Apartment buildings steadily became fancier as Margaux headed south, the iron balconies more ornate, the doorways and windows larger. Lemming even recognized a few street names –

rue Lafayette, boulevard Haussmann. There were more people around, including caped French policemen, often in pairs, looking shifty.

Margaux stopped at a large crossroads, near a theatre, the Salle Gaveau, outside which a crowd of people, both uniformed and civilian, was forming. There were posters on either side of the entrance, and Lemming recognized the smiling, and apparently bleached, face of Maurice Chevalier, alongside his melancholic counterpart, the dark-haired, bleak-souled Edith Piaf. Here were two French entertainers who had clearly decided to entertain all-comers, including those who were imprisoning and shooting their compatriots.

'We're getting close to the Bristol,' Margaux said. 'From now on, we speak French to one another, all right?'

'Jawohl,' Lemming agreed.

He definitely knew this area. They were close to the Champs-Elysées and the Ritz – which, tragically, everyone now knew as the Parisian social club of the SS. It was also notorious as the love nest of Coco Chanel, who had set up home in the hotel with the Nazis' head of propaganda in France, a man called Dincklage. It was even rumoured that the SS had recruited her as an agent.

Oh well, Lemming thought, one thing was for sure – Chanel's name would be mud after the war, and no one would want to buy perfumes that stank of Nazism.

There were cars on the road now, most of them Nazi, and for the first time Lemming and Margaux had to wait to cross a street. They did so standing beside a crowded corner café. Again, Lemming felt a twinge of nostalgia, blended with envy and disapproval. Men and women, civilians and uniforms, French and German, were sitting intermingled on the terrace, while a white-aproned waiter flitted amongst the plumes of cigarette smoke, like a bomber trying to avoid searchlights.

Smoking on terraces, Lemming thought, that's all Paris has been doing ever since 1940. A pleasant way to spend a war. And how come they have so much tobacco?

They crossed the road behind a limousine that was carrying two puppet-like Nazi officers, and entered another street that Lemming recognized. This was the rue du Faubourg Saint-Honoré, home to the French presidential palace, the former British Embassy and the original Hermès boutique, where he had frequently bought scarves for women, either to thank them for their bad behaviour or to apologize for his.

They were also only a couple of hundred yards from the Hôtel Meurice, the Nazis' military headquarters in Paris, so uniforms were everywhere, both patrolling with rifles on shoulders, and simply ambling. Margaux and Lemming were by far the worst-dressed people within a square mile, and Lemming definitely the most unkempt. He limped more heavily than ever.

Only now did he begin to question this need to get into the Bristol, a building right at the heart of Nazi France. It was like two pheasants choosing to waddle into a gun club.

Soon they were standing only feet away from the entrance to the hotel with its long, art nouveau glass awning. It was a fairly normal-looking, though undeniably fancy, apartment building built of cream stone. There were striped sunshades over most of its windows, and a higher-than-usual number of balconies.

A top-hatted commissionaire was idling on the steps in front of the gilded revolving door.

'Comment allons-nous entrer?' Lemming asked Margaux. How were they going to get in?

Normally, Lemming was the type of man who had commissionaires saluting him from five yards away. Not any more. He felt horribly conspicuous on the opposite pavement, staring at the building like a cat burglar planning his climb up the facade. The only fortunate thing was that there were no Nazi sentries outside the place.

'Allume une de tes cigarettes,' Margaux said. She wanted him to light a cigarette.

'Pardon?' Under normal circumstances, there would have been no need to remind him, but now he was trying to economize them for moments of true crisis.

'Allume!' she ordered, and he obeyed, remembering to appear half-paralysed.

Now he understood. His long, difficult pantomime with the matchbox and cigarette case earned them time to observe the building.

'Merde,' she finally said, and walked back the way they had come, pulling Lemming with her.

'Où allons-nous?' Lemming asked her, remembering that he had once asked the very same question of a woman whom he had met on a street corner in this very same *quartier* of Paris.

'Rear entrance,' Margaux whispered, in English.

Lemming seemed to remember his conversation with the *Parisienne* taking a similar turn.

Margaux walked around the block, looking for any sign that one of the doorways led to the service area of the Hotel Bristol. It wasn't until they were directly behind the hotel, in a parallel street, that they came across a wide alleyway.

A man in flat cap and blue overall coat was pushing a handcart towards the gateway. It was loaded with potatoes and onions.

They stopped, apparently admiring a display of drawings by Jean Cocteau, one of the Nazis' favourite French artists, in a gallery next to the alley, and watched the vegetable deliveryman open the gate to go in.

'Allons-y,' Margaux said, and obeyed her own instructions. Lemming took a long, final drag of his precious cigarette and followed.

It looked as though she had picked the right place. The alley was lined with empty crates that, according to their labels, had previously contained wine, olive oil, vinegar, sardines. Not spectacularly luxurious, but not a symptom of famine, either.

There were men and women coming and going. A young man with flamboyantly oiled hair was counting money as he walked towards the street – a waiter and his tips, presumably. A pair of girls were wearing maids' uniforms under their coats. An empty handcart was coming towards them, pushed by a bulbous figure in a stained white overall, most likely a butcher who sampled his own wares.

Margaux was striding confidently onwards, with Lemming in tow, limping slightly. No one challenged them until they reached a gate that led into a shadowy courtyard. The gatekeeper was a small, middle-aged man in a black jacket, with a braided cap to lend him authority.

'Oui?' he said, blocking their way.

'On vient chercher du travail,' Margaux answered. They were looking for work.

'Il n'y a pas de travail ici.' At least the man looked sad about it.

'C'est pour mon fiancé,' Margaux said, nodding towards Lemming. 'Il a été blessé à Dunkirk.' She was citing a war wound.

'Mais il n'y a vraiment pas de travail ici, mademoiselle,' the man repeated.

Margaux begged to be allowed to go in and ask, otherwise her poor, honourably wounded fiancé would be sent to do factory work in Germany.

She was an excellent actress, and even Lemming was convinced that he was about to be whisked off to slave labour in a munitions plant. Which might very well happen if his true identity was discovered. Unless he was simply tortured then shot, of course.

He stared the gatekeeper in the eye, trying to picture one of these fates so that he would look suitably fearful.

'Boh!' the man huffed. He told them they could try, with the same optimism as a golf caddie letting a novice player drive towards a bunker and a bottomless lake.

He said they should ask for the *'secrétariat'*, and pointed them towards the door where the staff were entering and exiting.

'Et maintenant nous cherchons la maison en briques?' Lemming asked Margaux, as they walked on.

She didn't understand.

'Maison en briques. Brickhouse,' he whispered.

'Tu as ton couteau?' she asked. Did he have his knife?

'Oui. Pourquoi?'

'Please stab yourself.'

She pushed open a door and suddenly Lemming was transported back in time about five years.

II

It was an enormous, colonnaded courtyard lined with ornamental trees and laid out around one of the few Parisian lawns that had not been dug up as a vegetable patch. Several times before the war, Lemming had lounged beneath a parasol in this courtyard, enjoying a cocktail in the company of someone attractive, fascinating or both. He wished that he could sit down with Margaux, order drinks and talk about something other than death and treachery.

'Je peux vous aider?' A young man in a short white jacket had stepped out from the colonnade and was asking whether he could help them, in a way that suggested he preferred not to.

Lemming clicked into pre-war mode.

'Non, merci,' he said, making to swan past the youngster as if he didn't exist. It was a technique that had worked for him everywhere in the world, except Soviet Moscow.

It didn't work in wartime Paris, either.

'Vous allez où?' the white jacket asked, more challengingly now.

'Nous avons rendez-vous,' Margaux said.

'Avec qui?'

'Monsieur Brickhouse,' Margaux replied.

'Qui?'

'Monsieur Brickhouse,' Lemming repeated.

'Qui?'

'Brie-kooze?' Margaux improvised.

'Ah, l'écrivain anglais?' The English writer.

'Oui, moi aussi, je suis écrivain,' Lemming said, motioning towards his unshaven chin. He thought that literariness might be a good excuse for slovenliness.

The young man stared at them, in much the same way as the older gatekeeper had done a few minutes before.

'Venez avec moi,' he said.

They crossed a hallway decorated with heavy crystal chandeliers and fleur de lys tapestries that would have made Louis XIV feel at home, and entered a large wooden lift. The young man said nothing as they climbed, the lift creaking ominously, to the fifth floor. He opened an iron trellis and ushered them out into a thickly carpeted corridor.

'C'est là,' he said, knocking on a door, and leaving them to it.

Margaux and Lemming raised eyebrows at each other as the young man walked back along the corridor and took the staircase. That had been suspiciously easy.

'We'd better not hang around,' Margaux said, as soon as they were alone.

The door opened to reveal a face that all England knew.

'Bon-jaw?' Brickhouse asked, his china blue eyes expressing mild curiosity from the centre of a perfectly bald head. He was holding up an unlit pipe as if he thought Lemming and Margaux might be about to offer him something to fill it.

'Plum,' Lemming said, holding out his hand. Brickhouse looked mildly astonished to hear his nickname. 'It's Lemming, Ian Lemming.'

'Good lord.' Brickhouse transferred his pipe from right to left, and shook Lemming's hand. 'Does this mean the war's finally over?'

'No, unfortunately not,' Lemming said. 'May we come in and explain?'

'Of course, dear boy, of course.' Brickhouse stood aside. 'Aren't you going to introduce me to your delightful companion?'

Lemming let Margaux introduce herself, not knowing what name to give. He did not even hear her reply, because he was too busy admiring Brickhouse's luxurious internment cell.

They were in a broad *salon*, furnished with three red velvet settees and, making up the square, a large antique writing desk, in the middle of which sat a modern typewriter. It was loaded with paper. So Brickhouse was working.

The room was so big that it had two chandeliers, but they were idle, and the soft lighting came from brass lamps set on side tables. The dim remaining daylight was also coming in through three enormous floor-to-ceiling windows. As a wartime refuge, it was far cosier than a London bomb shelter.

'Sit down, have a drink, Thelma's gone out, help yourself to a cigarette, how is your dear brother Philip?' Brickhouse was chattering away as if this were a routine social call. The war seemed to have made him much more garrulous than before.

'Philip's serving out east,' Lemming said, opening the lid of an ornately carved oriental cigarette box. It was full, and he almost gasped at the riches on offer. It was like being gifted a stack of casino chips when you had just bet your last money on a losing hand. He lit one and inhaled greedily.

'I heard about Mark, a terrible shame,' Brickhouse was saying. 'But then 1940 was such a beastly year, don't you think?'

'Beastly, yes,' Margaux said, impatiently. She did not seem to be a fan of Brickhouse-like dithering. 'Now can we –?'

'Excuse me,' Brickhouse said, and went to open one of the doors leading off the sitting room. He returned carrying a panting Pekingese dog. 'I do wish Thelma would take her when she goes out. The staff are delightful, but they tend to kick up a fuss whenever there are fresh claw marks on the doors.'

'Mister Brickhouse –' Margaux began.

'Call me Plum,' Brickhouse said, settling into a sofa with the dog on his lap. 'Now what are you doing in France? Don't tell me you've been interned, too? Goodness, yes, Ian, you look as though you've just been evicted from that awful place in Silesia where they locked me up. Honestly, these Nazis really do take the B. They're completely beyond the P.'

'No, we haven't been interned,' Margaux said. 'We need to ask you –'

'Oh no, not about those confounded broadcasts I made on German radio? They were a moment of profound goofiness. How could anyone think that I approve of these brutish warmongers? Hasn't anyone read The Code of the Roosters, in which the abominable Roderick Spade gets biffed on the noodle for leading the fascistic Blacksocks? Frankly, in all of my books, the only constants are friendship and honour. They're more binding than marriage, sex or anything. To quote the timeless Æneid: "Always be honest with yourself, know your own motives for what they are, good or bad, make your own decisions firmly and justly – and you will be a fine, strong character, of some real use in this muddled world of ours."[11] That's my philosophy.'

Sitting beside Margaux, Lemming could feel her quivering with what he took to be a mixture of impatience and fury.

Lemming, on the other hand, was enjoying himself. It was like listening to one of the books he had read as a younger man. Here was this Buddha in a well-cut but aging suit, whom everyone accused of being a traitor, but who was the most genial presence Lemming had ever encountered. His caressing fingers were even soothing the Pekingese, that most brattish of dogs, into staying calm. Of course, kindness to dogs did not mean that Brickhouse was not a traitor, plotting the downfall of western civilisation. Traitors did not have to be brutes. Even an evil genius could be genial.

'We need to ask you something,' he told Brickhouse.

'You'd like to borrow a razor, is that it? Well, go ahead, be my G. The bathroom's through there.'

'No that's not it,' Lemming objected, but Margaux gripped his arm.

---

[11] Brickhouse's reference to 'the *Æneid*' was in fact a joke, and he was quoting Enid Blyton's novel *Summer Term at Saint Clare's* which had been published a year earlier.

'Actually, Ian, that might be a very good idea. Unshaven, you do rather stand out in a crowd. And while you're shaving, I can have a serious chat with Mister Brickhouse.'

'Oh.' Lemming was seized by a very Brickhousian mixture of emotions. While being slightly offended by the suggestion that he did not need to participate in the tactical discussion, he was also relieved that he would not have interrogate this most charming of men.

To cap it all, right now the mere idea of applying hot soapy water to his face was even more pleasurable than the prospect of a quadruple gin, a naked woman or, yes, even a cigarette.

He went through the door that Brickhouse had shown him, crossed a small corridor, and found a marble bathroom loaded with more towels than he had seen since he once opened an airing cupboard in a Turkish bath. Perfumed tablets of soap were languishing in at least four or five dishes.

He had left the doors open so that he could eavesdrop, but heard little over the clunking of the hot water pipe. France's plumbers might not be away at war, but they apparently had more urgent things to plumb than Plum's hotel.

Shaving was blissful, but painful. Plum's blade was not very keen. Presumably because it had to cope with his scalp as well as his jaw.

It was as Lemming was towelling off his face that he heard a voice that was too male to be Margaux's, and too French to be Brickhouse.

Of course. In the enchantment of meeting Plum again, Lemming had forgotten the danger. Brickhouse, like his books, seemed to make you forget about the unpleasantnesses of life.

Lemming considered urgently who the voice might belong to. The most likely answer was that the excessively helpful young man in the white jacket had betrayed them. Or that the trap mentioned in the 'prune au lolo' message was closing.

Uncharacteristically, Lemming had brought his coat into the bathroom, and silently lifted his knife from the pocket. He decided to take the razor with him too. Even partially blunt, it would do damage.

He could not hear exactly what was being said, but the French voice sounded assertive. Threatening, even. He listened more closely. There was only one French voice, but that did not mean there was only one Frenchman. Lemming would need to use the element of surprise if he was to gain the upper hand over more than one of them.

He thought quickly. If he went back into the sitting room through the same door, he would be several yards from the settees where Brickhouse and Margaux had been sitting. Even the *victor ludorum* at long jump could not hope to leap far and fast enough to disarm two *gendarmes* or *Milice* men.

The best thing to do was to get out into the corridor. They would not expect an attack from there. Treading as softly as possible, he left the bathroom. Yes, to his left was a door that had to lead out into the main corridor. The floor was parquet, so he took one giant stride and was out the door before the wood had stopped squeaking. There was no time to lose. He dashed along to the other entrance door and knocked loudly.

'Qui est-ce?' a French voice asked from inside.

He knocked again.

The door was pulled open, and the helpful young man's face appeared. Although Lemming was holding a blade in each fist, instinct made him punch instead of stab. His knuckles connected with nose, and the young man was propelled backwards. Lemming leapt over his falling body and into the sitting room.

'Oh, it's you, Ian. What have you done to poor Jean-Marc?'

Brickhouse was still sitting on his sofa, tickling his dog. Margaux was sitting on hers, looking more impatient than ever. And a tall, slim man in a pinstripe suit was standing between them, looking confused.

III

Lemming helped the young man to his feet, apologizing profusely and offering to fetch a towel to staunch the lad's bleeding nose. His victim refused, obviously too angry at the assault on his pride and his previously unsullied features.

Margaux explained the situation to Lemming in hurried sentences. The man in pinstripes was the hotel manager, and his whole staff was staunchly anti-Nazi. The young man had escorted them to Brickhouse's room to get them out of sight of any guests less sympathetic to the allied cause. And Margaux's brother was currently hiding in the basement.

Lemming took all this in. But stalled at that final sentence.

'Your brother?'

'Yes.'

Yet again, Lemming was dizzy. This was, in its way, even more astonishing than the idea of self-guided bombs.

'Isn't he in a Stalag? I thought ...' He did not know what he thought.

'Yes, Patrick is here,' Margaux said, 'and I'm afraid the Gestapo won't be far behind.' Lemming now saw that what he had taken for Margaux's impatience when he re-entered the room was pain.

'And we don't want the Gestapo here,' Brickhouse interrupted. 'You know, the hotel has been hiding a charming architect bod, Monsieur Lehrman[12], since 1940. We can't have him carted off now. Who knows what would happen to him. He's Jewish, don't you know.'

'How on earth did Patrick end up here?' Lemming asked.

---

[12] This was true. The architect Léo Lehrman lived in room 106 at the Hôtel Bristol throughout the Occupation. The 200-odd staff kept the secret. In return for his accommodation, Lehrman planned the hotel's refurbishment, which was carried out after the war.

'That's what we have to find out.' Margaux seemed to shiver as she said it.

'Venez.' The pinstriped manager had been nodding throughout the conversation in English. Now he was keen to get them out of the room.

'You have to go?' Brickhouse was looking lost.

'Yes, thanks for the shave, and give my love to Thelma.' Lemming shook Brickhouse's hand, as if trying to keep up the sham of a social call.

'I'll pass it on, dear boy. Though of course I won't mention your visit to another soul. M's the W.' He escorted them to the door. As they scurried towards the lift, Brickhouse never stopped talking. 'Well toodle pip. Drop by after the war, won't you? And bring a cigar or two.' The man's whole brain was an escapist.

In the lift, the manager explained that the English airman had arrived an hour earlier. He had simply stumbled in via the front entrance and begged for refuge for the night. They had hidden him down in the *chaufferie* – the boiler room – while one of the staff went to find someone who could help. It was the first time anything like this had happened.

The manager got out of the lift on the first floor, asking them to deal with the matter as swiftly as possible. The young man in the formerly white jacket (now artistically spattered with his nasal blood, in an abstract way that would have horrified Nazi art critics) remained to show them the way.

Leaving the lift, Margaux swore as vulgarly as she had done that day in London while struggling with her umbrella, but this time with far more feeling.

'I think I should talk to him alone,' she said as they trotted through the warm basement corridors.

'I think you shouldn't,' Lemming said. If her own brother was involved, he reasoned, her loyalties would be more stretched than ever. 'I think both of us need to be in full possession of the facts,' he added. 'With any luck, we'll both be writing our reports on all this. And one thing I've always hated is incomplete intelligence.' That was what had caused the debacle at Dieppe.

'C'est ici.' The young man told them. He was pointing to a thick metal door.

'Let me go in first,' Margaux said.

Lemming opened the door and ushered her in.

The heat was oppressive, as was the noise. The source of both was an immense cast-iron boiler, like something salvaged from a cruise liner's engine room, that was roaring and clunking against the right-hand wall. Beside it, packed tightly into the space between the floor and a ten-foot ceiling, was a motley heap of wood – logs, lengths of plank, smashed crates.

The room was roughly fifteen feet square. Most of the floor space was taken up with a long cylindrical water tank that was painted a dirty cream colour. Out of the top sprouted a fan of thickly lagged pipes that reached up to pierce the ceiling at various points.

There was no sign of an RAF fugitive.

'Patrick?' Margaux called out the name as if she did not want to believe he would be here.

'Patrick!' Lemming barked it as an order.

'It's me,' Margaux said.

A head poked above the far end of the boiler. Lemming instantly saw the resemblance. Patrick was fine-featured, his hair the same deep chestnut colour as Margaux's. He sported a negligible growth of beard that looked soft and boyish. His eyes showed exhaustion, though no more than many of the combatants' eyes that Lemming had seen since 1940. Men returning from action kept that insomniac look for days. Lemming thought he probably had it himself by now.

'Margaux?' Patrick looked almost frightened to see his own sister. He stood up. He was in his shirt sleeves, sweat-stained RAF sky blue.

'We've come from London to fetch you,' Lemming said, to reassure the lad.

'Let me deal with this,' Margaux told him. She beckoned Patrick out, as if she wanted to embrace him.

But when he emerged, in his dark blue trousers, carrying a thick leather coat – an amateurish attempt at camouflage – she kept her distance.

'You've got to tell us what happened,' she said. 'Quickly.'

'There's no time, you have to get out of here,' Patrick said. He shared Margaux's crisp vowels. He spoke, in fact, like a younger Lemming. 'You have to leave, now.' He was almost pleading, looking alternately from Margaux to Lemming.

'First you have to explain,' Margaux said. 'What happened? Your plane was shot down, we know that, then what?'

In reply, he just shook his head. He looked as though he was about to weep. His shoulders slumped, and Lemming thought he was going to topple over.

'You were captured?' Margaux prompted him. 'They forced you to help them?'

He shook his head again.

'You have to tell me,' Margaux said. She gripped his upper arm and squeezed.

'You don't know what it's like,' he said, almost inaudible above the noise of the boiler.

'They tortured you?' Margaux said.

Lemming looked the young man over. He seemed to possess all his fingernails. He was able to stand straight enough, unlike most people who had suffered interrogation at the hands of the Nazis. He had a cut on one cheek, but his face had suffered less damage than the young lad whom Lemming had just punched. In fact, for a man who had baled out of a plummeting aeroplane and then been captured by the *Boches*, he was looking decidedly sprightly.

'They would have done,' Patrick said. 'They would have done.' Now there really were tears in his eyes.

'So they forced you to help?'

Patrick looked up, pleading again.

'I didn't really help. All they did was release me, and then dump me in the middle of the night near a town or village. They told me to look for somewhere to hide. They said they'd be watching, and if I tried to run, they'd shoot me then execute twenty RAF chaps in the nearest prison camp. So I had to go to the local café and ask for someone to shelter me. And as soon as ...'

His voice trailed away.

Lemming could imagine the scene. The person, or family, who took Patrick in were raided, their house ripped apart, everyone carted away. He had seen the results in Normandy. Suddenly, here was another young man he wanted to punch.

Margaux was breathing deeply – examining the features of her brother.

'What about the walnut?' she asked.

'Walnut?' Patrick was bemused.

'The message in the walnut in Le Touquet? Telling us to come to Paris?'

Patrick shook his head.

'But you must have written it,' Lemming interrupted. 'Only an Englishman would have known the slang.'

'What slang?'

Lemming explained about the 'hotel lolo', and Patrick snorted something approaching a laugh.

'That must have been Ernst.'

'Ernst?' Margaux did the honours.

'Kriminalrat Ernst, the chief Gestapo officer up there. A real rat. Lived in London before the war. Fluent in English, French, Flemish, Dutch, or so he says. Knows every European swearword in the book. Boasted about it. Said he's using his languages to wipe the shit off Europe's arse from Brittany to the Hook of Holland. Claimed he's their "big cheese" on the Channel coast. Bastard joked about it. Said it was "ze importance off being Ernst". He was very chummy – when he wasn't threatening to have me shot or cut off my fingers.'

Patrick was close to tears again.

'We'll have to have him dealt with,' Margaux said.

Patrick sprung to life.

'Well if you wait too long, he might very well turn up here. You've got to get away. He was the one who dropped me off near the Bristol. They must be watching the place. They'll raid it as soon as anyone fetches me out.'

For several seconds, the three of them stood motionless, silenced by their thoughts. Lemming was trying to imagine this Ernst, the Gestapo linguist capable of setting a trap in fluent English slang, a message containing the nickname of an author and a music-hall word for breasts – a sure-fire lure to any English person who read it. Ernst was a dangerous enemy. These Nazis might be thugs, but some of them were savagely intelligent.

The door opened, and all eyes turned to the man who entered the room. He was tall and wore a smart overcoat and well-brushed black felt hat. He took one step in and stopped dead, either because of the thermal shock or the surprise of seeing so many people.

Then Lemming too experienced a kind of thermal shock. A bead of sweat ran down his forehead.

It was the man on Brighton station. The one Margaux had pretended to greet like an old friend.

But if Lemming was surprised, Margaux was horrified.

Lemming understood why. This had to be the man whom Patrick had now lured into the Gestapo trap. Naively, the hotel manager had sent for someone who could help the British airman. This was him. And now he was snared.

As they all were.

Margaux and the newcomer wasted no time on how-are-you's. They went into an instant huddle, conferring inaudibly below the boiler's racket.

This left Lemming alone with Patrick, like two chaperones at a lovers' tryst. Though that would have provided them with a natural bond, whereas here there was none.

'Did your chap Ernst mention Brickhouse to you?' Lemming asked.

'You mean PG Brickhouse?' Patrick shook his head at the apparently irrelevant question. 'No. And he wasn't "my" Ernst.'

'Well, he certainly wasn't anyone else's.'

Irritated by the boy, Lemming went over to where Margaux and her friend were still conferring. They both looked at him as if they resented the intrusion, and cut short their conversation. Just before they did so, Lemming thought he heard the man say 'penis'. Which was inappropriate. These Frenchmen, honestly.

'Adieu,' the man said, raising his hat half an inch towards Lemming. He gave Margaux the swiftest peck on the cheek, and left the room.

'Can you wait for me outside?' Margaux said to Lemming.

'Why?'

'Please, Ian.'

The look in her eyes told him not to argue.

Without glancing back at Patrick, Lemming left the room and closed the door behind him. The corridor was blissfully cool, and empty. The man from Brighton station had already disappeared.

Lemming wondered what Margaux would be saying to Patrick. The big sister's moral lambasting, no doubt. Though this was surely much more serious than any sisterly moralizing since Queen Mary Tudor warned young Elizabeth not to get too Protestant.

And the worst thing was that Margaux would almost certainly have to abandon Patrick to his fate. She would then have to sound the alarm somehow, alerting all known Resistance contacts not to go to the aid of a young, dark-haired RAF man. Which was pretty hard on any other young, dark-haired RAF men who baled out in the near future.

After little more than five minutes, Margaux came out of the boiler room. She was looking shaken.

'Let's go,' she said.

'You're leaving him here, then?'

'Yes. Let's go. Please, Ian.'

'We could always try to get him out,' Lemming offered. 'Perhaps they won't be watching the rooftops.'

'Let's just go.'

She was looking so distressed that Lemming could not help becoming the parfit gentil knight.

'Why don't you leave, Margaux, and I'll try to smuggle him away?'

A single tear slid down her cheek. It got as far as the corner of her mouth before she wiped it away with a hand.

'No, Ian,' she said, with forced calm. 'I gave him my cyanide pill, put it in his mouth, and held his jaw closed for him. It's like you said, working with the Nazis is a stain that can never be erased.'

IV

The young man with the blood-stained jacket was waiting by the lift. Margaux blurted out swift instructions to him. He was to tell the hotel manager to call the *police française* immediately and report that a strange man had been seen coming into the hotel, and had taken refuge in the *chaufferie*.

The lad frowned at this instruction to betray an ally.

'C'était un traître,' she said, simply.

Lemming's mouth was still drooping open at the murderous efficiency he was witnessing.

Margaux asked the young man the best way to get out of the hotel unseen. He told her that the alleyway into the courtyard was where people came and went most frequently.

'D'accord, et merci pour tout,' Margaux thanked him.

The young man nodded and smiled.

'Et toutes mes excuses,' Lemming added, gesturing to the nose and the jacket. All his apologies.

In return he received no smile.

The stout gatekeeper in the braided cap was still on duty at the tradesmen's entrance.

'Alors?' he asked them, and saw Margaux's obvious distress. 'Ah, tant pis,' he added. Too bad.

Lemming told him they would return next morning to ask again. He thought it best to cover their tracks.

'Bonne chance,' the man said. Good luck.

The long alley seemed to be empty, though if Patrick had told them the truth – and surely they could credit him with that – it was almost certainly being watched.

Lemming resumed his limp, and he and Margaux made unhurriedly for the street exit, watching and listening carefully. It was dark now, and the alley was deep in shadow. There were plenty of places to hide a Nazi snoop.

'Demain matin, tu vas t'habiller mieux, chéri,' Margaux said. She was telling her supposed fiancé to dress more neatly the next day.

'Oui, oui,' Lemming agreed. He was still in shock about the true nature of the woman now gripping his elbow.

The street was dark. Only one in two of the lamps were lit, and faintly. As soon as they were out of the alley, Margaux tugged to the left. She clearly knew where they were going. Lemming had no idea, and did not dare ask.

There were few people about, no doubt because of the approaching curfew. Two uniformed Nazis were walking quickly along the opposite pavement, but seemed to be involved in a loud and cheerful German conversation. Probably not on the lookout for escaping Resistance agents.

A couple were wandering slowly in front of Margaux and Lemming. The male was short and wide, engulfed in a large coat and wide-brimmed hat, she was taller, in dress and jacket, trotting on high heels. She was complaining in plaintive French, 'jamais' (never) this and 'jamais' that, 'jamais, jamais'. If he had been in the man's place, Lemming thought, he'd have told her sharply: 'jamais' say 'jamais' again.

In any case, the couple looked genuinely married, frighteningly so.

Then Margaux dug her nails into Lemming's arm. She must have seen something. She changed direction brusquely, heading towards a small, dark street on their right. They crossed the road quickly although there were no vehicles approaching. It was getting difficult for Lemming to maintain his limp.

'Run!' she suddenly whispered. 'Run!' She shoved him forward, and Lemming needed no third bidding. Clicking once again into *victor ludorum* mode, he sprinted along the dark street, listening to the slap of his footsteps echoing against the walls, and expecting them to be interrupted at any second by a gunshot.

'Arretez-vous!' The shout was French. Without a German accent. Even so, Lemming ignored it and carried on running without looking back.

Only fifty yards later did he wonder where Margaux had got to.

The French policeman had been waiting a few steps from the exit to the alleyway. He had been briefed to stop everyone coming out, and demand their identity papers. If they were not members of the hotel staff or accredited tradesmen with business at the hotel, they were to be arrested.

The odd, shabby couple had looked suspect, and he had been about to intercept them when they turned in the other direction so suddenly that he had been taken by surprise. And when they started running, he knew he was on to something.

'Arretez-vous!' he had ordered, grappling with his holster, and setting off after them down a narrow side street.

The limping man had metamorphosed into a loping sprinter, and was already twenty metres away, but the woman was much slower. She had tripped on the kerb. He caught her easily, and shoved her against a wall. She would tell him who the running man was and where he would go to hide. He was out of sight now. In any case, it was probably the *Anglais* they had been using as bait. He would be picked up by the Gestapo soon enough.

'Tes papiers!' he ordered her, adopting the familiar, scornful *'tu'* form.

She looked calm for a young girl who had just been caught helping a British airman, he had to grant her that. She was rifling methodically through her small handbag. Too small to hold a weapon, he noted.

'Vous aimez travailler pour les Boches?' she asked, in a polite, matter-of fact voice. She was asking whether he liked working for the enemy.

'Ta gueule,' he replied, an efficient way of telling her to hold her trap. 'Et tes papiers.'

'Ca va mal finir pour vous,' she said. It was going to end badly for him.

'Et pour toi?' he asked, rhetorically. They both knew how it ended for Resistance workers.

Finally, she pulled out an identity card and held it up.

'Voilà, monsieur l'agent,' she said. She was looking him in the eye defiantly, almost triumphantly.

Then her eyes seemed to blink, and his own vision suddenly faded. He felt himself falling over.

'You took your time,' Margaux told Lemming, who was rubbing his knuckles yet again. That punch to the policeman's temple had been one of the hardest he had ever delivered.

'Let's go,' Lemming said.

After his sprint, he had got almost to the end of the short street before turning round to see Margaux being grabbed by a *gendarme*, who was pulling out a pistol. Sticking to the shadows, he had crept back and caught the distracted policeman from behind. A cowardly blow, but a vital one.

'We can't leave him here,' Margaux said. She was looking around, checking for other passers-by. There were none for the moment.

'We can't take him with us,' Lemming said.

'No, I mean, he's seen my face. He's seen my identity card.'

'So?' Lemming asked, but he already knew what she was going to say.

'Have you got your knife?'

'I can't stab an unconscious man,' he objected. 'In any case, what about reprisals?'

It was well known that the Nazis executed groups of hostages every time one of theirs was killed.

'They won't take reprisals for French policemen. Oh, for heaven's sake.'

She knelt down beside the *gendarme*, who was lying on his front. His feet were twitching. Leaning forward, she gripped the man's chin in one hand, the back of his head in the other, and twisted sharply. Lemming heard the neck give a sickening crunch. The *gendarme* went limp. She rolled his body into the shadows.

'Now let's go,' she said, getting to her feet. 'We have to get to the river.'

V

Lemming forgot to limp. In any case he was in a daze. This young woman, this *girl*, had just killed two men in cold blood, in the space of little more than ten minutes. And one of them was her own brother. With her bare hands, too, if you didn't count the poison. And she must have been carrying the cyanide the whole time. Presumably she would have slipped it to Lemming if he had become a risk to her security.

Who *was* she?

They moved swiftly, ducking into doorways whenever they heard approaching feet or vehicles. There were few. This was not a residential area, and people had little excuse for wandering these streets unless they were in uniform.

Luckily, the chic buildings had deep doorways. A pair of soldiers, rifles on their back, came within yards of them as they held their breath, pressed against the art nouveau ironwork of a tall front door. Ordinarily, Lemming would have been tempted to take Margaux in his arms and kiss her, purely as camouflage in case they were spotted. But now he feared what she might do to him if he tried.

The most dangerous part of their walk to the river was crossing the Champs-Elysées. It was wide, dark, and almost deserted. It came as a shock to Lemming, who had known that same avenue crowded with revellers, teeming with cars. The City of Lights really had been snuffed out.

There were bound to be even darker forces posted along the avenue because of the heavy military presence at Concorde, where the Nazis had their HQ. Lemming and Margaux paused to collect their thoughts in the corner of the gardens at the Rond-Point des Champs-Elysées, a large roundabout.

'There's a Métro station just opposite,' Margaux whispered. 'We'll make directly for it, go down the steps, then come straight back out again.' She seemed to have an instant plan for any situation.

Gripping his arm, she set off across the avenue. A car was coming towards them from Concorde, its dim headlights barely illuminating the road surface ten yards beyond its bumpers. It had to be military.

If the driver saw them, he did not care who they were. Neither, apparently, did four soldiers who were on the opposite side of the roundabout, lazily watching the street.

'Ignore the Métro,' she said, branching off left, away from the soldiers.

Lemming followed her lead, like a blind man being escorted to an urgent appointment.

They passed a theatre, dead and dark – so not all of Paris's actors were putting on shows for the occupiers.

At last they were at the river, with only an avenue and a tree-lined garden to cross. Here too, Margaux took things calmly, pausing to study the pavements, the road and the garden before starting to cross. The only sign of life they saw was what looked like a caped policeman on a bicycle, heading slowly away from them towards Concorde.

On the skyline, Lemming now saw the Eiffel Tower, a mere shadow pointing up into the luminous grey of the sky. It too looked dead, as if waiting patiently for the old, lively Paris to be revived.

'There are barges moored over there,' Margaux said. 'We have to choose one and hijack it.'

'What?' The evening had just taken yet another turn towards the surreal.

'You'd better take this,' she said, pulling something out of her coat pocket. 'And for God's sake use it if I tell you to.'

It was a pistol. Presumably *gendarme* standard issue, the former possession of the man lying dead near the rear entrance to the Bristol. Margaux had clearly had the presence of mind to steal it.

Lemming stashed it in his pocket, along with his knife. He was becoming a walking armoury. Though she was the deadly one. It was almost comforting to know that he had all the weapons, in case he became a liability and Margaux tried to bump him off too.

They crossed the avenue and the gardens, and stopped by a low wall on the riverside. They could see several long industrial barges moored along the quay. One was gliding upriver, creating a splashing bow wave as it fought the current.

A few yards away, there was a flight of stone steps leading down to the bank. A man in a flat cap and short jacket was walking from the base of the steps towards the nearest barge.

'He'll do,' Margaux said, and set off.

Lemming pitied the chap already. Almost half the men who had crossed Margaux's path this evening had ended up in the queue for the pearly gates. Was this one to be next?

'Monsieur!' she called, as soon as she was on the quay. The man stopped and turned. He had a large dark moustache over a smaller beard. He did not look at all suspicious or worried, and kept his hands in his pockets.

'Oui?'

Margaux waited until she and Lemming were right beside the man before speaking again.

'Vous allez au Havre?' she asked. Was he going right along the Seine to its mouth at Le Havre?

'Non, pas du tout,' he said.

'Si.'

'Non.'

Oh no, Lemming thought, we're in for one of those nursery arguments again. He pulled out the pistol.

'Si,' Lemming repeated.

The man laughed and shook his head. Lemming's toy was not going to fill up his fuel tank, he told them.

Margaux changed tactic. Pushing aside the barrel of Lemming's pistol, she quickly told the man that they had to get to Le Havre, to the coast. He shrugged as he listened, and replied that he and all his neighbours were stranded in Paris for lack of fuel. Only essential traffic was being permitted on the river, and that meant carrying loads for the *Boches*.

'Et moi, collabo, jamais.' He would never collaborate. The only way to get on board one of those barges, he said, was at the loading or unloading points, and they were bound to be guarded.

Lemming looked out beyond the moored barges towards the river. The boat they had seen before was now passing under the Pont des Invalides, just upriver. He could hear the low thrum of another boat coming from that direction.

'There's another way,' he told Margaux. 'Come on.'

He pointed towards the bridge, and she seemed to understand.

They ran along the quay towards the Pont de l'Alma. It was only about forty yards, but they were both breathing hard when they came to the ramp that led up to street level and the bridge. They had done far too much running and not enough eating or sleeping over these past few days.

There were a few people to their right, but they were on the terrace of a large *brasserie* that seemed to be lit by old-fashioned flaming torches. No one was on the bridge.

'We have to jump,' Lemming said.

'If we miss, I hope you can swim as far as Le Havre.'

'It's downstream. We'll float there.'

They moved to the centre of the bridge and looked down towards a barge that was approaching fast. Its long load compartment, running most of its length, was covered by dark tarpaulins. With any luck those would break their fall, without trampolining them off the boat and into the fast-flowing, and no doubt chilly, river. It was about fifteen feet down. Lemming had done parachute training exercises from greater heights. He supposed Margaux would have too.

When the nose of the barge was almost out of sight below them, they leapt, Margaux first, then Lemming. There was a rush of air, a spine-jarring thud, and then Lemming was entangled in Margaux's limbs, his feet in the air, her head and arms across his chest. The bridge swept past over their heads.

'The cockpit,' Margaux gasped. She, like Lemming, had had the air crushed out of her lungs by the fall.

Lemming's instinct would have been to lie low, but he realized that she was right. The bargee would almost certainly have seen two stowaways arriving from mid-air. He might be preparing to repel boarders – or report them.

They crawled to the side of the tarpaulin and ran along deck to the cockpit. Inside, they saw a woman of about forty, her hair tied in a light-coloured scarf, desperately trying to lock the side door.

Margaux barged it open. Lemming followed her into a cramped area that smelt of damp and oil. The woman was alone and looking scared.

'Qui êtes-vous?' she demanded, her already red cheeks flushing furiously.

'Conduisez, madame,' Margaux said – drive. She pointed to the unattended wheel. The last thing they wanted now was to crash into the bank. 'Calmez-vous,' she added, as the woman grabbed the wheel and corrected course.

'Qu'est-ce que vous foutez?' the woman asked, wanting to know what, loosely translated, the fuck they were doing.

'Nous sommes de la Résistance,' Margaux said, and Lemming pulled out the pistol to prove it. She explained that some 'amis' had seen them jump on to the boat, and if they got into any trouble, those same 'amis' would make sure that the bargees were brought to justice.

The woman quite reasonably asked what they wanted of her.

'Nous allons au Havre,' Margaux said.

The woman objected that she was on a return trip to Rouen, only about two-thirds the way along the river. She had no fuel to go further.

Margaux thought about this.

'Rouen, c'est très bien,' she concluded. She asked whether the woman's husband or any other family members were on board.

'Mon mari dort,' she said. He was asleep. 'On fait Melun-Rouen-Melun sans arrêt depuis trois jours.' They had been on the river non-stop for three days.

Lemming asked whether she had anything to eat or drink. He was suddenly feeling ravenous. It had to be all this unplanned athletics. And the nervous energy of causing multiple deaths.

'Pas beaucoup,' the woman said, but Lemming did not believe her. If you were on a long trip like this, you stocked up. And if you were doing *collabo* work, you got fed.

He went down a narrow set of steps into a galley area. Beyond it was a door, presumably leading to the cabins. There was a key. Lemming locked the door and pocketed the key. The husband would have to knock to come out. Or barge his way out. Very apt.

Rooting around, he quickly unearthed bread, sausage, cheese and wine in a larder cupboard. Grabbing as much as he could carry, he went back up into the cockpit.

Margaux was re-assuring the woman that all would go well if she dropped them off outside Rouen and then kept quiet about it.

'C'est notre bouffe, ça!' the woman objected, seeing Lemming in possession of her 'grub'.

In his best Churchillian French, he reminded the woman that the Nazis had stolen much more than a meagre meal from France. However, in a spirit of reconciliation, he offered his hostess a slice of her own sausage. When she refused, he thanked her for her generosity, and she huffed.

Lemming and Margaux chewed on what tasted like, and might well have been, donkey that had died of starvation. Lemming said that he had locked the door to the cabins. He saw the woman listening.

'Is it all right if I put my hand up your skirt, my dear?' he asked her, smiling pleasantly. 'Then maybe we can go and join your husband in bed?'

The woman's face was blank, though still as reproachful as it had been since they boarded.

'Don't think she understands English,' he told Margaux. 'And I've got some questions for you.'

'Now's not the time.'

'Yes, if I may be so bold, it bloody well is the time.' He smiled at the woman as if to reassure her that her captors were not having an argument. 'Two men are dead and we're running – or barging – for our lives. And I'd like to know exactly what's going on.'

'I don't think I have all the answers,' Margaux said, looking more sad than secretive. He guessed that she too must be in shock at the turn events had taken. Killing a brother was something that Lemming could not even begin to contemplate.

'You know more than I do,' he said, 'and there are some things I have a right to know, especially if they might cause me to get shot or tortured or both.'

'Ask, and I'll see if I can answer.' She took a decidedly unladylike slug from the wine bottle, grimacing as she swallowed. Lemming understood why. It certainly wasn't the kind of French bottle he would have taken home for his cellar, except perhaps to de-scale the water pipes.

'All right, first of all, why do you think they sent us to the hotel?' Lemming asked.

Margaux turned so that her back was to the woman at the wheel.

'I can only think that the Gestapo are annoyed because the hotel has kept its nose clean all these years.' She was speaking softly above the hum of the engines. 'It's the only one of the big Paris hotels that hasn't taken in Nazi lodgers. The management must be suspect in the Gestapo's eyes. I'm guessing they were using Brickhouse's name as bait.'

'You don't think Plum can really be that much of a traitor, do you? He wasn't in on the plan?'

Margaux considered this. 'Honestly, no. I think that if they ever do put him up against a wall, Allied or Nazi, right until the last second he'll be telling the firing squad to mind their ears because this is probably going to make a frightful bang. I'd say he's incapable of actual treason. Deliberate, anyway. And compared to every one of the French writers currently pontificating about the meaning of existence in Parisian cafés, while being published by collaborating publishers, he's an angel, a sort of ancient cherub.'

Lemming was very relieved to hear this.

'What about the French chap who turned up. He was the man from Brighton Station, wasn't he?' he asked.

'You recognized him, then?'

'Yes of course.'

'You didn't recognize him from anywhere else?'

'No.'

'He's also the sommelier at the Rose de Picardie.'

'Our restaurant?'

She nodded. 'La Fleur du Mall.' She shook her head. 'So it's true what they say. People like you never really look at the staff. They're just a means to an end.'

'All Frenchmen look alike to me,' Lemming said, but he felt chastened. She was right. Male serving staff rarely earned an attentive glance from him. 'Is he your boyfriend?'

Margaux stifled a bitter laugh.

'That's the story of all your dealings with the opposite sex, isn't it, Ian?'

'Well he is French. And I wouldn't blame him. Besides, I overheard him talking about his penis.'

'What?' Margaux laughed out loud, and the woman at the wheel looked across as if these two intruders were completely insane. 'Not a penis, you idiot. He was telling me to go and hitch a lift on a River Seine barge, a "péniche". Honestly!'

Again, Lemming felt chastened. 'This is why I never eavesdrop. And why I'm never jealous. You always end up looking a fool.' He took a mouthful of the wine as punishment. 'Wait a minute, though,' he added. 'That sommelier chap is a Gaullist, isn't he?'

This seemed to prove his and Rashbrooke's suspicions about Margaux's ultimate loyalties.

'He is, yes. But we do work together sometimes, you know. We are on the same side.'

'Until he reveals all our secrets.'

'That's why I got him out of that hotel. He knows the names of a dozen of his agents in Paris, each of whom probably knows a dozen more. If he's caught, their whole network goes down. That mob are as centralized as the French national pétanque association. That's why I told you that so many lives might be at risk. I knew he was going to be in Paris and might get sucked into our business. Believe me, though, he has no idea what my real name is.'

'Do I?' Lemming asked.

'I don't know. Do you?'

Lemming thought so. He had seen her file. He had read about her family. It couldn't all be fiction, could it?

'I'm very sorry about your brother,' he said. 'I know you must be hurting terribly. But I admire you for what you did. You showed incredible quick thinking and decisiveness. I'm not sure I could have done it. But you had no other choice.'

Margaux was breathing deeply, as if she had been transported back into the *chaufferie* with her brother.

'Thank you for saying that,' she said. 'And I think you're right, you wouldn't have done it. If I may say so, you're much too soft for this business. I must beg you never to come on a mission with me again.' She said it almost glibly, but Lemming could see that she was serious.

'Apart from not wanting to knock off a policeman in cold blood, I think I've done all right,' he defended himself.

'It's not just that. What do you want to do about the people in Biville, for example?'

'The old couple and the boy? You're not thinking of having them bumped off?' Lemming truly thought she might, if she had to.

'Of course not. But I'll be passing on their address to my superiors.'

'What? You'll put them on some list? You'd risk the lives of those old folks – and the kid?'

Margaux looked suddenly furious with him.

'I'm not sure you fully realize what's at stake here,' she said. 'Our airmen are getting shot down over France every day. They need safe addresses. As do our agents. And when the invasion comes, there is going to be one hell of a battle for the north of France. Do you think we should write to your old couple warning them when it's about to hit? Should we give their address to bomber command, so they're sure to avoid the old couple's house when they're trying to flatten the Atlantic Wall? Of course I'm grateful that they risked their lives to help us. But are their lives worth more than those of all the men who will be landing on the beaches or parachuting in behind enemy lines? And did those old folks risk their lives more by lending us bicycles than almost every single British male over the age of 17 has done almost every single day since 1939? For your average soldier, sailor or airman, the war effort isn't about lending someone a bicycle and then expecting a medal as a Resistance fighter. Our people get bullets and shells fired at them every day. You may not have heard about it, Ian, but there have been dozens, perhaps hundreds of deaths amongst the troops just *rehearsing* for the upcoming invasions. So please don't try to make me cry about one old couple who *might just* be in danger *if* between now and the invasion another agent like me has to look them up and ask for their help in some way.'

Lemming and the woman behind the wheel were both staring at Margaux in shock. The woman, because Margaux's voice had risen to an uncharacteristic falsetto climax. Lemming, because he realized that he was actually scared of this girl.

No woman had ever managed to unnerve him the way Margaux now did. He had frequently been accused, flatteringly he thought, of being a ladykiller. Well, Margaux was a genuine lady killer. A female assassin, a feminine bumper-off. Even members of her own family were not safe in her hands.

She seemed to recognize the effect that she had had on him.

'I don't think you truly understand my job,' she said, more calmly. 'A secret agent in the field has only one duty. That is to survive long enough to carry out our mission. And we will do anything, *anything*, to achieve that goal.'

'In that case, don't you think you ought to have tried to bring your brother in, so that we could find out exactly what he knew? About this Ernst chap, for example.'

The fires in Margaux's eyes were burning again.

'Don't ever doubt me,' she said. 'Don't *ever* accuse me of doing less than I possibly can for my mission. Do you know what I did as soon as he had convulsed himself to death in front of me?' She let the image sink in for a moment. 'I shoved, right up into his cheek, beside his clenched teeth, a small roll of silk marked in invisible ink with the details of an exit route out of France. A false trail, leading to a French publisher who has been printing pro-Vichy books all through the war thanks to Nazi patronage. With any luck, the Gestapo will find it and arrest the publisher, and Patrick's death will protect real agents, as well as landing a notorious collabo in the merde.'

These two French words gained the bargee woman's attention again.

'What do you want us to say about Patrick when we get back?' Lemming asked.

'What do you mean?'

'How much do you want to reveal about what he did? You know, family honour and all that.'

Again, Margaux was incensed.

'You think I'd lie to cover up my brother's cowardice? We have to report *everything*. One lie could put the lives of countless others at risk.'

'Very well.' Lemming wondered how far *he* would go to protect a brother's reputation. Not that one of his brothers would need it ... 'Did you know that Patrick might be behind the betrayals of the Resistance network?' he asked. 'I mean, before we left England?'

Even as he finished asking the question, Lemming saw the volcano preparing to erupt again.

'Of course not!' Margaux hissed. 'Do you think they'd have given me the mission? Do you think I'd have accepted it? No, it was coincidence, horrific happenstance, like two brothers shooting at each other in a civil war.'

The sick look on her face convinced Lemming that it was all true. And if she really had been unprepared for the surprise of finding Patrick at the Bristol, he admired her even more for her deadly decisiveness.

'In a perverse way, it was better,' she said, more quietly. 'At least I got to wipe the black mark off the family name myself. Partially, anyway.'

There was a banging from below decks. The husband had woken up.

Margaux grabbed the pistol and told the woman to come and explain to her *cher mari* why he would be staying quietly in his cabin for the rest of the night.

'You *can* steer a boat straight, can't you?' she said over her shoulder as she went below.

No woman had ever spoken to the adult Lemming like that. He had not heard such scorn for the male species since he was about fourteen, when a much older girl, the daughter of a friend of his parents, had mocked him for getting his watch caught in her brassiere strap as he struggled to undo it.

Oh well, Lemming thought as he took the wheel, it looked as though Margaux was one woman who had definitely chosen not to let him anywhere near her undergarments.

And for once, he truly regretted it. This was no trivial encounter at a cocktail party. His growing professional admiration for Margaux, and his subsequent fear of her, had now turned to awe. Not only for the professional agent, but for the woman.

When she went to bed with a man during wartime, he thought, it would be an extreme experience, enjoyed in the full awareness of life and death. There would be little or no romantic attachment. It would be purely, urgently, sexual. And as ephemeral as the physical sensations it provoked.

This, he realized, was because a woman like her, a secret agent in the field, could never really fall in love, or let anyone fall in love with her. The very existence of that love would make both her and the man vulnerable. If her lover was captured, she might do anything to save him, putting her mission at risk. But if he betrayed her, he had to die. So the true secret agent was doomed to be alone, and profoundly cold at heart.

And in a way, Lemming told himself, he was similar. Whenever he had a truly romantic entanglement, he felt weakened, vulnerable, and less able to act freely. Yes, he told himself, he was in some ways very much like one of those secret agents. Not that he would dare say so to Margaux.

VI

It was well past dawn by the time they got to Rouen. Lemming and Margaux had taken turns sleeping in the corner of the cockpit. Lemming had smoked one of his last two cigarettes, having failed to requisition any from the bargee woman. Her husband kept them down in the cabin, she insisted.

The bargee woman had stayed at the wheel all night, though not without complaints. She was, it turned out, Belgian, though her husband was French, and they had been working the Seine for more than a year, mainly Rouen to Paris, carrying any load they were offered – 'nothing military, though,' she assured them. Not that they believed her.

Margaux told the woman to take them past the port, so that they would be able to get on a boat going to Le Havre.

'Mais il n'y a plus de pont,' the woman said. Downriver, there were no more Seine bridges to jump off.

'On s'arrangera,' Margaux said. We'll sort it out. Lemming didn't see how, unless she had an inflatable bridge tucked away in her blouse, along with the cyanide pills, silk documents and who knew what other items of secret agents' trickery.

The port of Rouen was busy with ocean-going ships loading and unloading in dock. Cranes were lifting sacks, crates and vehicles. There were fuel tanks, giant silos – presumably for grain and building materials – and a pyramid of dark wooden barrels. Lemming suspected that a lot of this merchandise would be getting exported from France to supply Germany and its armies. There was little chance that the Nazis were importing Bavarian beer and Ukrainian cereals, even for their own troops. Occupation was about old-fashioned pillaging. Rumour had it that even the Louvre was half-empty.

It was satisfying to see that some of the silos were truncated, and a whole row of cranes bent and twisted. Bombs had been holding up the pillaging.

The port was heavily guarded. There were sentries everywhere, and a military zone with hangars containing what looked like torpedo boats. Lemming thought he recognized a minesweeper, with its long rear deck, and a submarine hunter, armed with a barrage of depth-charge cannons. He would have loved to stop off and do a spot of diving around their hulls, with a few of those new limpet mines.

The barge pulled alongside an empty quay just beyond the port. There was a long brick warehouse on the riverbank, but it had been damaged in an air raid, and looked abandoned.

With the motor idling, Margaux took the woman down into the galley to brief her and (through the locked door) her husband about what to do next. They should go about their ordinary business, Margaux said, as slowly as possible so as to hinder the *Boches*. One day soon, she told them, an immense allied army would invade. There would be a million Americans, for example, sailing into every port on the coast from Bordeaux

216

to The Hague, from Nice to Marseille, and they would sweep the Nazis out of France, Belgium and Holland. Then it would be wise for bargees to figure on the official list of Resistance workers if they did not want to get shot as collaborators. And when Margaux and Lemming escaped from Le Havre, they were going to put the names of their bargee hosts on that Resistance list. Of course, if they did not escape, the real Resistance in Paris, the people who watched them board the barge, would put them and their boat on the collaborators' list.

So all in all, it was best that the bargees said nothing to anyone. In any case, the British and the Americans now had spies in the *gendarmerie* and even in the Gestapo, so anyone denouncing Resistance workers would be identified and later left to the mercy of the million Americans.

Up in the cockpit, holding the wheel so that the barge stayed close to the bank, Lemming listened to all this, and thought how wonderful it would be if it were true.

What was true, he knew, was that the French would believe anything about Americans. He had seen their mystic charms work a thousand miracles in Le Touquet. Anyone with a New York accent and a big cigar was treated like a millionaire, and any half-way good-looking Yank could play the Hollywood star. One excitable French girl had even assured Lemming that Ernest Hemingway wrote 'the most perfect English in literature'. She had intimated that she would have been far fonder of Lemming if he had been a writer with a Midwest drawl and a Cuban pimp's moustache.

They jumped ashore and ran to hide in the abandoned warehouse.

'So we're getting a boat to Le Havre?' Lemming asked.

'Of course not. We're heading for Dieppe.'

'Dieppe?' The name did not conjure up pleasant memories.

'Or thereabouts. With any luck, we can make it back to our dinghy.'

'And paddle across the Channel?

'And get picked up. I gave René a message to radio out.'

'You trusted him?'

'Enough to tell him to radio out that "forget me not" wanted to be picked up at point and time of entry sometime in the next three or four days. It won't mean anything to him.'

'You think he'll do it?'

'Just in case, I also gave the same information to our friend the sommelier.'

Lemming took all of this in. While he had been dashing along like a rugby player charging for the touch line, she had been playing chess, planning three or four moves ahead.

'And you didn't tell me, for the usual reasons,' he stated.

'Yes, but now that we're on the final sprint, you deserve to know. If you can make it to the dinghy, and paddle a mile out to sea, there might well be a submarine waiting to say hello.'

'And if there's not, I keep paddling.'

'Unless you know a shoal of friendly haddock that will give you a tow.'

There were plenty of people in the streets, almost all of them civilian. The wide boulevard running into the centre of Rouen was crowded with handcarts, bicycle carts, gas-driven lorries, horse-drawn wagons, even the occasional car. Along the pavements there was a constant flow of people on their way to and from work, or carrying large empty bags, as if off to market. Schoolchildren too, in their blue coat-length overalls, carrying satchels, looking like miniature solicitors on their way to court.

These civilians all walked unseeingly past one of the tall totem poles of black-on-white Nazi signposts: 'Sanitätspark', 'Luftwaffenlazarett', 'Ersatzteillager', 'Unfallmeldestelle'. [13]

Keeping well away from the port, Lemming and Margaux climbed a wooded lane into leafy, almost rural suburbs, where some of the houses had large gardens and even orchards. Here, people were tending their vegetable patches, and Lemming

---

[13] 'Medical area', 'Luftwaffe hospital', 'Spare parts depot', 'Accident report station'.

raised his eyes at Margaux, asking whether they should inquire about transport. She shook her head and carried on.

After half an hour, things got more industrial again. There were small factories and fenced-off yards.

'The road north is not far from here,' Margaux said. 'Watch out for bikes to steal.'

'Bikes?' Lemming was looking at the sky. Tall, angry-looking clouds were streaming overhead. Unless he was mistaken, the Atlantic was sending them some of its vast supply of moisture.

'I don't think I want to trust anyone here,' she said. 'You know that Rouen is where Joan of Arc was burnt by the English.'

'I see your point.'

'Before that, she was captured by French soldiers and handed over to the occupier, which was us at the time. So in a way, Joan of Arc is the patron saint of Resistance fighters handed over by their own countrymen to the enemy.'

There were no likely targets until they reached an area by the railway. Smallish apartment buildings, three or four storeys high, were intermingled with larger houses. And fewer people were in the streets, as if the residents had all gone to work or school.

Lemming began to scale the walls of front yards, and nose into tenement halls, while Margaux kept watch. After fifteen minutes of fruitless prowling, they came across a modern brick house with a garage set back from the road. The house was empty, and the garage door opened easily, with a little help from Lemming's shoulder. Inside was a delightful little two-seater Citroën 5 HP, a car Lemming knew well. Its square profile was a common sight on the roads around Le Touquet in the 1930s. It was the car that every old doctor, banker and small-town bureaucrat drove.

This one had not been used recently. Its crimson bonnet and chrome headlights were dusty, its black roof was streaked with green mould.

Lemming called Margaux into the garage. She kicked the car's tyres almost scornfully.

'Forget it, Ian. Where are we going to get the petrol?'

But Lemming was already lifting the bonnet and unscrewing the petrol cap. He tapped the tank and peered in.

'There seems to be a bit of fuel in there. How far do we have to go? Forty miles?'

'The tyres are flat.'

But Lemming had already spotted a foot pump at the back of the garage.

'We'd be too conspicuous,' Margaux said. 'No French people drive cars these days.'

'This little machine does 50 kilometres an hour. If we take the back roads, it will get us to Dieppe before anyone notices us.'

'If you can start it.'

Lemming hunted around the garage, opening cupboards and boxes. He found some dusty bottles of what smelled like calvados. He wondered whether the engine could cope with, say, forty or fifty per cent alcohol mixed in with the petrol already in the tank. A Citroën carburettor was an efficient gadget. It was worth taking a chance. He poured a full bottle into the tank, and prayed.

After twenty more minutes of pumping and tinkering, with Margaux keeping her nose to the garage doors, Lemming was ready to crank the starting handle.

It turned once, to no effect. A second time, and it was like flicking an empty lighter. Lemming heaved a third time, and the engine gave a single puff of protest. Summoning all his strength, he wrenched again, with two hands this time, throwing his whole body into the movement, just as he had done when putting the shot at Eton, or punching that Parisian *gendarme*.

The engine turned over, puffed, coughed, and then awoke fully, like a smoker emerging from sleep. The car began to shake on its high suspension.

'Vive la France,' Lemming said, and climbed up behind the wheel.

Margaux checked that the coast was clear then opened the garage gates, and they were soon chugging through the northern quarters of Rouen, looking like a rather scruffy doctor and his nurse off to attend a patient in the country. They hardly attracted any attention from pedestrians, even from a policeman who was standing outside a shoe shop, talking to an old man in a leather apron. As Lemming had said, these cars had been very common at one time, as familiar a sight as a Parisian poodle trotting with a *vieille bourgeoise*.

Arriving at the main road north, they saw a column of military vehicles – whole truckloads of troops – heading straight for Dieppe. They crossed over, and headed further east than they wanted, along smaller lanes and through peaceful villages.

Afraid of running out of fuel, Lemming drove as gently as an old lady's chauffeur, using the gears to accelerate and letting the engine ease its way up inclines. He realized that he was enjoying himself. He had long dreamt of returning to the roads of Normandy, and even though he was travelling some fifty or sixty miles per hour more slowly than in his fantasies, this was fun. Cows and sheep looked up as the Citroën passed, no doubt unused to motor traffic, and people in fields and gardens waved at the cute little car.

Once, as they were leaving a large village on the edge of some woodland, a lone policeman tried to flag them down. It looked as though he had been inspecting the crater left by a stray bomb – a large muddy hole in the middle of a grass pasture. Either that, or the Resistance had blown up a collaborator's horse. The policeman was walking back towards the gate when the car passed, and he gesticulated as if he might want a lift.

Margaux waved back apologetically – sorry, no time to stop, her body language said, our patient is at death's door, or about to give birth, or somewhere in between. The man shouted what sounded like abuse, but took no further action. Luck seemed to be with them.

'What if we get stopped?' Lemming asked her, above the coughing but steady note of the engine.

'You have an identity card that says Biville. We're on the road to Biville.'

Lemming did not want to resume the argument about putting old people at risk.

'Maybe it would be better if you just shot whoever stops us,' he said. He handed her the pistol.

They were crossing the Béthune river, about fifteen kilometres south of Dieppe, when they saw that they were driving straight towards an army camp on the other side of the valley. Its wooden huts covered several fields, and even from a distance they could see uniformed Nazis walking about, sitting by camp fires and standing guard on the perimeter fence.

They could not turn around, even though their current trajectory was going to take them right through the centre of the camp. The public road divided it almost exactly in half.

Lemming changed gear and let the car potter at about fifteen miles per hour up the hill towards half a dozen or so Nazi guards, a couple of whom were watching the approaching vehicle along the barrels of Spandau machine guns.

The car was now travelling pretty well at walking pace, and the guards, all in their square helmets, belted overcoats and black jackboots, were staring at it as if a ballet dancer carrying a cardboard sword was marching towards them. A mixture of curiosity and military derision.

One of them, carrying a machine pistol, stepped out into the road to confront the ponderously approaching Citroën. He had time to examine the blankly staring faces of the occupants and the quivering red bonnet of the car that was idling towards him no faster than a strolling lamb.

He was very young, maybe seventeen at most, and his helmet looked too big for him. He gave a small grin when he saw Margaux close up. But he did not hold out an arm to stop the car. Instead, slinging his machine pistol backwards, he stepped to one side and then, as the Citroën edged past him, he slammed his weight against it.

He was actually giving them a push, and laughing to his comrades. Another of them broke away from his guard post and began shoving from the other side. Now all the guards were laughing. One of the Spandau barrels was actually bouncing up and down as its custodian bellowed with amusement.

The car began to gain speed. The road was levelling out, and after a few yards the two pushing soldiers left off and cheered their own success.

'Merci, merci!' Margaux shouted, giving them a royal wave out of her window.

'Feef la France!' a German voice replied, causing even louder hilarity back at the guard post.

'Charming boys,' Lemming said, 'for a bunch of murdering, warmongering Nazi thugs.'

'Yes,' Margaux agreed. 'Did you see the camouflage netting on their huts and vehicles? Probably almost invisible from the sky. We'll see if we can't send them an RAF thank-you note one of these nights.'

The car finally died only a few miles away from Biville. It refused to make the short climb over a river bridge, and rolled to a stop on the edge of what looked like a field of potatoes.

They manoeuvred it so that its nose was pointing south. It would look to curious eyes that they had been driving away from the coast. Then they began to walk. It was early afternoon.

'If the dinghy's still there, we can paddle out tonight,' Margaux said.

'And if it isn't?'

'Then it isn't.'

VII

Taking no chances in daylight, they hid in the corner of a field, between a thick hedge and a young walnut tree. Rain was spitting, so they burrowed into the hedge as far as they could. They had several hours to wait until dark.

Conversation was sporadic. They were tense at this final stage in their long ramble across France. Now was crunch time. Escape or fail.

Deep inside, Lemming felt sure that these would be his last hours of freedom. Or of life itself. They might well be caught by a patrol before they got to their tidal cave. The dinghy might not re-inflate. Even if it did, the submarine might not turn up. If the sub surfaced on time and in the right place, it might get shot at, as it had before. And all that was if the dinghy was still there. If it wasn't, the future looked even less certain.

'We can steal a rowing boat, anything to get us out there,' Margaux said. 'We could even take a log if we get desperate.'

Growing up in Scotland and having been educated at public school and in the Alps, Lemming had got used to cold baths. But he knew that even he would not last long in the Channel in April. Margaux would probably last even less, despite women's fabled layer of protective fat.

He preferred to think of other things.

'I have one more question for you,' he said. 'You didn't answer it before, and you don't have to now.'

'I know I don't.'

'That day by the Houses of Parliament, with your umbrella. Were you waiting for me? Did you pick me up deliberately?'

Margaux laughed.

'Of course I did.'

So he had been right all along.

'Why?'

'When I heard you were coming along on part of the mission, I wanted to know what kind of man you were.'

'Did you go out for dinner with Major Maclean and Group Captain Basil as well?'

'No need. They were tried and tested in action.'

'Ah.'

'And I'd heard about you from friends at HQ. I thought it might be fun to get a closer look.'

'I see.' This was more flattering.

'Yes, from what I heard, I was afraid you might be maverick enough to go chattering about the mission to all and sundry.'

That was less flattering.

'Oh. And did you decide I was a maverick?'

'I thought you desperately wanted to be seen as one. But you seemed reliable enough,' she said. 'It was very amusing when you got all cloak and dagger about crème brûlée. You even started scribbling notes. What was that about?'

Lemming remembered. He had meant to draft a memo about it for the rear admiral, but events had overtaken him.

'It was just an idea I had,' he said, 'to use flames as camouflage. One could cover a building that might be a potential enemy target with a layer of combustible material – over a non-inflammable surface roof, of course. Then, if you set light to it, you might convince the enemy that the target had already been hit. They would leave it alone.'

He was quite proud of the idea. He would definitely write that memo.

'I see,' Margaux said. 'So you *do* go chattering to all and sundry after all.'

Lemming felt a rush of anger. She had tricked him.

'After these few days in France, you're hardly all and sundry,' he said. 'And if my idea gets out, I'll know whom to shoot.'

Margaux pushed aside the leafy bough that was separating them. She looked Lemming in the eye.

'I'm sorry, Ian. I was only teasing you. And it was unfair to ask you about your crème brûlée idea. Don't forget, I've been trained in extracting information from men. I am a professional Mata Hari.'

'In all ways but one,' Lemming said.

Margaux laughed, but cut off the conversation. She was clearly no longer willing to engage in any innuendo with him.

Lemming leaned back into the springy hedge and closed his eyes. If he was going to do any swimming tonight, he would need all his energy.

It was dark when he awoke, with a twig poking painfully into his cheek.

Margaux was shaking him.

'Time to go sailing,' she said.

They climbed out of their hedge and began walking along a pitch-dark lane towards the sea. A salty wind was gusting in their faces. It reminded him of when he had stood on the deck of the submarine.

Somewhere in the distance, they could hear engines, but the vehicles did not seem to be getting nearer. Meanwhile, planes were flying overhead, but high, and slowly. The signs were good. The war was keeping its distance.

The lane began to slope down towards the sea. They climbed over a gate so that they could walk on the field side of a tall hedge, parallel to the road – just in time, because footsteps were approaching along the lane, from the direction of the coast. They waited until the Nazi patrol, or pair of eloping lovers, or whoever it was, went out of earshot.

After ten more minutes they were at the clifftop where they had landed a few days before. Ahead, silhouetted against the bright, softly crashing sea, they could see the bunker that had slumped over in the landslide.

This was the crucial moment. If their dinghy had been discovered, there might well be guards or booby traps.

'I'll go down and check,' Lemming whispered. 'If you hear shots or an explosion, something will probably have gone wrong.'

In reply, Margaux gave his arm one of her trademark squeezes.

On hands and knees, he slid forward over damp grass, listening intently. Now he knew how mice felt in a field patrolled by owls. There was no sound except the sea, muffled by the cliff. No movement except his own, and the fluttering grass just below his face.

Clinging on to tufts of weed and outcrops of stone, he clambered down the cliff. The tide was higher than when they had landed, but not fully in. The waves were wetting his ankles as he edged towards the sea cave where they had concealed the dinghy. At any moment he expected a searchlight, a torch, a German command or a gunshot to halt his progress. None came.

Water was slapping loudly against the base of the cave walls, and his feet were already frozen. He was not going to be able to swim a mile out to sea and wait around for a submarine, that was for sure.

Digging blind, he lifted boulders until his fingers met rubber. Yes, the dinghy was here. A wave of hope and relief made his head spin.

'Name?' a voice whispered.

He thought he was hallucinating.

'Do not turn around. What is your name?'

This was it. The voice was too stilted to be English. And Lemming could not remember the name on his identity card.

'Henri,' he guessed.

'Commander Lemming?' So his whole cover was blown.

'Non, pas du tout,' Lemming said.

'It's me, sir, Sergeant Carrell.' The voice was still whispering, but it had relaxed now, and the full Jamaican accent had bloomed.

'Carrell?' Lemming turned. He wanted to hug the man. 'You've come to fetch us? Have you got a boat?'

'Just my dinghy … You said "us"?'

'Yes, Margaux, er, Warrant Officer Lynd, is up on top.'

'That's excellent news. We three were the only ones who got ashore, sir.'

'What about the others?'

'Aborted the mission and went home.'

'Leaving us behind?'

'Probably thought we were dead.'

Lemming wondered if he had been reported 'missing in action'. It would be almost glamorous.

'You've been here ever since we left the sub?' he asked.

'Yes, sir. I radioed in as soon as I landed. They were going to try and pick me up, but then yesterday base camp told me that two forget-me-nots were on their way here, so I stayed on.'

'You have a radio?'

'I'm the radio operator, sir. Didn't you know?'

'Of course. This is wonderful, let's go and break the good news to Mar, er Warrant Officer Lynd.'

The two men took as many precautions getting back up as Lemming had taken on the way down, though it was reassuring to have a fully trained survivor on call, with his Tommy gun and commando knife. Lemming felt almost carefree as he crept back to Margaux's hiding place behind a grassy bank.

He went in first, so as not to frighten her.

'Sergeant Carrell's here, he's been expecting us,' Lemming whispered in her ear.

'Thank heavens.'

Carrell joined them, and it reminded Lemming of a midnight rendez-vous in his school dorm, to share forbidden cakes. The three of them gripped arms in a heartfelt reunion.

Carrell whispered his story. He had been hiding out in these fields ever since the night they landed. He had not been able to carry out his own mission.

'Not your fault,' Margaux said. 'You were alone. You would have got caught. How did you survive?'

'I'm used to foraging,' Carrell said. 'When I was younger, I used to go and spend whole weeks on a beach near Montego Bay. Eating fish, birds, coconuts, anything I could find. I used to collect tropical shells and sell them to a merchant in Kingston. Good money in it, for a kid.'

'Not many coconuts around here,' Lemming said.

'Raw turnips are easier to crack open,' Carrell said. 'I caught myself a seagull one time. And I winkled up some limpets and mussels from the cave while I was checking on the dinghies. Not as tasty raw as when I bake clams on my beach in Montego Bay, but not bad.'

'Well, you're a very brave man to have waited for us, Sergeant Carrell,' Margaux said.

'Just doing my duty, ma'am.'

'Beyond the call of duty, I'd say,' Margaux replied.

Great heavens, Lemming thought, she's flirting with him.

'And you have a radio?' she asked, sounding like a London debutante confirming that her dinner date owned a Bugatti.

'Yes. It's well hidden, away from here. Best not to risk sending a signal now. I know that the sub will be offshore tonight, tomorrow, the day after that. They got your message. Well done getting that through, ma'am.'

It was a mutual admiration society, Lemming thought. Perhaps I should go and find my own grassy bank and leave them to it.

He felt no real resentment. The two professional fighters were very similar – both of them matter-of-fact in the face of danger, both trained to kill with their bare hands, and without compunction. It would make for an exciting time in bed.

'Another hour or so and we should go and inflate the dinghies,' Carrell said.

'Anything you say, sergeant,' Margaux said.

Did that include, 'roll over and lift up your skirt,' Lemming wondered, but then realized he was acting like a jealous child, and killed the thought. He lay back and listened to them whispering in the darkness like old friends. Margaux seemed to be hungry for more details about Carrell's Jamaican beach hideaway.

Despite the darkness, Lemming could see a rapt expression on her face as she listened to Carrell's description. She looked as though she was imagining herself on that beach. Come to think of it, he could imagine her there too, in the briefest of swimming costumes, cracking open coconuts to slake her thirst beneath the tropical sun. No, not Margaux. Sharing a tropical beach with her would be a far-from-relaxing experience. He drifted off into a daydream, fitting beautiful faces he had known to the sunburnt body he would like to see on his own sunlit, deserted strip of sand.

VIII

Inflating the dinghies in the cave was tough. Their feet and fingers were quickly chilled to the bone. They had to work in the dark, taking turns to pump as hard and fast as they could.

It took a full half an hour to make their boats seaworthy. When this was done, they attached the two dinghies together with the anchor ropes. They did not want to drift apart in the darkness when it came to submarine pick-up time.

'I'll take Warrant Officer Lynd,' Carrell whispered.

'Yes, I expect you probably will,' Lemming wanted to answer. 'Or, more likely, she'll take you.'

But he simply nodded and grabbed a paddle.

The two dinghies set off together, silently gliding over the low wall of waves, and then out into the black swell of the Channel.

Lemming, alone in his boat, had the easier job, but it took all his strength to paddle against the wind, fighting to control his strokes so that he made as little noise and splash as possible.

He did not know how long it took before he felt three sharp tugs on the rope. This was the signal to stop and wait for the submarine. He replied by pulling on the line, and soon the two dinghies were alongside each other.

'Everything all right?' Margaux whispered.

Lemming nodded. 'Fine.'

'Shouldn't be long now,' Carrell said.

'Nothing to do but lie back and think of England,' Lemming said.

He thought he heard Margaux laugh.

The dinghies drifted a few yards apart again, and Lemming literally did lie back and think of England. His head resting on the hard, wet side of the inflatable, his backside soaked through, he thought fondly of his warm, crowded, smoky office.

Smoky, yes. He had one last cigarette in his case.

But no, he would resist the temptation. He suspected that the cigarette that he had smoked somewhere near this very spot a few nights ago might have been what brought down flaming hell upon the submarine.

He quashed his craving and pictured himself in his office again. The day after tomorrow, with any luck. He would be freshly shaven, recently fed, with a cigarette in his mouth and chilled alcohol warming his blood. He would be wearing a pressed uniform and a crisp shirt. His hair would be neatly oiled. And he would be typing his report about this mission, listing the secrets he had learnt and those he would like to decipher, describing the people who had helped to save him, and at least two who had died.

The endless slap of the waves behind his head sounded like the thump of his fingers on the typewriter.

Meanwhile, of course, Margaux would be in her office at SOE, or wherever she was based, writing her own version of the story. And although their opinions about certain events might differ vastly, the basic facts would have to match.

His report would need to stick rigidly to the truth. There would be no room for imagination, unlike some of his past memos, which had proposed ideas bordering on science fiction.

His few days with Margaux the lady killer would have to be described using undiluted, unadorned, straightforward fact.

Just thinking about it, he was already bored.

He mused on how much more stimulating it would be now if, for example, instead of waiting for a banal submarine – a suffocating metal tube that stank of diesel and men's sweat – he could be watching out for, say, a new type of rescue aeroplane, specially built to swoop down and retrieve a life raft from the sea.

He pictured the dramatic scene, and it instantly became real.

He would send up a balloon attached to the life raft via a guy rope that the plane could latch on to, with some kind of trailing hook that it would drag behind it.

As the plane passed overhead, the life raft would be lifted smoothly into the sky. The raft itself would have to be sealed and covered, of course, so that the passenger, or passengers, did not fall out.

Passengers plural, yes. It would be much more fun to be escaping with one of the glamorous bikini girls he had imagined on Carrell's beach – to be fleeing from Jamaica itself maybe, anywhere but this freezing Channel.

Come to think of it, the weather would not matter if the life raft were a fully self-contained survival capsule. Bulletproof, dry, climate-controlled, with a comfortable bunk for two. And it would be pre-stocked with essential supplies for the escapees. There would be chilled caviar, Champagne to toast their survival, at least a hundred cigarettes ...

FIN

The author would like to thank Ian Fleming for his books which, like so many thrillers written before the end of the 20th century, now seem to betray an undercurrent of outrageous political incorrectness, but which – at the beginning of the series at least – are some of the most entertaining and grittily written novels in the English language. George Orwell and Jane Austen would have approved of Fleming's linguistic economy and clarity (probably).

The author would also like to thank everyone who has worked on and/or supported this story, especially (not in any particular order): Ruth Murray, Helen Richardson, Natacha Henry, Carolynn & Phil Venables, Kerry Glencorse, the Friday Lunch Club and the Papermill and Newcastle crews.